THE GOOD-BYE ANGEL

THE GOOD-BYE ANGEL

HONEST CHEATS PLAY DIRTY GAMES CLEAN

IGNÁCIO DE LOYOLA BRANDÃO

Translated by Clifford E. Landers

DALKEY ARCHIVE PRESS
CHAMPAIGN AND LONDON

Originally published in Portuguese as *O Anjo do Adeus* by Global Editora, 1995
Copyright © 1995 by Ignácio de Loyola Brandão
Translation copyright © 2011 by Clifford E. Landers
First edition, 2011

Library of Congress Cataloging-in-Publication Data

Brandão, Ignácio de Loyola, 1936-
[Anjo do adeus. English]
The good-bye angel : honest cheats play dirty games clean / Ignácio de Loyola Brandão ; translated
by Clifford E. Landers. -- 1st ed.
p. cm.
Originally published in Portuguese as O anjo do adeus.
ISBN 978-1-56478-594-7 (pbk. : alk. paper)
1. Brazil--Fiction. 2. Noir fiction. I. Landers, Clifford E. II. Title.
PQ9698.12.R293A8413 2010
869.3--dc22
2010037559

Partially funded by the University of Illinois at Urbana-Champaign
and by a grant from the Illinois Arts Council, a state agency

  MINISTÉRIO DA CULTURA
Fundação BIBLIOTECA NACIONAL

Obra publicada com o apoio do Ministério da Cultura do
Brasil/Fundação Biblioteca Nacional/Coordenadoria Geral do Livro e da Leitura

The publication of this book was partly supported by the Ministry of Culture of Brazil,
the National Library Foundation, and the General Coordination for the Book and Reading

www.dalkeyarchive.com

Cover: design and composition by Danielle Dutton
Printed on permanent/durable acid-free paper
and bound in the United States of America

THE GOOD-BYE ANGEL

DECEITFUL MEN TRY TO BRIBE THE AUTHOR TO ALTER THE STORY

These events actually took place in Arealva and the city remembers them, even though it refuses to talk about them, just as it avoids speaking of the Hangman, the Terrorists Who Poisoned the Milk, the Bishop Who Went Crazy, or the Lynched Men. It's character-istic of this people to want to expunge memory. I haven't altered dates or changed names, despite many of them still being alive and others being my friends. Like Christina Priscilla, Adriano Portella's ex-wife, who doesn't appear here but who gave me an interview by fax[*] clearing up the disguised relationship between Antenor and her husband. Adriano wasn't elected[**] and moved to Florida after a noisy trial focusing on lobbying in congress. The amount of money startled the court and alarmed the press, revealing all sorts of secret financial machinations in the country's interior. Antenor, through the attorney Bradío, furnished the necessary proof to the court. If you go to Miami, look up Portella. He sells electronic goods to Brazilians and is opening a restaurant serving feijoada on Saturdays and dobradinha on Wednesdays.[***] He plans to open a pastry business and turn it into a franchise operation.

I interviewed Rita, Efrahim's daughter, who runs the Victoria I Aerobic Academy in Poços de Caldas.[****] From her comes the version of the Focal fire, just as her father told it to her. It was a trauma, the obsession of her life, a frozen instant in her existence. Tall, redheaded Rita left Arealva—Efrahim was afraid the Godfather would rape her. That's what he had promised her grandfather while playing cards. She admitted it: "My grandfather was a crook, we were poor because of him, it took my father a long time to get back on his feet." This city replicates the history of Brazil—it was settled by exiles.

---

[*]   Unfortunately, the chemicals in the fax paper weren't right, and Christina Priscilla's comments have disappeared into a gray stain.

[**]   I'm not getting ahead of the facts or spoiling any surprise. Portella is a minor figure, so don't worry.

[***]   Address: 9877-B Collins Avenue, next to the Bal Harbour Shop. Twenty-four-hour instant service. Portella has become an assiduous worker. (Who could have guessed?) It's likely that he'll make his fortune in the United States, the land of opportunity. His foreign bank accounts have never been discovered. (Because no one bothered. Did anyone try?)

[****]   Special discounts for readers of this book. Rua Guido Borim Filho, 450-A, Pinheiros Park, Poços de Caldas.

Bradío tried to prevent this publication. An enigma: how did he get access to my originals if they were locked in the bank vault? Unsuccessful in this, he then tried to bribe the author. We met in Apartment 316 at the Hotel Nove de Julho* and he offered a hundred thousand dollars if I'd increase his height by 13½ inches.** And if I'd remove all allusions to the sale of pre-written rulings to corrupt judges. Bradío was worried that after the book, no judge would buy his wares. Admittedly, he wrote brilliant decisions. As for the orgies, he asked me to *add* details; it would help his image if he appeared well-endowed and priapic.

I have kept the original without modifications, even under the threat of a guilty verdict; anything is possible in dealing with the justice system in this Brazil of ours. I have no desire to prejudice readers and warp the story of Arealva. I'm considered persona non grata in the city and have been told not to return, despite having been born there, near the port. There's a series of people claiming to be the models for the characters. It's not true. They're looking for their moment of glory, they want to appear, like Iramar Alcifes, who was ecstatic about being on various radio stations in São Paulo, and the juice manufacturer who lied to the country's most celebrated blonde host on national TV. Fortunately, both were unmasked on the air. I acknowledge that certain (minimal) situations were imagined in order to make the connection between facts that have remained unexplained

---

* Rua do Cão Que Caça, 564. Currently being remodeled.
** I admit it: I didn't accept because I knew he would cheat me; he wasn't going to pay. I think there was even a video camera in the apartment.

to the present. Documents and photos of Manuela disappeared from police and court records. Anyone taking the trouble to look through the files of newspapers, radio and TV stations will find empty folders. Alencastro, the owner of a TV station, handed everything over to Antenor, who tossed it into the Regattas and Navigators Club lake. A witness saw him. There are those who claim that Manuela never existed or that I was one of her lovers. A campaign is under way to discredit me, saying that I've gone mad, that I'm out for revenge. What for? I left the city because I wanted to, I return frequently, I have a house on the banks of the Tietê. True, I've been robbed many times.*

Actually, the disappearance of thousands of photos of Manuela remains a mystery. Alencastro denied giving Antenor the files. He stated that he got rid of only those belonging to his own TV station. But what about the others? Who ended up with the picture from the Carnival dance at the Scala in Rio de Janeiro, as famous as the Marilyn Monroe calendar, nude on a red satin background? Luisão, editor of O Expresso, could clarify so many things. But he died at the beginning of this year, murdered by a former reporter who escaped from the asylum where he had inexplicably been committed. Arealva attributed the crimes of the Good-Bye Angel to that young man, but this book will prove that the truth is different.

Antenor was greatly disturbed by the events of that weekend (which speaks well of his character) and obsessively quizzes everybody in an attempt to find out what happened. Everyone sidles away when he approaches. He doesn't believe a single word

---

* I won't give the address for fear of new break-ins.

in this book, which he termed a fantasy novel, and threatens to "punch out my lights": his very words. The Godfather was found dead dropped over Manuela's favorite snooker table (because of her, the skinflint had to replace the felt on all the tables) after setting fire to his own son's home. Someone very strong plunged a stake into his heart, exactly the way vampire hunters do. Tall and thin, without a shirt, his arms spread, he was compared by Iramar Alcifes to Jesus on the Cross. Indignant Catholics published a manifesto protesting the blasphemy, which only increased the audience for this venomous journalist who thrives on controversy. Lindorley, the crippled cleaning woman, was the one who found him. Squealing, she removed the old man's clothes and washed the body with the dirty rag that she dipped into bleach in a plastic bucket. Then she wrapped him in a sheet and held him in her arms for two days.

About Heloísa, after all, not much was known. Women who were what she was and who brilliantly transformed themselves by changing their identity know how to protect themselves. *A Lista* called her a pioneer and pathfinder, a builder of men and companies, giving an ambiguous tone to it all. She killed herself by sealing her head in a plastic bag used to wrap sandals. Yvonne, who appears casually in the plot, without much detail, a nebulous figure,* wrote to the newspapers for some months and demanded that the police intensify the search for her vanished boyfriend. She was found strangled (by the same ex-reporter?) in the tunnel of Focal, the cotton-oil factory that burned down in 1953, in

---

* She could have given meaning to Pedro Quimera's life, thereby avoiding dire happenings.

7

whose ruins* dwell ghosts and goblins, some of which perform miracles, recognized even by the bishop of Arealva, an intransigent and orthodox clergyman.**

---

* Finally bought out by Antenor's group, which is to start work on a shopping center. A lot of money passed under the table in the Municipal Council and the site had been expropriated by city officials for unpaid taxes. The juice factories will have to change the train tracks or pay tolls, which engendered a new legal battle that will delay construction of the shopping center. I'd be willing to bet that Bradío will write the judges' ruling.

** Pray for their souls or commission a Mass and you will be blessed.

1

Manuela died while her husband was on his knees drooling over thousand-dollar bills, muscles trembling in excitement, worshiping gold bars. Edevair set himself on fire at the very moment that the Great Leader of Profitable Knowledge, at the Coral Whale, purged from their minds any guilt about accumulating wealth, loving money, or lusting after profit. Two deaths in one night. And a violent storm, a small tornado, that knocked over antennas and satellite dishes, stripped off roof tiles, caused landslides, and destroyed most of the acrylic store signs, which were considered a contribution to aesthetics. It was a Saturday that would be remembered for years.

Manuela's death aroused irritation in some quarters, because as the news spread like some raucous nocturnal bird, the important events lost their impact. The golden anniversary dinner of Cyro, of the mill trust, emptied out as soon as the meal was finished. The Large Profits Dance to commemorate the collapse of the American acerola harvest ended. The cocktail party to mark the first Jet Ski competition of the Regattas and Navigators Club melted away faster than the ice in the whiskey glasses. At the banquet for political supporters of Adriano Portella, opponent of Antenor, Manuela's husband, it was the sole topic of conversation, eclipsing the collusion and alliances, and another meeting was proposed for the following week. The pre-Carnival festivities of the Getúlio Vargas Recreational and Cultural Club were interrupted for an hour while everyone went down to the square hoping to see Manuela's body. The one who profited was Efrahim, owner of the Crystal Night, the city's most elegant café, which was celebrating its tenth anniversary. Everyone headed there, with the result that at two in the morning he had to shut down the open bar, lest he go bankrupt.

This time the Good-Bye Angel has gone too far and is going to get caught, people commented. Or maybe he's taken a liking to such things and is starting to increase the number of executions knowing he'll get away with it because of police incompetence? Few knew the details; they didn't know that Edevair had committed suicide in front of witnesses and that Manuela didn't bear the Angel's usual signature, four stab wounds in the back forming the corners of a square and parts excised from the body: arm, leg, finger, ears, knee, breast, nose, teeth removed. And a small religious image stuck to the left cheek. A commonplace image, of the kind given at First Communion, showing an angel with huge wings hovering over an Alpine village. At the time of the first murder, ten years earlier, a man with a metallic voice had telephoned the district attorney's wife warning that the Angel of God or Executioner had come to Earth. She misunderstood. It wasn't from God but from the Angel, as he made clear in a phone call to the radio stations. Just as the Hangman had appeared at the turn of the century to exercise his craft he, the Executioner, had come to eliminate people that society doesn't need. "Neither society nor I," he emphasized in an ironic tone. "Sent by whom?" asked the assiduous reporter Dorian Jorge Freire. "No one must know from where the envoys come; it's enough that they come to fulfill their mission," replied the Executioner.

He finally made a mistake and he's going to get caught, everyone thought, relieved. Killing Manuela would cause Antenor to get the entire police force involved. Investigators would come from São Paulo and private detectives* would be hired. The husband would call on the FBI, Scotland Yard, the Sûreté, Interpol, his friends in the old National Intelligence Service, Naval Intelligence, and Army Intelligence, where he circulated freely. Since the seventies he was an intimate of the generals who frequently visited the city and occupied positions in his businesses. Unless

---

* Many believe that they exist in Brazil, and are good, the result of watching television.

Antenor was involved, in which case he was disinclined to solve anything. No one could ever figure out this man.

One a year. There were nine deaths, beginning in 1985, in the last week of president-elect Tancredo Neves's life in São Paulo. Shortly after the bearded spokesman announced on television the president's state of health, the Good-Bye Angel phoned the principal of Christ the King High School to communicate that his daughter was dead in the balcony of the Esmeralda theater, a fleabag movie house that showed fifth-rate spaghetti westerns on even days and gay films on odd days. The killer was the Angel, determined to cleanse the earth of filthy people. The Esmeralda, built for cinema festivals,* was once the most elegant theater in all of Latin America, with (rotten) papier-mâché palm trees and artificial fountains (today dried up) in the lobby that simulated a desert oasis. Everything went on there, as was common knowledge. At least to the habitués: drug dealers, whores, junkies, thieves, queers, cornholers for hire, voyeurs, street urchins, bums. And certain women who, disguised in wigs, dark glasses, and weird makeup, would spend hours going from seat to seat, servicing strangers, to the point that they would leave with cramped jaws. One of them created a huge scandal. Upon unzipping a fly, she recognized it belonged to her husband, who was at that moment in extremis, so to speak.

Once a year a person was killed under the same circumstances, with only the month changing. The Angel attacked in sequence. After the tenth victim, he would increase the number of executions.

---

* One of the reasons that led Pedro Quimera to move to Arealva—he wanted to see movie stars up close.

He made a point of emphasizing that he wasn't a political terrorist—he disdained politics, although many politicians were on the list. Nor was it moral or gender based, because he killed men and women, gays and lesbians, bisexuals and the impotent, the pure, the ingenuous (ingenuous types are a plague), and the corrupt. In short, he would kill anyone he pleased. He enjoyed killing, and all the explanations the media came up with were fertilizer for newspapers to sell copies, psychologists to gain publicity, and psychiatrists to attract patients. Nevertheless, as soon as Manuela was killed, the police and journalists did some calculations and realized that the murder didn't follow the chronological order strictly observed to that point.

Two bodies on the same square. A hundred yards from the historic and traditional 27th precinct, from whose cells had been torn the brothers lynched by the anti-abolitionists fifteen years before the end of the nineteenth century and where, after the coup of 1964, subversives* were tortured and killed. Woe to the bloody city! proclaimed *A Lista* in a headline the next day in an extra. Because whenever tragedies shook Arealva, the paper would revive the prophet Ezekiel and the curse that dated back a century. Ever since Father Gaetano, in 1885, heading for five-thirty Mass one morning, had found the bodies of the lynched men incinerated in front of the church, by order of the local authorities.

That morning, in a dramatic, peremptory tone, the priest refused to open the church doors. He wouldn't reopen them until

---

* Terminology from the 1970s. Subversives = the caste of society whose elimination was recommended by those in power, with the support of a good part of the population.

there was an end to the impious emanations of the crime anticipated by the city, which to a man had covered it up. Everyone
knew, but many went on trips, remaining away for weeks; others kept quiet and closed their windows, while the killers carried
out their mission. Father Gaetano outdid himself, carried away
by his own rhetoric; a great orator, one of the best, he was sought
out each year by various parishes to arouse the faithful during
Holy Week, able to enthrall multitudes with the Sermon of Seven
Words. He had before him a terrified city and a biblical theme.
Arms raised like the prophets in a Glauber Rocha* film, buffeted
by the cold July wind, in a pose like Captain Ahab in John Hus-
ton's *Moby Dick*, he hurled invective, cursing Arealva with the
words of Ezekiel:

Woe to thee, bloody city! I will even make the pile for fire great.
Heap on wood, kindle the fire, consume the flesh, and spice it well,
and let the bones be burned. Then set it empty upon the coals thereof,
that its brass may grow hot, and burn, and that its filthiness may be
molten in it, that its scum be consumed.

A *Lista* would recall once again, perhaps for the fiftieth time,
the priest's speech, of dubious authenticity, a tasty dish to feed the
myths circulating about the square. Two dead people in the same
place. Despite the rumors, which naturally pointed to Manuela's
husband, Antenor, as the main suspect (and with what pleasure
everyone did so), he had 350 witnesses to his presence at the Coral
Whale. Many of them were confused, declaring that he was in
the front row. It's likely that the habit of seeing the man leading,

---

* For young readers who don't frequent art theaters: the films of Glauber Rocha
(1939–1981) were mystical-violent epics, acted with pomp and affectation.

always at the forefront of any situation in which he found himself, had given rise to such statements. Actually, Antenor humbly (which wasn't his style) had declined the first row in favor of a businessman whose group, which includes a bank, would support him in the next election. He had contented himself with a seat in the third row. Modest but strategically located for the lenses of photographers and cinematographers.

There were also five hundred malcontents who saw him come in, forty minutes before the lecture began, under a fine, light rain. Protests began outside, shouts demanding that they abandon the cramped Whale and go to the large Sports Arena. They were unreconciled to missing the most highly anticipated evening in the last ten years, one surpassed only by Paul McCartney, who, sponsored by a pool of businesses, gave a show in the Memorial Musical Shell on the banks of the Tietê amid blossoming orange trees. This enchanted Paul, a defender of the environment. Only they didn't inform him that those businesses were the biggest polluters in the region. The perfume the night of the Beatles show will be talked about for many years.

Edevair's twisted body was removed from the square before the crowd left the Coral Whale and before the first Carnival revelers showed up for the "pre" at the Getúlio Vargas, an old dance hall. The liveliest, frequented on Tuesday nights by the best people. People considered it democratic to rub elbows with folks from the outskirts who reeked of cheap perfume and low-quality deodorants, wearing knockoffs of designer labels.

When they wanted to, the police at the 27th could act fast. There were lots of people who mattered at the Whale, and Edevair, the retiree who sacrificed himself uselessly, was put into a van and taken to the morgue, where he was tossed like a bag of manure onto a stained Formica slab, awaiting someone from the family to identify and claim him. No one could foresee, let alone imagine, that the body of Manuela—of all people, Manuela—would be found some hours later, igniting an earthquake registering to 20 on the Richter scale. The police concluded that the murderer must have left the corpse there at the height of the storm that began after Edevair had set fire to his own body, like the Tibetan monks of the sixties. The violent rainfall scattered the people, most of whom sought shelter in the dance hall; the Whale's doors were closed, so some squeezed into the How Come Pharmacy, which had only one of its doors open because the wind blew in a lot of water.

Why did it have to be in the square? Again! Always there! The abomination of the lynchings and the curse of the woman who confronted the Hangman will never end. A century-old malediction. It'd be better to raze the place, turn it into a parking lot. Years ago Adriano Portella tried to find a way to expropriate the square and build a shopping center and parking garages, part of a renewal project of the old downtown area that would have yielded a bundle of money. The initial comments about the killing of Manuela displayed perplexity, shock, skepticism. They recalled the general astonishment when people heard of the death of Tom Jobim, no one believing that Tom could die. There was curiosity about the way that Edevair had killed himself. Just as the stigma of the Hangman was beginning to be forgotten and everything was fading into the limbo of misty events, the fatal evening of 1910 came back, making people think that the wrongfully hanged woman was still imprisoned inside those thousand square meters of thick vegetation. The entire square block under the weight of a restless soul killed on a sunny day typical of Arealva.

Two deaths the same night, in the same place. And a storm unlike any seen for years in the city. Many people saw hidden signs in it! They would never be free. Nonsense, stop it, it's already been eighty-five years, said Dorian Jorge Freire, a journalist and rival of Iramar, a serious and respected man despite having been roguish in his youth. It's as plain as the nose on your face that "the lowlife" killed his wife. He was seen by three hundred people? At the Coral Whale? Bah! Anybody who frequents the Whale is one of his, cocaine from the same line! "When there are too many alibis, it's suspicious," commented Efrahim, an avowed enemy of Antenor, whom he invariably referred to as "the lowlife." Despite this, he had received an invitation for the night of the Great Leader but had sent it back. "As if I were about to spend two hundred dollars on con games. The lowlife promotes nothing but con games."

Efrahim became restive in his café, listening all night to the sound of people coming in. If normally the place was jammed, that night it was bursting at the seams after 2:00 a.m. It was impossible to find room, and groups spilled out onto the sidewalk. The patio in the rear was opened and packed. They were all awake, woken up by the fear of the rain and wind or abruptly roused from sleep by irritating phone calls. They roamed about to see the damage, while police and firefighters went into shantytowns, followed by TV cameras to record mudslides, flooding, and deaths. Little by little, in a natural accommodation to events, the small tornado was forgotten, something to be watched on the news, while the death of Manuela moved to the foreground, floating like the illuminated whale in the sky on St. Peter's Night celebrations, a light-filled colored balloon. Suddenly, as if a gust of wind had swept through the city and revived what had been forgotten, each one recalled a situation involving Manuela. The tiniest incidents, unremarkable while the person is alive, after death—if it's a violent one—take on the outline of hints, clues, signs pointing to what was going to happen, revelations about what the person was like.

No one spoke of Edevair, the human torch, however unusual had been his end. The omission wasn't conscious. A stranger, living on the outskirts, was of no interest. Poor people die all the time, at all hours, in every way. The news about Manuela, on the other hand, went from mouth to mouth. "She had to end up like that" was a sentiment heard everywhere, even in the absence of any concrete proof. She was the most accessible (albeit distant), impossible fantasy of men, the envy of every woman.

When the customers left the Coral Whale around midnight, they noticed movement in the square, some disturbance. But no one was concerned; it was always the scene for disturbances and commotion. Decades earlier it was reserved for a promenade by the blacks who tried to buy the Whale building for an exclusive club when the association was deactivated and the building abandoned. However, a judge declared it part of the historical patrimony and therefore it could only be bought through a public auction should the city decide to sell. In reality, it was an effort to obstruct the emerging consolidation among the black population. Some of them had degrees in law and engineering, and others were training to be teachers; in the schools, till then, blacks were only servants or janitors. Two were very successful in business on the outskirts; one of them had gotten rich by bringing Cadillacs to the city. The same judge, before he died, dictated the document that made it possible for Antenor to buy the Whale in the name of a philanthropic entity, an entity whose philanthropy never benefited a single person in need.

The square was littered with scattered branches, broken and twisted trees, the ground covered with leaves, papers, plastic wrappers, bottles, garbage swept up in the wind and rain. The fountain had overflowed, and dead fish were scattered everywhere. Inside, the audience had heard nothing, entranced by the magnetism of the Great Leader of Profitable Knowledge. A disused name, ugly, but a good thing, I love money, now more than ever, and I feel good about it, they concluded. Manuela's body had yet to be discovered, lying face down in the bushes.

When it was identified, at 1:05 in the morning, the police called a representative from the district attorney's office and asked him to go to the Hotel Nove de Julho, where everyone was having dinner, to inform Antenor, discreetly. Some of the policemen felt the husband was the prime suspect. They were excited at the prospect of getting their hands on that arrogant man who challenged everybody, bought city councilmen, bribed inspectors, bankrolled congressmen, went around defiantly armed, and ignored fines. Phantom invoices, illegal parceling of land, invasion of others' landholdings, tax evasion, dollars smuggled abroad, indictments of contractors, manipulation of Social Security funds, physical attacks on councilmen, firing two shots at a soldier of the Civil Guard, irascible security men, brawls at parties. Didn't Antenor have the audacity to piss on the foot of the federal congressman chosen by him who had voted for a law against the interests of the industries polluting the city? He must snort a lot of coke.* Who was the supplier of the upper class? They didn't know. Even if they knew, there was someone in the police who did know and kept his mouth shut. Just as they would keep quiet, receiving what the others received.

There was a rumor that Manuela was seeking a separation and was beaten daily by Antenor, which explained her enormous collection of dark glasses. Hundreds of them, by Hermès, Cardin, Ferré, Valentino. She traveled a lot, and in the last year she had disappeared, dropped out of circulation. She drank and was no longer being invited to homes. She was seen in her turquoise-blue Honda Civic, the socialite's car, wandering around rough neighborhoods in search of drugs and rough lovers; she likes smelly peasants and being trodden on by soldiers' boots. She would frequent the Godfather's pool hall, the Snooker, in the afternoon, in that period after lunch when even professional pool players, bums, and loafers are feeling drowsy, the time when the crippled cleaning lady was sweeping up in the main room. It was said that Manuela would play countless matches by herself, sometimes with the Godfather as her opponent. The windows

---

* I have listed here what was said in all the get-togethers, cafés, bars, luncheonettes, clubs, and banks; no one seems to like Antenor.

remained closed. It wasn't the first time that it happened. The older ones recalled that when she first came to the city, she was looked at suspiciously because she frequented the Godfather's establishment. Years later, accompanied by a nurse, she celebrated the same after-lunch ritual, with the room all to herself. Hadn't it been there, on a Good Friday, that the son of Cyro, owner of the wheat mills, had been hit on the head with a pool cue and gone into a coma? It was never made clear. The official version was that the seventeen-year-old boy was found dying at the edge of a cane field, victim of a robbery.

When the police in the square recognized Manuela, they were overcome with both happiness and fright. Working on the case would bring them fame: they would be in the newspapers, even while under a lot of pressure. And it would be complicated, once they penetrated (or so they imagined) that separate, isolated world of "the people who matter," as defined by the polemicist Iramar Alcifes. An indefinable feeling came with it: punishment. Manuela had gotten away with everything, led her life as she chose, with an apparent disdain for norms. Policemen, paralyzed by the wear and tear that daily violence imposes, nevertheless harbored deep-seated moral judgments. To do what they did, risking their lives, they cloaked themselves in the mantle of defenders of society, crusaders, vigilantes on the alert for lawbreakers. But most important of all were financial gains. Everything had a price: silence, hiding or planting evidence, misdirecting an investigation. The fright came from one simple question: who could have killed, and so ferociously, the most beautiful, luscious, funny, strange, crazy, challenging woman in Arealva—and why? Who was this woman? At that hour of the morning the heat was returning. And through the rain-washed atmosphere came the asphyxiating smell of orange trees.*

2

The Coral Whale had that enigmatic name because it was the revamped version of the Synodus, created in 1870 by the gathering of disparate individuals: abolitionists, alchemists, anarchists, cabalists, chess players, crossword enthusiasts, Egyptologists, esotericists, historians, mathematicians, philosophers, religious and political polemicists (there were many newspapers,** a tradition maintained even today), positivists, slavocrats, theologians, theosophists. The documents preserved in the Lev Gadelha Museum do not record who first gave the new name to the Synodus. There is, however, clarification as to the meaning of the name. The whale represents the entrance into the cavern. To penetrate into the whale is to plunge into the shadows and emerge renewed. The coral relates to the axis of the world with the nether darkness. "To light the darkness," reads the charter of the foundation.

The Whale's objectives were less than precise. As far as can be ascertained, a place for discussions, for men only, where the habit of conversation and debate was cultivated. Its library and reading room were famous. Nearly all the books were burned in May 1964

---

*   A poetic phrase to offset the violence.
**   These local papers have a good pressrun, despite the competition with those coming in from São Paulo and Rio de Janeiro.

by a group that invaded the association in search of subversive literature. The huge bonfire burned all night in front of the Getúlio Vargas Recreational and Cultural Club. Scorched copies can be seen in the museum. Members of the Whale wore a blue badge with a fish, just as the old Marian Congregations used the same badge with the Cross. The fish is the symbol of fecundity (of ideas, in the case of the Whale) and in China is the bearer of luck. There was, however, no such good fortune. At the turn of the century the Tietê overflowed its banks,* the waters claimed everything, and when they subsided, the Whale found itself deep in parched mud. Initiates of the Synodus scooped up that mud (clay, the beginning of man) and took it away in carts to the site at the highest point of the city, the location where the square would be laid out; for decades the major spot in the city, with a courthouse, church, Municipal Council, and jail. With the development of business and the first incipient industries, brought by Italian and Spanish immigrants, Arealva expanded away from the river instead of nestling on its banks. This was because the ports for loading and unloading rice and corn, the main products, were violent places, with prostitutes, raucous disturbances, dens of unsavory characters, smuggling—illicit dealings of every type.

Using the clay, they laid new foundations and raised solid construction with brick walls, financed by merchants for whom numerologists did calculations to foresee if the businesses would work out. Money and politics mixed inside the Whale, making it into a powerful institution that acted behind the scenes, a kind of Masonry.

---

* The Tietê was a living river then, not the open sewer of today.

When it was declared a public utility, in 1936, the Whale was under the control of the Spaniards ensconced in the scrap metal, used paper, and glass business. For unknown reasons, the Esperantists, who corresponded in the language created by Zamenhof, enjoyed a great deal of power. In 1941, an eminent group of townspeople departed for Europe to offer the benefits of Esperanto as a code language for messages on the front lines. The ship was sunk by a German torpedo off the Spanish coast. The names of these heroes are carved on a granite tombstone in the shape of a stylized ship sinking into a reflecting pool of blue water[*] across from a disused warehouse in the port area, the cultural center for a labor union. Actually, it's merely a large room with tables for pool and Ping-Pong, and some video-game machines. On the other side of the river, facing the monument, lie the ruins of the Old Red Fort. A mystery even today. It's not known when it was constructed, where the blood-colored stones came from, what military objectives it met, or when it was abandoned. Historians, members of the Whale, went through archives, ministries, military headquarters, libraries, and national museums, and found no trace of the existence of the fort, which was occupied in 1968 by a terrorist group that threatened to blow up the city on the day the repressive Institutional Act 5 was decreed. A troop from the Air Force made mincemeat of the guerrilla squad—none were ever identified.

During the Second World War, the initial objectives of the Coral Whale were forgotten, and the Synodus ceased to function.

---

[*] It was blue only at first; today it's green, stagnant. Even so, on hot days, street kids bathe in the pool.

There's a version that the Godfather tried to buy the imposing building (and why so imposing? people asked) to make it into a pool hall, his obsession and passion.* He was an audacious man who had made money buying up old railroad passenger cars,** disassembling them and selling items such as fixtures, doors and windows with beveled glass to antique dealers in São Paulo.

In 1946 the Whale was restored by an architect who copied everything and turned it into a replica of Villa Tabucchi, the grandiose mansion of an intellectual from Vecchiano, a small Italian village near Pisa. The restoration was financed by Ulisses Capuano, an industrialist who established the hat factory, the beer brewery—later taken over by Brahma—and the gigantic Focal: Fine Edible Cotton Oil, which burned down in 1953. Despite women never having been admitted, a sex scandal rocked the association, which was closed down in 1949 following a large demonstration in favor of the return to power of the deposed dictator Getúlio Vargas. In those days, the word *scandal* had strong connotations in a conservative society, leading to the suicide of two women. The gilded plaque with green letters over the door is rusted, leaving only the letters

C R A L W H L E

---

* It would be in reality a casino, such as existed in Águas de São Pedro, Poços de Caldas, and Urca.
** This is how he tells it. There's a rumor that he stole property from the railroad with the complicity of one of its managers, whom everyone nicknamed the Hungarian, heaven only knows why.

A Lista, in 1957, published an article saying that one of the secret objectives of the Synodus was the discovery of the bones of a whale that, two hundred years ago, had become stranded at the sandy port. Immense, at least to those people who had only seen whales in engravings. Grounded, it survived by being fed by the people, who tossed fishes into its mouth and took turns wetting it down so it could stand the heat. To protect it from the sun, they had erected an awning made of 150 bedsheets, and in this way the whale stayed alive for a time, an attraction and focal point of picnics. Somewhere in the river are buried its monumental bones. From this came the name of the city, according to writings in the museum: Ossos de Areia, or Bones of Sand. Because the village prospered dating from this event, the whale became its talisman, a good-luck charm. As it grew and became the fifth largest city in the state, it was decided that Bones of Sand was a provincial name and it was changed to Arealva, which still doesn't please the majority of the people who matter. They'd like a more imposing name with an American accent, something like Minneapolis, Milwaukee, Cincinnati. The argument is that, because of the heavy commerce of juices between Arealva and the United States, it would be useful to have cities with identical names so they could be designated sister cities. Iramar Alcifes, ever the contrarian, suggested Whalebones or Sandbones. The implacable journalist Dorian Jorge Freire published a piece with sixty suggestions offered by city councilmen.

There's a belief that whoever discovers the bones of the beached whale will find luck and fortune. They will cause his enterprises to prosper, make him win the lottery two hundred times, realize huge profits in business, take out loans from state-run banks without having to repay, and dominate politics. An expression emerged when Antenor married Manuela: to find the whalebones. From that time on, it entered into common parlance. And that Saturday, when Manuela's body was discovered, the expression underwent a modification: Antenor lost the bones. Many were rooting for him to lose them.

Once the heavy rain was over, the night turned hot again, with the result that there was no empty bar or beer hall with room. The club's swimming pool remained open, speedboats streaked across the lake, oarsmen practiced their rowing skills on the Tietê, the squares were packed, bikers' hangouts were hopping, imported cars slid silently along, to the despair of those who loved the mighty roar of engines. News of Manuela's death began to circulate. People listened in silence, not moving, paralyzed. Not believing. There are situations that are never going to happen, that transcend the realm of possibility. Dorian uttered the best phrase: "And I didn't even know that Manuela *could* die." Who killed her and why?

Little by little, telephones began to ring. Agitated cell phones. In every bar, restaurant, club, house, fast-food stand, and hotel they rang in a crescendo. As the news spread, the lines to police stations became jammed; the newspapers didn't answer calls. Editors were called, and they answered enraged. The Sunday editions were ready; it was a real headache. Like a flood in which the water comes down, claims everything, sweeping aside whatever is in its path, news of Manuela's death went from mouth to mouth. There's a certain satisfaction when someone well-known dies. That's when the person becomes common, just like us, vulnerable. An underlying envy of power and glory exists, explained Dorian to a radio station (he was always the first to be interviewed), and the death of a well-known person provides a bit of relief from the load of resentment—why did he get ahead and not me?—and jealousy. It would be no exaggeration to say that the entire city, or at least those who mattered, as defined by Iramar Alcifes, was awake, wanting to go somewhere, meet with someone, to talk, listen, ask questions, gossip, get clarification. All of them dominated not by horror or piety but by irrepressible curiosity that made them abandon guests at parties, spring out of motel beds, get up from their sofas without turning off the TV. Running, without knowing in what direction they should run. Frenetically, with but a single question in their minds: Did Antenor kill her? Or one of her lovers? The Good-Bye Angel? Was it drugs, a kidnapping? Silencing a witness? Revenge? Whom did the police suspect? Why was she killed?

Many refused to believe it, thinking it a hoax. Especially those who had cell phones, because there was always somebody calling for no reason. Others, like Efrahim, took the news skeptically. Another of Antenor's ploys, he contended. Some demanded confirmation. A cortege of cars headed for the square, which the police had cordoned off. It was impossible to approach it; people had to get out blocks and blocks away and walk. The crowd was growing. Everyone was excited by the prospect of seeing Manuela's lacerated body, because by then a thousand versions were being born—she had never been a woman to engender unanimity. Every minute gave rise to a new detail: fifteen stab wounds, thirty

28

gunshots, crushed by an automobile, her hands cut off, her eyes plucked out, her body set afire (here they confused Manuela and Edevair), her head smashed with a rock, her genitalia severed—shouted Iramar Alcifes—her belly slit open by a samurai sword, all her fingers amputated, and all her toes. Nothing was normal with Manuela. Exaggeration enveloped her even in death. She couldn't be murdered prosaically, it had to be extravagantly. Everyone asked about Antenor. Vanished. That was when the strange fact occurred concerning the pharmacist Evandro.

3

Antenor and his group revived the Coral Whale in 1974, the year they all made a lot of money with stockpiled gasoline, sold at exorbitant prices following the worldwide oil crisis. Taking advantage of the scarcity, they created a black market in which anyone who wanted fuel paid dearly. The dilapidated old Synodus plaque was recovered and placed on an interior wall. We cannot ignore the history of our city, declared Antenor. The phrase, along with everything else that he said and was published as a quote from him, came from Brídi, the media consultant hired in São Paulo. A discreet neon sign of lovely design, bearing the signature of Philippe Starck, was installed in place of the old corroded plaque. "And just who is this Philippe Starck?" bellowed a furious Iramar Alcifes. "Don't we have enough artists of our own? Why *design*"—he pronounced it *de-sig-nee*—"when the Portuguese language, so beautiful and rich, has the word *desenho* or painting?" At the time of the congressional investigation of the budget it was discovered why the society had been revived, but that's getting a bit ahead of the story.[*]

Self-esteem, self-help, or Profitable Knowledge, as the Great Leader termed it, was a popular topic. Books burst onto the best-seller lists, lecturers were scheduled for suitcases of money.[**] Not to mention the television program that, despite the hour and day—7:00 A.M. on Sunday—enjoys an enormous audience. Hundreds of successful people would testify about the transformation of their lives since they discovered the Knowledge. The majority of these men were unknown, but not the symbols that they exhibited—mansions on the outskirts of São Paulo, Rio, Ribeirão Preto, and Joinville. Imported cars, Japanese motorcycles, Jet Skis, boats, Learjets, American appliances and computers, digital watches with everlasting nuclear batteries, five-story apartments with Persian rugs, cellular videophones, Japanese sound systems, scotch whiskey, designer fountain pens, Hermès neckties, German white wine in blue bottles, Italian suits and shoes, shirts open to show hairy chests, gold chains, blonde women in flashy dresses and eight-inch heels. How not to give in? Videos, initiation meetings, notebooks, exchange of know-how, and franchises.

Thousands were on the waiting lists for the Key-Gatherings for Personal Success held at luxury hotels in the countryside, closed for confidential ceremonies, like the spiritual retreats of the forties and fifties and the short courses of the sixties and seventies.

---

[*] The object of an investigation in the Municipal Council. It was never concluded and no one was found guilty, which obliges us to refrain from comment.
[**] Literally. The greenbacks go inside elegant Samsonites.

Those taking part did not reveal what went on there; after all, they were paying rather dearly to gain access to highly effective formulas. They spoke in a particular code using normal words, but with a connotation different from the usual, which situated them in a universe of their own. They would emerge energized, ready to confront without guilt both life and monetarism. The anguish dissolved about speculating in currency, gold, the dollar, stocks, investments. It was as if they had been thawed in a microwave.

In a state of grace, 321 attendees left the Coral Whale, strolled contentedly, mildly intrigued by the throng in the square. But it could be a vendor, a preacher—there were so many new religions— a poet, a small political rally of popular parties. They didn't even see the lights of the police car; the Whale was at the extreme opposite end. And there was the garden with hundreds of topiaries, each trimmed in shapes that ranged from stars to various animals, the products of the gardener's personal collection of fables: insects, birds, planets, unknown animals, rockets, airplanes, tables and chairs, busts, and chalices, which generated extensive coverage on the *Fantástico* show every Christmas.

No one had said that the gardener's masterpiece had been removed from the square. It had taken him six years of effort, infinite patience, behind barriers to which no one had access until the day the scandal erupted. The gardener had managed to reproduce, in a living sculpture employing different types of vegetation, Courbet's *Sleep*, painted in 1866 and property of the Musée du Petit Palais in Paris. It was the pharmacist Evandro who identified the work, having published an article on Courbet in *O Expresso*. However, what was later rumored and was the beginning of a campaign to destroy the sculpture is that those two nude women, languidly intertwined on a bed, were Madeleine,[*] Iramar Alcifes's wife, and his lover, a young woman from Rincão who, thanks to the radio program, had been chosen Miss Arealva 1990.

In reality, it was difficult to recognize any face, but the controversy surrounding *Sleep*, starting with an anonymous phone call, resulted in the discovery of the fact that Iramar had been impotent since the age of fifteen, when the tire repairman at a gas station raped him in the basement of an old theater converted into a storeroom for a textile factory. It was there, among thousands of pieces of every type of cloth, that Iramar had his initiation. This was one of the reasons that he never changed a tire, in addition to avoiding the Street of Elegant Commerce, a name preserved from the 1920s. Elegant it wasn't, a collection of cheap stores, cheap fabrics, plastic shoes, pay-by-weight restaurants, locksmiths, vendors of Arab fast foods, pastry shops, government lottery agencies, illegal lottery sites, and cubicles for electronic betting. The smell of rubber and of fabrics disturbed Iramar, upset him, left him beside himself. He would suffer attacks that appeared epileptic but weren't. He would have these attacks in front of the microphone when he became too nervous; he was an apoplectic sort. His few intimates said that Iramar's virulent attitudes on his programs came directly from these mental disturbances, provoked by the rape and by everything he had suffered at the hands of Madeleine, with whom he was in love. Situations that didn't make a man's life

---

[*] Her mother was a reader of Proust and loved the Madeleine cookie that provokes the sensitive memory. She always lamented the marriage of her daughter to Iramar, an ignoramus who sucks his teeth after meals.

easy. A half-man, as she told anyone who would listen. And they all would.

It was a memorable lecture, affirmed all the privileged who were there. Iramar, even showing his press pass, hadn't been able to get in; it was a closed function, which outraged him. But he heard the report of third parties. The speaker, pointing the gold bar in his hands at the audience like a remote control, howled hysterically.

Kneel down before the golden calf!

Bow your heads in acceptance. The sole truth of the millennium!
In his right hand, the gold bar pointed toward the men. In his left, a diamond, shown to the women. Who knew how many carats it was?

This is the salvation of mankind!

Leaning forward, drawn by that bar, his nose touching it, trying to smell it, Antenor was in a state of grace.

This is why I came into the world. To teach you!

To free mankind from the worst of all vices. To eliminate the guilt that the love of money brings to people. Know this! It is the great revelation. Christ became enraged with Judas only because he considered paltry the amount for which he was sold. He felt disdained, diminished.

The audience was startled. Some got up, went to the office and demanded their money back. Economics is one thing, blasphemy is something else! Antenor didn't budge. He wasn't bothered by moral or religious issues and ignored ethics. Some claim that at that very moment he knew his wife was dead but feigned veneration of gold so the audience could witness it. How could you contradict 321 people? (We're excluding the 29 who walked out.)

"It was worth every penny of the two hundred dollars I paid to get in," declared the lawyer Bradío, known for having gotten Evandro acquitted on twenty-eight different occasions and who had come from Rio de Janeiro in the same Learjet that brought the Great Leader of Profitable Knowledge. They had tried to convince the Leader of the need for a second session, but he had only three hours, the exact amount of time he spent in the city. He left, disappointing the organizers and those who hadn't been able to get in. He didn't even consider staying at the Hotel Nove de Julho, a decadent structure dating from the time when the city produced rice for all of Brazil. Its restaurant, restored with material from the first-class dining cars of the defunct railroad, was a pleasant spot with a great deal of atmosphere. Its chef had come from São Paulo after retiring from La Casserole, fearing the violence in the city.

For months the great lecture on Profitable Knowledge was all people talked about in Arealva. Antenor had spent a week between Rio de Janeiro, São Paulo, and Belo Horizonte, in talks trying to find an opening in the Leader's schedule, which wasn't impossible. Thirty thousand dollars will stretch any amount of time, especially when the whole thing would take only three hours and a Learjet would pick up and return the Leader. These conditions were made known because Antenor (Bridi, actually) had a precise approach to marketing. Each listener would pay two hundred dollars, which left a profit, deducting the speaker's honorarium and expenses for the decorations, of sixty thousand dollars. The plane was a loan from an acerola grower at no cost to him; everything was accounted for and deducted, taking advantage of legislation on cultural sponsorship. Bradío, though rather unstable, was on permanent retainer.

The dinner was included in the expenses, even without the presence of the speaker. What the entire city asked was this: at the moment they were enjoying the delicate and fragrant salmon carpaccio on a bed of arugula, did those men know that Manuela was dead? Not all of them! Still, no one doubted Antenor's involvement. For most, the lecture was merely a cover to camouflage the crime and provide an alibi. What could be proved? And how? What police officer would have the courage to summon to the precinct the men who had set up the dinner?

Evandro, the pharmacist, whose pharmacy was on one of the corners of the square, saw when the police withdrew, after the body of the man who set himself on fire had been removed. A boy with burnt fingers appeared and asked for a salve; he applied a picrate and the boy left, his hands smeared with the yellow lotion. Suddenly, Evandro heard the police siren near the Whale Ship, the best known of the topiaries in the square. Soldiers scurrying, gesticulating frantically, someone approaching. At that moment, Dona Idalina came into the pharmacy for her nightly injection. The only way she could sleep peacefully, without being troubled by nightmares full of men making indecent proposals. The injection took a long time; first Dona Idalina had to be calmed down, as she was afraid she might faint and the pharmacist would take advantage of her. Evandro was used to this, for he had been observing this ritual for five years. His life had become a series of permanent ceremonies. What he couldn't explain was the loss of the notion of time, because—between the removal of Edevair's body and the discovery of Manuela—many hours went by.

Dona Idalina left, slowly, in the direction of the nearby two-story house. She barely had strength to climb the stairs; she had been known to fall asleep on the last step, awake with bodily pains, go down and get an injection of Voltaren. Evandro went to the door. The light rain was still falling, and in front of the Whale Ship he could make out a swarm of blinking red lights, disjointed sentences, a policeman cordoning off the area with sawhorses and tape. Curious, Evandro advanced, excusing himself, shoving, an uncomfortable feeling in his kidneys. As he was known, they let him through. The police greeted him, thinking he was there officially. Thus he arrived at the exact moment when the body was being turned over for identification. The police photographer's flash lit up the scene. A spotlight was turned on, information was shouted. Evandro looked at that face and at the bystanders. He was dumbfounded, his fingertips tingled. The face seemed to widen, explode. And then he heard, again, repeated by a policeman, "It's Manuela, what a juicy piece! What a waste! And I never had her!" The name echoed through the square. Evandro fainted and was carried back to his own pharmacy.

HOW CAN MOSQUITOES POOP UPWARDS?

1

Evandro opened his eyes and saw he was lying on a bench. He recognized the ceiling of the pharmacy. Old boards covered by thick coats of yellow paint marked by thousands of black specks. Mosquito poop. How can they poop while upside down, their feet gripping the surface? he wondered in the evenings in the deserted pharmacy when he would sit and look at that ceiling, his curse. He had been there for nineteen years. Since the day those time-worn boards had been painted by Gentil, the same man who had done for Evandro's father the posters for the movie theater, reproducing vague semblances of the actors' faces. The painter was disappointed. He considered painting ceilings a lesser task, but he was a steady worker, an elderly man who would find no other work if he left the film exhibition business that Evandro's father had run since the 1920s. Though the old man did try. He wanted to draw the great men of science, like Eilhardt Mitscherlich, discoverer of selenic acid and the Law of Isomorphism. Or Eudoxus of Cnidas, the Greek astronomer and mathematician who, 350 years before Christ, discovered that the 365-day year has six extra hours. Or Sir Thomas Clifford Allbutt, inventor of the thermometer. Evandro grew excited about the idea, having those people overhead, like the ceiling of the Sistine Chapel. He was surprised: where did Gentil acquire such knowledge? Evandro's father brought the two of them back to reality: paint carefully, in yellow, without wasting time, this is a store for selling medicine, sick people don't care about art.

It was his mother's idea for him to become a pharmacist—she didn't want to die without seeing her son graduate from college. In those days she suffered from granuloma inguinale and had pustules all over her body. Believing that his mother would die soon, Evandro agreed, certain that the fate that pointed him toward the pharmacy was temporary. His studies concluded, he received from his father the space facing the square. It had been a storage room for films when, in addition to showing them, the old man was the leading distributor in the region. Three doors and numerous shelves, a good boost for starting out in life. Faded photos of stars like Lilyan Tashman, Bessie Love, Winifred Greenwood,

Viola Dana, Nita Naldi, and Laura La Plante covered the walls in back and Evandro made an effort to discover who they were and what films they had made, but the local cinematheque was just beginning and limited itself to a few productions filmed in the city in the late forties.

His mother hadn't died. She had gotten used to the pustules, which didn't cause any pain, and spent her time in a chaise longue whose brightly colored print fabric was replaced yearly. There she would receive visitors for canasta and lots of Cuba Libres, constantly complaining about migraines, gastritis (she burped frequently), and her husband, who would fuck women in the armchairs of the Esmeralda's VIP balcony, on the sofa of the manager's office (which she refused to enter), and in the case of some of the more depraved, standing up in the bathroom, which had been a sensation in the city because of its pink lights over the mirrors, an illumination that eliminated facial wrinkles.

When Evandro first opened the pharmacy, there were still no buildings around the square, with their galleries full of stores, precursors of shopping centers. It was a temporary installation, an ephemeral arrangement, bearable long enough to save up the money that would take him to Europe. Part of those savings would come from the pharmacy. Another part, from the jewels that disappeared from his mother's chests. She knew about it. A secret accomplice, she was always asking her husband for necklaces and bracelets, earrings and brooches, pendants and tiaras, a way of expiating his guilt over adultery, as she would tell her friends, all of them drunk on Jamaican rum and sweet vermouth, in the evenings.

Evandro was sure he would be leaving soon, eager to live in Paris. His dream was to start at the Jeu de Paume* museum, copying the Impressionists, then later find his own style. The influence of fascicles sold at newsstands. He was ready to suffer, to go hungry. Every great artist needs a personal tragedy to stimulate creativity. And what profound drama does Arealva offer me? Even the name of the city is small, provincial, despite its airs of grandeur. He had only one friend, Evangelina. Skinny, stoop shouldered, with two enormous pointed breasts, she wore glasses with lenses like the bottom of soda bottles. Possessor of a monumental voice, she was part of the Gilda Parisi Municipal Chorale. Go to São Paulo, everyone advised her, make a career, get a scholarship, study in Europe, sing on television. Shy, she tried to get sponsorship from a juice manufacturing firm but received the reply that culture was pineapple, acerola, orange, and passion fruit—and if they gave grants, it would be to technicians.

Evandro and Evangelina would spend the night at the pharmacy, into which came fewer and fewer people. Most of them drunks, adolescents wanting condoms, poor people looking for hair straightener, youths in alcoholic semi-comas after the dances at the clubs and associations in the neighborhood. How the pharmacy managed to stay in business was the question, although most attributed it to his mother's jewels and an allowance reluctantly given by his father to his fortyish only child. For some time he had undertaken decoration projects for stores and bars but had been squeezed out by the interior decorators' lobby in São Paulo, which had more

---

* He is unaware that the Impressionists were transferred to the Musée D'Orsay, on the Left Bank, a restored railway station.

name and power. Evangelina worked as a bookkeeper for a hamburger franchise and as soon as she left at four thirty would head directly to the pharmacy, where they would sip whiskey with Pedialyte, which when chilled has the pleasant taste of coconut water. The salesmen couldn't understand how they sold so much of that energy drink. The pharmacy never closed, even though Evangelina was terrified of holdups; the area was crawling with bums. Things improved only when there were meetings at the Whale. Then, the police would assign a squad to protect the people who matter.

But every night—it was a mystery, at eight o'clock sharp—Evangelina and Evandro would climb the hill that led to the north of the city and go into a house that everyone considered strange. They would return later, around midnight. The house was a defunct gas station that Evandro had bought in ruins (it cost a bracelet and two earrings, gold and diamonds), remodeled its interior while maintaining in front the two red and yellow pumps for which Shell had offered a fortune, with the intention of placing them in an American museum. No one went in there; Evandro had no maids, bought his food already prepared, frozen. Once a month he would go to São Paulo, returning with large packages transported in the luggage compartment of the bus. Packages in brown paper that aroused the curiosity of the drivers at the bus station, anxious to guess the contents. They ventured indirect questions: Did you buy a TV? Evandro was evasive: A few small personal items that I can't find here in town. And the drivers, with the pride typical of Arealva: What can't be found here in the city, the best in the central eastern region of the state? But the conversations never went anywhere. Evandro would begin looking out the window as if he'd never seen that landscape he'd been familiar with for forty years. Small houses, incomplete, unfinished—one lacked stucco, another the roof; there were only the slab, window frames made from boards taken from crates, shacks of tin, and plastic and piles of sand and bricks that waited year after year for an upturn in finances, an end to inflation, miraculous economic plans. The poor outskirts surrounded Arealva in the shape of an L, to the west. Going toward the north, one made his way into the middle class, and turning to the east, would enter the region of those who matter.

Evandro planned, once in Paris, to live in La Ruche, the famous building that had been home to ateliers of all the artists—Chagall, Picasso, Soutine, Miró. He would go hungry like Hemingway in the twenties and Henry Miller in the thirties. One of them sat in cafés drinking red wine and writing stories, and the other hammered away infernally at his typewriter in his room at the Villa Seurat, going out at night in search of women whom he would later transform into characters. Evandro soon realized there was no climate for Modiglianis drowning in alcohol and tuberculosis (what did he die of? he wondered, and Evangelina promised she'd do some research). No woman would ever be the equal of Anaïs Nin. "And why can't I be your Anaïs?" asked Evangelina, who could find in the library no reference to this woman who dwelled in Evandro's dreams. "You can't because you're very ugly, you're poor, you don't write diaries," he answered, overcome by sudden fury, irritated with Evangelina and with the yellow ceiling full of mosquito poop. He bought a VHS of *Henry and June* and watched it every night, grasping Evangelina's neck and pointing to Maria Medeiros: "That was Anaïs! You think she's like you with those plastic breasts?" Evandro knew—and from that knowledge was born his despair—that there were no more Henry Millers or James Joyces, the latter so skilled in marketing himself, inventor of fellowships for writers to be able to write calmly without having to worry about survival. Paris was no longer the city? Where, then? Berlin, London, New York, Calcutta, Medellín, Botucatu, or simply Arealva, where he was inexorably burying himself?

"Are you all right?"

"Seems like it."

Evandro sat down, startled, looking at the paunchy black policeman in the ochre uniform of the Corporation, a municipal security force linked to the Civil Police.

"What happened?"

"You fainted."

"I fainted?"

"You took one look at Dona Manuela and went out like a light!"

Evandro didn't remember leaving the pharmacy, or crossing the cordoned-off area, much less having seen Manuela. Around him, a small group of the curious.

"Manuela, Mr. Antenor's wife. She's dead."

"Dead?"

"She was found underneath the Whale Ship. Murdered!"

One of the best known bushes in the square. It had taken the gardener years to trim the shape of a whale next to that of a ship. A sculpture out of scale, like a *naïf* canvas, a good hiding place for sweethearts to have sex, adolescents to smoke pot, and muggers to conceal themselves. Uncontrollable shuddering took hold of the pharmacist, who saw a sweaty fat man with a cigarette in the corner of his mouth. Evandro recognized Pedro Quimera, a frequent customer of the pharmacy, an odd sort, a mouth breather, constantly tired, unprotected. His pockets were always full of lottery tickets. Evangelina gave him a hard time but she gave everybody a hard time; perhaps it was a defense mechanism because of the ugliness that left people aghast, except when she sang. Then she was transformed and attracted the public.

"What happened?"

"I don't know . . . I fainted . . ."

"Did you see anything, Evandro?"

"I don't remember. Should I have seen something?"

"The pharmacy was open. The doors face the Whale Ship."

The potbellied policeman was listening to the conversation, with a suspicious demeanor.

"I didn't see anything. But I know who did."

Evandro thought the reporter had something of Sydney Greenstreet about him, without the elegance of the actor in *The Maltese Falcon*. He always associated people with films. That was why he liked Quimera, who knew actors, directors, and actresses from several eras. The reporter had been the only one to recognize the sets from *Gilda*, the Charles Vidor film, in the project Evandro had done for the Crystal Night. A perfect copy that would leave the art directors of Columbia Studios with mouths agape.

"Who saw it?"

"The Nighttime Shoeshine Man. He was by the door waiting for the rain to stop. Suddenly, he ran to the booth, I was giving Idalina her injection. I never saw him so frightened. It can only be because of that. He must have seen it!"

The paunchy policeman ran out the door. Quimera appeared to awaken. He was an intelligent man who suffered from an almost apathetic temperament. Nothing interested him. One night he told Evandro, "Something, someday, will change me. I'm what I don't want to be and don't know how to become what I should be." He was unparalleled when he tried to express himself, without others understanding. A man by himself remains the same his whole life if he refuses to see that moment in which everything opens up and he need only have the courage to cross the line. Anxiously, he asked:

"Where did the Shoeshine Man go? Where can I find him? Where does he live?"

2

Edevair caught the bus in Vila dos Remédios. He showed his retiree card and sat down, placing the plastic gallon container on the pile of newspapers in his lap. He had gone out that hot night determined to make the sacrifice that would cause Brazil to tremble and focus its attention. It was 10:00 P.M. when he got to the square. Edevair was alert, certain that there was nothing else to be done.

From the building at the rear of the square came applause, from time to time. He focused his clouded vision on the neon sign, not understanding what Coral Whale meant. With a silly name like that, it must be a boardinghouse for students; the city was full of them. Edevair saw people leaving the site, irritated. He was unlucky in his choice of day and hour. How could he have foreseen, first, the sudden summer rain that flooded neighborhoods, swept away shacks, and destroyed trees in the square? How could he have imagined that on this, his night, which he had thought about for months until gaining awareness of the necessity of what he was about to do, Manuela was going to die?

Edevair didn't have the slightest idea of who she was. He might have accidentally heard her name or seen her picture in the papers or on the TV news. He wasn't the type of man to buy *Caras*, that new magazine that was causing a sensation. He didn't hear the comments about Manuela's daring to allow herself to be photographed in a bathtub, amid foam produced by Revlon bubble bath, hugging her husband Antenor, who was fifty-something (he said, but his real age was unknown, and there was talk of a few plastic surgeries), muscular, suntanned, habitué of fitness centers.

During Carnival, Manuela had paraded with the Olodum group, in Bahia. She had been in the Sambadrome in Rio and in skybox #11, belonging to a famous illegal lottery boss,* had taken off her blouse in front of TV cameras. She was unlucky, for that same night the president of the republic paraded with an anonymous woman wearing no panties, catching the attention of TV and all the photographers. Unresigned, at the dance at the Scala she took off everything, leaving only her Cartier** watch and her tiny panties. Antenor exhibited the photo published in the magazines, because Manuela's breasts were perfect and he took great

---

* It may have been someone else, but "illegal lottery boss" lends it a certain atmosphere.

** This is not a matter of product placement. The watch was in fashion, and Manuela was wearing what columnists proclaimed as being "in," an expression no longer used by the best people.

pride in them. His enemies were unsparing: he's a cuckold and advertises it. She was well proportioned, even though evil tongues asserted that prior to Carnival she had been to Dr. Pitanguy's plastic surgery clinic.* "This city has more wagging tongues than a truck distributing fruit to the juice factories at harvest time," commented Iramar Alcifes, the provincial pseudonym of a journalist hated by those he called "the corrupt elite" (the people who count and who keep count, as he explained acidly) but loved by people on the outskirts, who read his column every day in a sensationalist paper and listened to his four shows daily on the radio.

What the newspapers later had to say was pure speculation, sensationalism, the stuff of novels. They wrote that, in the moment when Manuela was dying, Edevair was sitting in the square, facing the Cathedral, observed by a crowd of people taking advantage of the cool of the trees and the colorful fountain. He yelled for the people to come closer. "A sarcastic irony of the great God who has forgotten the poor," wrote Iramar, in his cliché-ridden style.

Edevair, carrying the gallon container, newspapers, and rolled-up light cardboard, went from bench to bench, polite and gentle. Inviting sweethearts, adolescents, and elderly couples who had probably been sitting on those benches for decades, enjoying happiness (I regret having to quote Iramar so much), to take part with him in a moment of repulsion and indignation. No one paid much attention. The square and streets were full of bums, the unemployed, and crazies, especially after the freeze on money that the government imposed in March 1990.

---

* Address: Rua Dona Mariana, Botafogo, Rio de Janeiro. I consulted Dr. Pitanguy, but he never reveals the names of his clients.

Edevair sat down on the pile of newspapers, observed disinterestedly by a group of adolescents who were talking about motorcycles, skateboards, and the Jet Ski competition at the Regattas and Navigators the next morning. He shouted: "Come here, please!" No one paid any attention. He shouted two, three times; people imagined he was a Saturday preacher. Edevair opened the container, poured the gasoline over his body, wet the newspapers, and struck a match.

A few seconds were enough to turn Edevair into a human torch. At that moment, the rain began. A violent, unexpected summer cloudburst. The people scattered in confusion. Disturbed. Undecided whether to run for shelter, because there was heavy hail, or to help the old man. There wasn't much left to help. Edevair was frail. His glasses had twisted over his eyes. The flames resisted the water for some minutes. When they went out, they left a charred stump. A boy, before running away, approached and grabbed the scorched poster, burning his fingers. A light blue piece of poster board, with red letters written by a thick Pilot pen:

I AM 74 YEARS OLD   TIRED OF GETING UP
EVERY   AT THRE   IN THE MOR   STANDING
IN LINE AT THE COUNTER   A NUMBER
AND COMING BACK 2 OR 3 TIMES   BEING
MISTREATED   RICH PEOPLE WHO NEVER
WORKED   LIKE ME   46 YEARS
EDEVAIR CASTELLI LOPES, RETIRED, ELETRICITY
CUT OFF, ULCER   HISTERICAL WIFE AND
ZERO IN   BANK.

When the photographers arrived (it was Saturday, so it took some time), there was nothing left. The 27th had removed everything. After all, those who mattered in the city were at the Whale, but there were people outside. Cinematographers and photographers recorded the black stain on the stones.

When the Great Leader's lecture ended and the audience left the auditorium, it was no longer raining and the night was cool. No one had paid attention to the storm because of the excitement stemming from the adoration of gold, diamonds, and the dollar. Few even knew about what happened. Some, led by Antenor, took the Leader to the airport and then went to the Hotel Nove de Julho. Others went to the Crystal Night, vying for impossible tables at that late hour. The café was the city's nerve center, its pulse. Everything converged there, concentrating on Efrahim, the owner, a man who moved in all social classes. Groups spread along the sidewalks, glasses in their hands, waiting for tables to become available on the terraces.

Close to 2:00 A.M., the ones from the sidewalk burst noisily into the café. They were talking loudly, going from table to table, gesturing wildly, and as they leaned over this or that table everyone rose, and within a few moments the entire café was astir. Which startled Efrahim, who by nature was extremely calm, always rubbing one hand slowly against the other.

"Manuela is dead!"

The phrase circulated, women dropped their glasses,* and men downed their whiskey in a single gulp. Some ran to telephones, others took out their cell phones. The sidewalk filled up, cars pulled

---

* Nobody actually drops their glass that way, not even in soap operas.

away, accelerating quickly. But others were arriving, so the café remained packed, with uneasy people coming and going, entering and leaving. That was when Efrahim decided to announce that the birthday party was over and that from then on everyone would be responsible for his own bill. At almost five in the morning, the last "forgetful"* left.

Still dark, it was misting. Efrahim told the manager to leave the place the way it was and send the employees home. When he left, there was a small group on the sidewalk, discussing whether they should go to Antenor's house. "And do what?" asked the deputy mayor, a young millionaire, the owner of a used-motorcycle agency. "Where can Manuela's body be?" two tipsy women in long dresses wanted to know. One of them headed a social assistance league that received money from the state government that went directly into her own account. "Maybe Antenor needs us," said the district judge,** "he must be devastated." Efrahim listened from underneath a tree, one of the last in the old downtown. All of them were being removed to widen the avenue. In the air, the acrid smell from the juice factories, which ran day and night. He loved the city just before daybreak. When he first came to town, the son of Capuano, an immigrant, his first job had been on the graveyard shift at the multinational passion fruit factory.*** He

---

* "Forgetful" is waiters' slang for those who forget to leave, to ask for the check, to have one for the road.
** I omit his name because he is a respectable person who would not like seeing his name among so many lowlifes. He suffers because of his colleagues co-opted by Bradío.
*** Efrahim's father forced him to start working very early in order to learn the value of money. Because of this, the Count was disgusted by events to be related here subsequently.

never forgot walking through the empty streets, happy to have work. Then he heard a familiar sound, wood on wood.

"Aristeu!"

The Shoeshine Man rapped his brush against the wooden box, as he customarily did when he tended to his customers, beginning at 7:00 P.M. He looked at Efrahim, at the group, at the people approaching him.

"Help me, Count!"

"Count" was Efrahim's nickname, because of his calmness, always in dark glasses, rubbing his hands against each other, dressed in Armani suits, shiny shoes.

"Help you?"

"You've gotta hide me!"

"What did you get yourself into?"

"Help me!"

"Is someone going to get you? Silence you for good?"

The Count had an ironic temperament and took pleasure in needling people, whoever they were. Those around him laughed.

"It's 'cause I saw him! The man!"

"What man? Have you gone queer?"

"I saw him. When he got out of the car. And he took Manuela's body. Behind the Whale Ship."

"Who was it?"

"It was raining hard. I was in the pharmacy. Evandro's. I saw the car stop. The man got out. He looked around. There was still an awful wind. It was ripping branches off the trees. He opened the trunk. He took out Manuela's body. He left the square and went away."

"You've been snorting more than you should, Aristeu!"

"The Godfather saw me. It was just me. At the door of the pharmacy. Its lights were on."

"The Godfather? Are you sure? Listen to what you're saying! The Godfather?"

"The Godfather! I saw him! It was him. The pharmacist was giving a shot. To Idalina, the needle woman. He stopped the car. He looked straight at me, like he was saying: you know what'll happen if you talk."

"I know a place! Nobody will look for you there."

He picked up the Nighttime Shoeshine Man's box and took it into the Crystal Night. "It's empty? You already got rid of everything tonight? Is there anything but a brush and shoe polish in here?" He came back carrying a shot of gin. Shoeshine Man was wet; where had he gone after the rain? The Godfather? How valuable would that information be? The Count knew Shoeshine Man; he wouldn't get anything further out of him. He was someone used to confidentiality and knew what opening his mouth meant, because of what he did. Never had a client of the Shoeshine Man found himself suspected of anything, even if he'd been arrested several times. He was protected, although conscious that his impunity depended on silence. People were still murmuring: could it really be the Godfather that the crazy saw? Nobody took the Shoeshine Man seriously, except for those who needed him, and many did. In recent times they were running scared, because he kept a small electronic notebook in which were recorded all the names, who owed, who paid, who placed orders. The group dispersed, with the exception of the district judge. Efrahim pulled Shoeshine Man aside and whispered in his ear.

"I'm going to take you to the cotton-oil factory. There's a hole underneath the rusted-out press. People are afraid to go there. Tomorrow I'll come for you and bring food. Don't leave the place. I have to figure out what to do, where to send you."

"As long as they don't send me to the Floral Mansion. Not there, for the love of God!"

"Keep quiet, you've said too much already. You're getting to be senile. Come on, let's go to the factory. As soon as the people leave."

"What about the ghosts, Count? What if the mad locomotive engineer shows up? Or if the locomotive comes through? Right on top of me?"

"The living kill a lot more than the dead."

"The Godfather! He's gonna kill me, Count."

When Efrahim looked, the judge seemed to be listening.

3

For many years the city would remember the next day, October 18, known as The Sunday of Manuela. A historic date, set aside in all our calendars. In the same vein were: The Lynching Night; The Thursday When the Hangman Arrived; The Night of the Great Fire in the Cotton-Oil Factory, which left ghosts wandering about the ruins and where no one dares enter; The Afternoon the Train Crashed into the Station Bar, killing thirty-seven people; The Night the Terrorists Poisoned the Milk from the Dairy Farm; The Friday the Bishop Went Mad and Brought Christ Down from the Cross with an Axe; The Noon the Bomb Destroyed the Vault at the

Bank of Brazil and all the money was carried off by subversives; The Saturday the Ninety-Mile-an-Hour Wind Tore the Roofs Off Half the Houses.

The Crystal Night reopened at nine thirty in the morning, as it did every Sunday. Efrahim ordered a cleaning-up. He was unsure whether the normal Sunday brunch crowd would appear. It did. Earlier than usual. Many had tried to go to Antenor's house. There was a single wide, landscaped avenue that went to Hydrangea Gardens, closed off by police barriers, which led to a traffic jam.* The newspaper offices were opened, editorial staff convened. Extra editions were expected, the dream of romantic editors. Those old extras that were quickly sold out. It had been years because of the growing popularity of television since extra editions circulated, sold on the streets by a legion of young newsboys.

There was no Sunday atmosphere; it seemed like a normal day. All that was missing was for the shops to open their doors. Restaurants foresaw a great deal of business. Two events at the same time. It was too much! Manuela dead and a man self-immolated right in the square protesting against the government. Ideologies and arguments reawakened in the editorial rooms. Who should get the front page? The bourgeois woman or the massacred man of the people? Arguments between militants of workers' parties, the habitual socialists on duty, middle-aged editors, more mature—and therefore cynical about the role of the press—the conservative editorialists and the wild-eyed men who incline toward anarchism.

---

* A notable traffic jam because of the Mercedes-Benzes, Mitsubishis, Hondas, Alfa Romeos, Camrys, Toyotas, Renaults, Audis. In the interior, the people are either indifferent—in order to avoid the impression of provincialism—or extremely curious.

"A dazzling* woman or some poor devil without a pot to piss in who was foolish enough to set himself on fire like those human-torch Buddhist monks of the sixties? And let's not forget that socialite killed in Búzios in the seventies. What was her name? It was worth thousands of lines, hundreds of pages, we sold papers like crazy. Angela something. Go hit the archives, we're going to show that Brazil hasn't changed, still male chauvinist and rife with impunity! Manuela. Was it her husband who killed her? Did she commit suicide? Let's look into the old man. Blame the government for his death. Make it into a national case, bring the people out into the streets, stir up the student radicals. Where are the feminist organizations in Arealva? How can we link the two cases? Why not put them both on the front page?"

Manuela was the lead story. Sleepless reporters, rousted out of bed, returning from dances and bars, had to think fast. What interest could Edevair arouse? The public doesn't like stories it already knows, doesn't want to hear about its own misfortunes. The retiree's tale was all too familiar. It happened every day, with your neighbor, your father-in-law, your mother. The only difference was the fireball into which he had transformed himself. This was the reason for excitement. Nevertheless, no photographer got there on time. If one had, it'd be a full-page photo, sold throughout Brazil, and eventually picked up by the international agencies. The photographer would get rich. The impact would bring down the government, ministers, the mayor. "For those who don't believe such things happen in Brazil," sighed the diaphanous Angelica.

---

* A word that Luisão loves, much used in the 1950s.

Manuela was a delicate dish, as tasty as the salmon carpaccio at the Nove de Julho. A woman everyone saw but about whom they knew so little. Married to an older man who had the reputation of a lecher. She would disappear for weeks at a time, then reappear, racing down the streets in her turquoise Civic or her showy red BMW convertible. Manuela, an irascible woman: had slapped the ticket taker at the movie theater who had the audacity to say she had a lover in Belo Horizonte. The woman who bought her makeup in Rio de Janeiro, had a rented apartment in Miami, went skiing in Las Leñas, gambled in casinos in Aruba. The pious woman who never missed a novena in the Church of St. Judas, in São Paulo, taking three candles as tall as she was. Who had challenged everybody by exhibiting her breasts with silicone nipples, the women claimed. Who gave enormous tips to manicurists, fitness instructors, clerks at boutiques, and masseurs, but who could also get them fired over some complaint. And who got people fired for the sheer pleasure of it.

Every newsroom had bulging folders. The negatives in which Manuela appeared would have covered the Arealva-Manaus highway.* No photo, however, older than twelve years, when she had met Antenor, marrying him a year later. They could have gotten married sooner, but it took place at the Spring Dance, in September 1983, at the club. As proof of his great love, before the dance began, Antenor, wearing an outfit purchased in Europe, had to jump into the chilly swimming pool. "If you jump in, I'll marry you," she shouted, and he went into the water.** He didn't hesitate. The end of the playboy,

---

* The highways are in terrible shape.
** Innocent acts of madness, absolutely ingenuous, just imagine. Almost childish!

discredited before his friends, the Group of Perverts. Famous for one night having dumped hundreds of pounds of strawberry-flavored Tang into a neighborhood's water tank and then calling people to say that the blood of Jesus was coming out of the taps. People fled into the streets, falling to their knees in prayer.[*]

An extra edition would be a juicy morsel that Sunday when the population was in the streets, filling the club, the Crystal Night, and the Regattas, and all the restaurants had placed tables outside. A newspaper to be sold in the neighborhoods.[**] Who wouldn't be curious to see the ruined body of one of the most beautiful women in the city? Everyone was expecting fantastic revelations about a mysterious life. There was still no photo or information. Nothing but word of mouth, busy telephone lines, cell phones tied up. Television and radio set up outside the entrance to Hydrangea Gardens, the condominium where Antenor lived. Everything blocked off. The police opened the apron for certain autos to enter. By the make and the license plate it was easy to tell who they were: CEOs, businessmen, bankers, politicians. What about the other cars with smoked glass? Whom were they carrying? Plates were jotted down for the newsrooms to investigate. Except that it was Sunday, so they wouldn't find out until tomorrow, if they could be identified at all. A green and white helicopter descended inside the walls. Half an hour later it left. Was it Antenor fleeing? To Miami, London, Paris,

---

[*] The Group of Perverts could provide material for a novel or a film that might be directed by Mario Monicelli, of *My Friends*.

[**] Commercial contacts were set in motion to arrange ads or sponsorships from businesses. An impasse resulted. If they took out ads, Antenor would oppose them; if they didn't, they would make enemies of the newspapers. *O Expresso* played hardball, truly blackmail.

Bangkok, Salzburg? Was he accompanied by his psychic? The two were inseparable. Had the psychic foreseen Manuela's death? Or had the copter come to pick up one of the rich people who had nothing to do with the case?

Extra editions were decided on. People were dispatched to gather statements, to research Manuela's life. "Who was she, beyond the rumors, the gossip, the unsubstantiated talk? Did she have some close female friend? Who'd she hang out with? There was an old nurse, a faithful retainer, and they would go everywhere together, but she disappeared after the death of the son. What've we got on the death of that son who drowned in a swimming pool? Who was the doctor who treated her? Find Maciel, the gynecologist who lost his license. He was always at her side; they were supposedly lovers." All the newspapers had the same idea at the same time. But friends' phones didn't answer. Reporters went to clubs, churches, squares, homes. Maciel had no address and his place of residence was unknown; he would appear around town and then vanish. "A total eclipse in high society," commented the editor of O Expresso, one of the oldest papers. Founded at the time when the city was the gateway to the west of the state, for anyone crossing to the state of Mato Grosso, or going north to the state of Minas Gerais or south to the state of Paraná. Expresso had begun as an intercity rapid-delivery company and was today an intricate holding company that ran one of the best-selling dailies. "If her friends don't want to talk, let's hear from her enemies. And if no one talks, we'll run an edition with just pictures, Brazil is crawling with illiterates. I want the sexiest photo you can find." It was still the one from the Scala dance—so recent, so stunning, at the height of her physical form and beauty, as Iramar* characterized her in his morning program. Even he, always so angry, had spared Antenor. Lawyers hurried to newsrooms asking for time, care in the coverage. If the request seemed about to be refused, the men displayed mysterious, sealed briefcases.**

Pedro Quimera entered the newsroom after a thirty-minute nap. He felt sticky, but the water in the kitchenette where he lived was out. He was worked up at the prospect of breaking the Sunday morning tedium. Anybody who wasn't a member of a club and didn't own a car or motorcycle had nothing to do but watch television with its rural, ecological programs, children's cartoons, Catholic Mass or preachers of ever-newer religions. There was arena soccer and team handball, but you had to rent the space months in advance because they were constantly sold out. And if there was anything Quimera hated, with that huge body of his, it was exhausting himself in the sun, sweating, running, getting tired, panting. A plastic surgeon had recommended liposuction, to be paid in installments, but the thought of being sucked through the belly with a vacuum horrified him. Even his relationship with Yvonne left him bewildered. How could she like him, with his misshapen physique, the object of jokes in the newsroom? But she had admitted being excited by fat, flabby skin, by the thought of being crushed underneath.

---

* Iramar, who enjoys attacking famous people to gain listeners, never uttered an original phrase.
** Politicians have a strange fear of mysterious briefcases. Do you remember the famous TV debate between two presidential candidates in which one of them lost his courage—and the election—when he saw the briefcase his opponent was carrying?

On Sundays, another prospect that irritated him was drinking beer in a bakery, eating slices of salami, cheese wraps, greasy sausages, or snack foods that gave him heartburn just from looking at them. On the outskirts, people were playing football, singles vs. marrieds, with the veteran teams of bald and potbellied men, heart attack survivors and retirees, eager to demonstrate that they were in good shape. The calmer ones contented themselves with dominoes, checkers, canasta, horseshoes, or bocce. Activities not in the least exciting. A completely unknown facet of Quimera's personality* was his participation in the secret Organized Antifans Group. Ever since he was hit in the stomach by a stone thrown by a fan of the Arealva Football Club, a second-division team, Pedro had suffered from gastritis, which bothered him greatly, always imagining that he had bad breath when everything started burning inside him. At an AFC game against Palmeiras, in the war between cheering sections, he realized there were people who were rooting against both sides. He approached and saw that these individuals identified themselves by a small wristband on which was written "Cat." He followed the group, learned of its aims, and adopted the cause with such dedication that he ended up as regional leader. The Cats attack aggressively, slashing the tires of buses, planting bombs in the clubs, tying foul-smelling ribbons next to the nostrils, forcing people to drink from polluted rivers. But when out of earshot of whistles, the sound of boot against leather, curse words, Quimera is calm, relaxed, laid-back.

Luisão, the editor of *O Expresso*, believed in the images propagated by film and literature. He liked to role-play. He would yell,

---

* A man hides so many things!

hurl insults, slam down the telephone, bang his fist against the desk, and the only reason he didn't rip up copy was that it was composed on computers. But he was famous for tearing poorly written articles into tiny shreds. He wore glasses on the tip of his nose, kept a cigar in the corner of his mouth, and used an incredible green eyeshade straight out of an American film of the forties, written by Ben Hecht.

"I've dug up a lead," said Pedro, sitting uneasily across from Luisão. At the age of thirty-one, he still wasn't sure he wanted to be a journalist, while the other man was, and one of the best, independent of the fantasies he employed to create his image.

"You dig it up with your hands or did you need a shovel? Are we talking go-cart or Formula 1?"

"I have some good information! I got it from Evandro, of the How Come," said Pedro, ignoring the sarcasm. When he sweated, he noticed nothing. He felt bad.

"Evandro? The ET? Now that I think about it, from his pharmacy you can see everything. The Whale Ship's right across from it."

"He fainted when he saw Manuela!"

"Strange! The guy's weird, always with that skinny woman with the big tits."

"But he knows something."

"Manuela used to spend a lot of time at the pharmacy," commented the diaphanous Angelica, who bore that name because her mother had fallen in love with the TV series *The Marquise of the Angels* during her pregnancy.

"Right there in downtown? That pharmacy only deals in Lexotan, Prozac, Valium."

"And she stuffed herself. Lately she was walking around like a zombie."

"I have to send a reporter."

"It's my find," protested Pedro.

"Did you pay for it?"

Luisão had both disdain and admiration for Pedro Quimera. He gave him a hard time even about his name, although in moments of good humor he considered it poetic. The reporter was dawdling, came in late, missed work, and was slow to write. Still, once he made up his mind, he wrote sensitive texts, knew how to manage sentences, even if he did make up a lot. He fabricated too much, had gotten into two lawsuits, and had been warned: once more and he was through! He didn't seem worried about it. Luisão attempted to observe him, trying to discover what made Pedro tick, where he wanted to go in life. There were no clues; he gave the impression of swimming against the tide, without noting the direction. Now and then, a flash of excitement would appear in his eyes.

"I'm the one who found the lead!"

"I can't send a jerk-off, because I don't know when you'll come back with the material. But did the pharmacist say anything? Maybe this'll be your day. Maybe you'll catch the Good-Bye Angel."

"The Angel's an obsession, huh?"

That morning, Luisão was in a bad mood. He had been called away from the bar, where he was stuffing himself with greasy fried chicken drumsticks.

"The Nighttime Shoeshine Man saw the guy! The one who took Manuela out of the car and put her behind the bush. He was in a Civic."

"The blue one? The socialite's car?"

"Don't know. With the heavy rain you couldn't see anything. He wasn't a strong man, he had problems dragging the body. It was pulled by the feet. The head must've really been messed up."

Pedro Quimera was making it up. Having fun. What he said had a logical basis: someone had had to drag the body.

"I'm going to check with the coroner to see if they've let in the press. The body is locked up, under guard. You go chase down the Shoeshine Man. Maybe we can figure out what's with this guy! Anybody know where he lives?"

No one in the newsroom had any idea. He always appeared after seven at night, banging his brush against the side of the box and playing a tiny harmonica. But the brush didn't control the rhythm, it was a nervous tic, or perhaps a trademark. He circulated in bars, at the door of clubs, in video arcades, and complained that today's youth never shined their shoes. He hated sneakers and had tried to attack kids because of them.

"Alderabá! What about Antenor? Did you find the man?"

"He disappeared yesterday. No one saw him after the orgy at the hotel. I went by the coroner's. He'd just left. The reporter from Sunrise Radio said Antenor got into a fight with Morimoto, the coroner."

Alderabá was the best reporter in the city. Clever and pushy, he had worked for the magazine *Manchete*, in Rio de Janeiro, and his greatest glory was having helped find the clue leading to the hairdresser killer of Claudia Lessin, the young woman who died from drugs.

"Interview Morimoto, he'll open up. He's from the Portella crowd."

"He's vanished too. The big thing in the city today is disappearances. Bradío announced a press conference for noon."

"That sly fox was at the orgy in the hotel."

"One of these days, that'll be the hot news, the Nove de Julho orgies. Talk about decadence, a bunch of potbellied guys in their fifties screwing call girls!"

"What about Maciel?"

"He was seen last night, at the pharmacy. Seems he was at Evandro's house in the evening."

"At that gas station? What's there?"

"And where was Manuela seen?"

"She was at the Crystal Night. Everybody was there, it was open-bar, after she left her husband."

"Hunt down Antenor. Maciel. The Shoeshine Man. I want everyone on it. Alderabã, you have to get into Antenor's house somehow. Go to the lake, rent a boat. Didn't you get into Cumbica Air Base when Jânio resigned? Aren't you famous for being the only one who did?"

"At the time, he was only eighteen and didn't give a shit. Today he's a doddering old man."

The success of Alderabã, a journalist from the old school, was a source of irritation to the younger reporters.

"Who can arrange for me to get into the Regattas? It's the only entrance to the lake. Those people are very snobbish."

"See if Alencastro's at home. He's a member and has a boat, and he's a friend of ours!"

"The forecast is for more heavy rain!"

"I want Antenor, the Shoeshine Man, I want stories. Interview Manuela's girlfriends, get what you can from the pharmacist. Find Morimoto, put the squeeze on the café owner—she practically lived there, in that room in the rear."

Luisão was excited; he was an editor from the old times whose blood circulated best when he smelled a good story. He pointed to Pedro:

"Go have a talk with the Godfather."

"The old guy from the Snooker? What can he possibly know? It's another world."

"Manuela frequented the Crystal Cue, years ago, when she first came to the city. That was when she became famous; the Crystal Cue would be filled with people who wanted to see her play—she was really good. Nobody knows where she came from, who her family is. Now's a good time to research that in the civil registry. Look up the marriage papers, go through the public records, she's got to have been born *somewhere*."

"The Snooker? Who would've thought it. That hole?"

"It was once the nicest playing area in the region. A lot of dough was spent there. Find out what Manuela was doing in that place . . . Maybe there's something else around. Do a story about the afternoons of a lonely young woman in a pool hall."

"If you know so much, why don't you do the story?"

"I've done enough articles in my time. Because there are articles that I can't do and others that I can't publish."

Pedro Quimera had a flash. He would like to be Luisão. What did he know but couldn't tell? What was the relationship between the Godfather and Manuela? A shady old man, supposedly a millionaire, a usurer, a picturesque figure in the city, feared for reasons that were far from clear. Luisão sometimes wondered about his strange ties to Pedro. He considered him enigmatic, never saying what he felt, coming across as submissive, but at certain moments it was apparent he was furious. He dreamed about winning the lottery. He tried endless combinations of numbers, roamed around the city, one bet at each lottery outlet. On weekends he would make plans on how to spend the money and give TV interviews. His fear was that he would win, only to have the manager of the lottery agency run off with his receipt.

In recent times Pedro was obsessed by the notion that he was turning into an invisible man. People looked at him without seeing him. Even Yvonne hadn't located him at the shopping center one night, looking everywhere, when he was right in front of her. Was this a new ability he had acquired, or was he losing his personality, gradually disappearing?

He spoke of an Yvonne, who must be his girlfriend, but she'd never been seen with him. Luisão believed that in his ingenuousness, with his sly face, Pedro could convince the Godfather to talk. He might be able to discover what Manuela did at the Snooker those afternoons with the windows closed. Luisão had been the first to publish an article about her in *O Expresso* and had felt that Manuela was dissimulating, giving evasive answers. Maybe she wasn't all that intelligent, just a society doll.* Then a custodial worker arrived with a copy of *A Lista*. With two photos on the front page. A close-up of Manuela and Edevair burning. How had they gotten it?

---

* Another expression from Luisão's vocabulary. Would a glossary at the end of the book be better, so the new generations can understand?

CHAMPAGNE AT THE GARDEN WATERFALLS

1

When *A Lista* hit the streets, it was the only one out, and people fought over it. The paper normally sold less than two thousand copies, between members of unions and class-based organizations, retired railroad workers and pensioners of the defunct Highway Department. It was purchased from inertia, put under one's arm and then forgotten. At the time of college entrance exams it enjoyed good sales with its listing of successful candidates, since there are eight universities in the region, some of them created to provide sinecures and to further political ambitions. The name of the news-paper reflected its origins. It had begun as a bulletin that listed the names of successful candidates in the examinations for jobs with the railroad, the savings bank, and the revenue department in the thirties and forties. It would also publish ads when large firms at the time—the factories manufacturing tin cans, shoes, hats, hand-kerchiefs, scissors—needed workers. The first news items and ar-ticles came out when the leaders of class-based organizations saw they had no access to the major newspapers for discussion of wage grievances or complaints about work conditions.

A Lista sold seventy thousand copies in the sixties and seven-ties, when Arealva broke out of the lethargy in which it had lived for decades, beginning a developmental process driven by the concession of free land exempt from taxation for twenty years. When that period ended, money began to flow and the city was named number three in economic growth,[*] an attractive site for investment. Seeing *A Lista*'s success, the larger papers entered the sector, opening space to areas previously forbidden. *A Lista* sur-vived with official notices from the city government, small classi-fied ads, funeral announcements, and subsidies from minor politi-cians who couldn't find space in the media dominated by Antenor and Portella. *A Lista* was shut down in April 1964, despite having supported the military coup that took power, and was reopened in 1970. The newspaper changed hands and ideology, becoming reactionary, the mouthpiece of evangelists who later abandoned

---

[*] That designation, conferred by an important economic periodical, cost the city government millions, stated Adriano Portella. Tape #12 of the recordings made in Miami.

it in favor of a television station; once again combative, it merely gained the nickname "chameleon."

Its extra edition showed a front page divided in two. On one side, a man on fire in the public square. On the other, Manuela, smiling, in a string bikini, by the pool at the Regattas. The burning man was merely a crude montage done on a computer. On the 11:00 A.M. program, a disagreeable appetizer for the corrupt, Iramar bellowed, as advertised, "We're going to run a Roto-Rooter through the sewers of the corrupt elite! The death of this socialite will be the key to prison for lots of people!"

The rabble was beside itself with joy. The ones who mattered turned off the radio. Not that they customarily listened to Iramar, but on that Sunday there was no information, so the thing to do was to try to find out if news would be coming from somewhere. What had promised to be a peaceful day, with the Jet Ski competition, had changed. Anxious phone calls. Antenor's telephone line gave a continuous busy signal. Even the unlisted numbers. The phones must be off the hook. Veritable pilgrimages headed for the clubs. There, by piecing together bits from various persons, stories were woven. Which of them was true? No one cared. No one ever cared. Truth is put to use according to convenience; it's either accepted or rejected if it doesn't serve our purposes.

Access to Hydrangea Gardens was becoming worse and worse. The thermometers in the Alfa Romeos read: external temperature, 99 degrees. What about the funeral? Will it be today? Has the body been released? There was an enormous amount of curiosity. Everybody was itching to see the body of Manuela. Was it at home or still at the morgue? Was Antenor obstructing the investigation? Was Manuela disfigured? In such heat, putrefaction must be setting in. After all, she had died the night before. At what time? Only the coroner knew. Cell phones going crazy. There was no way to move ahead, back up, or escape along the jammed sidewalks. People began arriving from the outskirts. Watching planes at the airport, the usual pastime, had been forgotten. Fragments of conversation. The condo barrier lifted, the people murmured, shoved, squeezed, necks craned, some were leaning on others. They wanted to see who came or left.

People were formulating a way of getting past the security guards and making a dash to Antenor's house to catch a glimpse of the most splendorous garden in the city, with its mazes of vegetation. To see whether it was true that there was a waterfall. Natural on normal days, it flowed champagne or beer on party days. And the 830-yard slide that ended in the pineapple-shaped swimming pool. Antenor had begun his fortune by selling scratch-off lottery tickets on the beaches of Rio.* The garden had been designed by a landscape artist from Rio de Janeiro, paid for with money embezzled from Social Security. Only *A Lista* had published this information, and there was a lawsuit pending against it, brought by the attorney Bradío.

No, this morning there would be no naked people in the pool, as was murmured. Manuela wasn't alive to show her body to friends. And what about the grotto dedicated to St. Lucia? Could it really perform miracles, as employees, fired for telling reporters about

---

* There are so many versions that I get lost. It can't even be proved that Antenor was ever in Rio de Janeiro. There's one version that claims he was in a reform school.

Sunday mornings, claimed? The grotto was built by Antenor, in gratitude for not having lost sight in his right eye from the bullets he took soon after marrying Manuela. Bullets fired by Dr. Maciel, handsome and elegant in those days, courteous and oozing with good manners, so much so that he was in charge of the ceremonies for City Hall and the Chamber of Commerce when governors, ministers—he received two presidents of Brazil—or foreign entrepreneurs came to town.

A yellow car, falling apart, stopped behind the last car in line, announcing: "Pure cream of corn! The best pamonhas from Piracicaba." Snow cone vendors watched the shaved ice disappear under green, yellow, blue, and red syrup. The speakers of a hot dog cart, at full volume, played Chico Buarque's "Geni," until a security guard made him turn it off. "It's a lack of respect."

Quimera wandered about, observing the multitude. Any mass of people threw him into a panic. The smell of sweat and cheap perfume, mixed with the unbearable stench of sugarcane rum coming from the fields, made him nauseous. He had considered writing about the curiosity that tragedies arouse in crowds but changed his mind. Sweat soaked his shirt; he felt ill. He thought about his utopia, the dream of being admired, of being successful. He looked at those people, thirsty for Manuela's blood, and thought that, once he achieved success, he would need all his cunning and wit to maintain it, because in Brazil they always try to bring down anyone who makes it, and they employ all their wiles. Perhaps because he thought that way he admired—never admitting it—Antenor and his businesses, his purported coups, the life he led, the strange and beautiful wife he had. Now, certainly,

Antenor would capitalize on popular emotion, would turn the table and make himself the victim, because in Bridi he had the best adviser to take him to the governorship. Pedro knew that Bridi was preparing a program of modernization of the country to be revealed gradually by the press. Authority, opening Brazil to foreign capital, admission to the First World, and total denationalization were points that were occasionally leaked, finding their way to the media at the opportune moment. Quimera decided to go to the Snooker. He walked half a mile, until he came to an intersection and caught the bus. He collapsed onto the seat with such force that the fare taker asked, "What's with you? You nuts?"

Unlike that upscale condominium,* a highly protected island, the old downtown area was deserted. He passed the Lev Gadelha Museum and thought about going in. It must be cool in there, it was the coziest place in the city. Quimera was usually the sole visitor to the museum, the display rooms were empty. There was talk of closing it down, relocating it on the outskirts where real estate was much less expensive, in order to take advantage of the monumental site and erect skyscrapers and galleries full of small boutiques. The project existed, a copy of La Défense, in Paris. The stumbling block was a legal document, exceedingly well worded by the Hugo Fortes legal firm, one of the most powerful in Brasilia. The old millionaire Lev Gadelha, crazy about ancient science, who read hieroglyphics and Sanskrit, an adept of Esperanto,

---

* "Ghetto. It's a deluxe ghetto. The residents are superrich prisoners," argued Dorian Jorge Freire as he drank passion fruit juice with vodka, which made him recall his youth in Mossoró. Where he was born and to which he would return, resolved to begin a monastic life. "Only asceticism can save a man," he sighed.

had made his fortune manufacturing economically priced alcohol lamps sold in India, China and African countries. He had donated the building and hundreds of lots to the city, with the condition that for 120 years no commercial interest could take possession of them. But a legal consultancy hired by Antenor, Portella, and other businessmen was looking for a way to break the contract.

Pedro had gooseflesh when he thought that the old thirty-room house—it was rumored that Lev Gadelha, who had spent some years in Egypt, kept a harem—with thick walls, always cool, a backyard full of fruit trees, an anachronism in the middle of town, might disappear under bulldozers. The site occupied three blocks, and Lev Gadelha had built high walls, covered in ivy, between one block and the next, and because the garden was below street level, everything had been excavated, lowered. Quimera imagines a time when the display windows, which contain documents, historical objects from the city and Brazil, come to house jeans, shoes, panties, bras, purses, gowns, pants, videotapes. Where will the small four-hundred-year-old Chinese dragon, which has a room all its own, go? An object made of platinum and precious stones, hermetically sealed in a glass dome on a concrete pedestal, that continually nods its head, as if responding to a light breeze. Pedro is one of the few who are astonished at this mystery, moved by such preciosity.

He arrived at the Crystal Cue. He had never been to the place, situated between the railroad station and the municipal theater. He rang the bell, twice, five times. He heard a sharp noise, and the door opened. An old staircase, with a greasy carved handrail and worn steps, led to the upstairs floor. Walls of a faded red. From somewhere came the sound of an opera, Bizet's *Carmen*, though he preferred Otto Preminger's *Carmen Jones*, with Dorothy Dandridge.* He stopped, remembering Dorothy with a red rose between her lips, singing "Dat's Love." For a second he thought of the actress dying of cancer while still so young. In front of him stood a fat creature with very green eyes, blocking the way distrustfully.

"Who are you? We're closed. It's Sunday!"

"I want to talk to the Godfather, I'm a reporter."

"He's smoking his Number 6 cigar and won't see anybody till he's finished. Stay right there! Don't climb a single step, not one, or I'll tell him and he won't see you! You don't know the Godfather!"

She went up, limping and farting. She took some time returning and when she did, she was carrying a mug of beer. "C'mon, he gave the OK." Pedro entered the large room. He never imagined it was so big. He'd once read a puff piece about Arealva that cited the Crystal Cue as being similar to the Hall of Mirrors in Versailles. Pedro had vowed he'd see for himself, if he ever got to France. Peeling mirrors covering the immense walls, in frames made in Cuzco, dingy chandeliers, a huge balcony worthy of an English club. Atmosphere: art deco. Empty bottles, most of them rum, Paulista Fire, Egg Liqueur, Kimmel, Old Eight, vermouth, Jurubeba, cognac and beer, all on shelves that in a distant past were once silver-plated.

"And the Godfather?"

---

* In CinemaScope. Bizet was adapted by Oscar Hammerstein II. One of the scenes that I, the author, like best is Husky Miller, the boxer, singing "Stan' Up an' Fight."

The woman grunted, pointing to the old man who was smoking, leaning against the window that looked out over the Old Municipal Market. She observed Pedro for a time, then bent down to pick up a cloth, dipped it in a bucket, and began to mop the floor. The cloth was even dirtier than the deteriorating boards.

"What you want, boy?"

"Are you the Godfather?"

"To those who know me! Those who don't, call me by my name."

"Which is?"

"Only after you get to know me. What do you want?"

"To talk about Manuela."

"Talk about what?"

"They told me this was the first place in town she went into when she arrived."

"So what?"

"So you knew her very well, you've got a lot of information."

"And what's that information for?"

"For the paper! I'm a reporter. From O *Expresso.*"

"Ah, Luisão sent you? Why don't you write about him? He's more interesting. I'll help you. About that, I know a lot! If there's gossip in the Crystal Night, there's gossip here too. Different people, naturally. Long before the police discovered the body, it was known here that Manuela was dead. Write about Efrahim. It was no doubt him who gave Luisão the idea for you to come here. Why hasn't any Jew in the city ever complained about the name of the café?* Although, there aren't many Jews in this city."

---

* Finally, a reaction to the name of the café.

Pedro was bothered. The Godfather gave off a strange indefinable smell. He had the eyes of a rat, appeared to be very old yet at the same time displayed impressive firmness. There are people who spread anxiety around themselves, without our being able to determine what it is. A dry, authoritarian voice. The Godfather looked Quimera directly in the eyes.

"Tell me! Manuela! How did she die?"

"Murdered."

"Out with it! By shooting, stabbing? Poisoned, strangled, hanged, beaten to death, hacked with a machete, run over, raped? And what do I have to do with it? What's Luisão up to? He's like that"—rubbing two fingers together—"with Efrahim, the café owner. They're setting me up for something. How did she die, this Manuela?"

Pedro didn't have an answer. He could only think of pamonha. Was this any time to think about that?

2

The Crystal Cue was cold, as if it had air-conditioning. It smelled of cigarettes, alcohol, bodies sweaty from the tension of pocketing the right ball. Everything looked old. Even the walls showed streaks, like varicose veins ready to explode.

"Lindorley, pull me a draft. Lots of head."

The crippled cleaning woman turned with an expression of fury. She took the wet cloth from the bucket and splashed water on the wide floorboards.

"You know how I hate pulling drafts!"

"Nobody asked you! Bring two. For me and—"

"Pedro."

"I'm allergic to pulling drafts. I'm already doing a lot to be working on Sunday!"

The Godfather went over to Lindorley, cuffed her a couple of times, grabbed her by the nape of the neck, and placed her in front of the beer tap. Pedro Quimera was bothered. There were locations in the city whose existence he never suspected. He had heard talk about the Godfather, but everything was vague, reference to things that had no relation to him, connected to illegalities, violence, corruption. Till now the Godfather had just been a distant character belonging to another world, one he had never thought of approaching. The Crystal Cue, even in its run-down state, situated as it was in a dirty, polluted place, was coming back into style, frequented by those who mattered, in a wave of nostalgia and revivals. Beautiful people were there at night, and the photos in the society pages recorded a background with bums and petty criminals who seemed to be enjoying themselves. Even *Vogue* had contacted them to reserve the place for a shoot, planning to bring Cindy Crawford and Gisele Zelauy to Arealva. The Godfather was off-putting and at the same time fascinating. He seemed drunk, or could he be on drugs?

"All you need now to complete your meanness is to put Natchi Kingy Colee on the record player singing 'Faseenayshon.' You're bad, Godfather."

"And you're a stinking, ungrateful sow. You ought to kiss my hand."

"The hand of a leper, you're gonna get leprosy, Godfather. You're gonna get cancer. Tuberculosis, a real big-time case. AIDS. AIDS alone will kill you!"

"She's like that, but she pulls the best draft in the city."

By his vocabulary, he must be from the city of São Paulo, though he dragged his s's like a native of Rio. The reporter had the impression that the two of them enjoyed that mutual aggression. A game whose reasons they alone knew. Maybe even they didn't know. It was what it was and that's that. The problem is that we constantly try to justify our every act, gesture, or word. Not them. They just live, without worrying. The draft came and Lindorley displayed a docile acrobatic agility as she handled the tray, limping unmistakably. She gave the impression of a drunken sailor. The Godfather took a swallow, belched, sorry, banged his glass, toasting his companion. He stared at the cleaning woman as if expecting something more.

"What is it? What's the matter today?"

"Nothing. Thinking how I'm gonna kill you. Pouring boiling oil in the holes in your nose."

"The chair, bitch! The chair!"

"Sundays I don't have to carry the chair."

"When we got Sunday visitors, you do."

She grumbled, went around the counter, returned with a chair, the straw weave of its seat shining like new, and put it in place. The Godfather sat down, and she remained beside him.

"Well, Pedro?"

What now? What am I here for? thought Quimera. He should have asked earlier. But where, of whom? He had no idea what could be the relationship between Manuela, Antenor, and this decrepit man wearing clothes that had once been of good quality but were now covered with stains from cigarette ashes and burn holes. They seemed to belong to a world as similar as a nun and a rhino. Through the window came the sound of a piano. Someone playing scales, over and over.

"Lindorley! Go down there and tell that damned pig that I'm gonna put a bullet in that fucking piano of hers. I can't take it anymore, it's day and night. Four daughters, and the mother made them all play the piano. What was the bitch thinking?"

He spoke rapidly, running over words, foaming, saliva mixed with the creamy head of the beer. Very well pulled by Lindorley. I'm going to end up drunk, but I'll have another, pondered Pedro, who was starting to like this man, to respect him.* An uncommon person in this city of common people, all alike and as repetitious as the scales that fled terrified from the piano to take refuge in the Snooker.

"Speak up! What'd you come for? Why're you so quiet?"

"Why did Manuela come to this place first when she arrived? Did you know her?"

"I'd never laid eyes on her. She came here because it was her destiny. Just like it was her destiny to die yesterday."

He fell silent, lowered his head as if he were sleeping or deep in thought. Several minutes went by, with Pedro not knowing what to do, a bit fearful.

"And what went on here every afternoon? She was playing pool at a time when it was a game just for men. Did they talk about her?"

---

* Odd how these things happen. How to explain them?

"About who?"

"About Manuela."

"What've I got to do with Manuela?"

"You were going to tell me about when she first arrived."

"I wasn't gonna tell you anything, I got nothing to tell. You're wasting your time here."

The Godfather was breathing with his belly. Silence returned, prolonged, awkward, like two classmates at their first meeting. Quimera took a stab at what he couldn't see. There was nothing for it except to take a chance.

"I was told that you know the whereabouts of the Nighttime Shoeshine Man."

"And why should I know where the shoe polish owl is?"

"They say he's in hiding."

"You see how you talk? 'I was told.' Who told you? 'They say . . .' Who says what? You take me for an idiot? Think you can fool me? You're here for something. What is it?"

How easily he defeats me, admitted Pedro, this time without feeling disturbed. I'm going to do what I can; if it doesn't work, too bad! To hell with the story. I don't even know if I want to be a reporter.

"Lindorley! 'Fascination'!"

"Do it yourself!"

She tossed the record, an old 45 with an enormous hole in the middle. The Godfather showed his agility. He rose and caught the disc like a skilled goalie.

"One of these days I'm gonna break your other leg."

"I been waiting for that for years. That way you can put me out of my misery once and for all!"

"Lay your cards on the table, little brother."

"What do you know about Manuela?"

"What should I know? What everybody knows. A socialite. A beautiful woman. Intelligent, shrewd. An angel who had her wings broken by Antenor. She had a wonderful pair of shapely ankles. What was it the paper said the other day? A *social climber*." This last phrase was in English.

Pedro was startled. The man had pronounced the words perfectly, without the slightest accent. Like someone who knows the expression used by a newspaper. Pedro had studied English and knew the language well enough to perceive nuances.

"I went by the Crystal Night. And Efrahim told me that strange things happened at the Snooker, when she arrived in the city."

Pedro loved to make things up, based on the situation. There was something that men in the city like Luisão, Efrahim, and the Godfather knew. Some secret connection between facts. And they took pleasure in it. In withholding that knowledge. Like the Egyptian priests who possessed knowledge and, by playing the game, maintained power. It could cause one hell of a mix-up, reflected Pedro, light-headed from the beer. His stomach was empty and he wanted a refill. He had decided to play, without knowing which game or what the rules were. The Godfather was pacing around the room, Lindorley behind him, limping and complaining, carrying the chair. Pedro found the scene a bit odd. When the Godfather threatened to sit down, she very quickly placed the chair strategically. They didn't look at each other.

"They killed Manuela, Lindorley!"

"Killed her? You're lying, you bastard of a cow and a monkey."

"Murdered, really murdered."

Lindorley squealed and ran around the room, grabbing loose billiard balls from the tables and throwing them at the Godfather. Pedro Quimera had to duck; one of the balls could crack his skull. The stained mirrors shattered, bottles exploded on the shelves. Curiously, not a single ball struck the Godfather, nor did they appear aimed at him; they were an outburst of pain or rage.

"You no-good bitch. That's enough!"

The Godfather had a small snub-nosed revolver in his hand, which fit in his palm. Lindorley calmed down, went to the bucket, dunking and removing the dirty rag. The Godfather turned to Pedro as if nothing had happened.

"You ought to print Efrahim's story! Interesting, little brother, very interesting. Did he tell you? Did Manuela come here? Yes, she did. I didn't like the idea of women inside here. There'd never been one in here. They could jinx the games. Then the blind woman with a cue showed up, and then Manuela with the nurse."

"When was that?"

"It was . . . it was . . . Lindorley, another beer!"

The Godfather suddenly shed his decrepit posture and sat up straight in his chair, like a doll stretching. He was a tall man. His eyes had taken on a frightening liveliness. He tossed the cigar stub out the window. Now two of the sisters must be studying together, playing "Für Elise."

"You're not too clever. Efrahim didn't tell you anything. He couldn't! You're not a reporter! You're a cop! An SOB of a slimy cop who wants to implicate me in this Manuela story. There's corruption behind it, but go after the right guy!"

"And who's the right guy?"

"Find out for yourself."

"I'll confess, it wasn't Efrahim! I got it from a conversation at the door of the Coral Whale, weeks ago."

"The Whale, the Whale. The ones who go there are bigger crooks than the poor bastards who come here to play Life."

"Why don't you tell me more about Manuela? I have the feeling that it does you good."

"Does good! Does good! How's it do me good? What do you know of me? You've never even seen me!"

Nevertheless, the Godfather didn't seem irritated. He remained agitated and Quimera felt he'd struck a nerve, but he had no idea of how to continue. There was something involving this man, and if Pedro was sharp, didn't lose his focus, and kept on maneuvering, he would be digging the tunnel in the right direction. Tunnel. He loved films where the characters dug tunnels to make their escape.

"What about Antenor?"

"What about him?"

"Did he used to come here?"

"He was never here! He's a filthy piece of crap. Stuck-up. Thinks he's something he's not."

"You seem to hate him."

"He doesn't exist. Doesn't run in my circle. Why talk about Antenor?"

"He's the husband, a VIP. A suspect."

"You think they're going to get their hands on him? A future senator?"

"Senator? They're going to nominate Portella, everybody knows that. He's strong in the interior, in the party, the administration's behind him, even the president is coming to campaign for him. As for Antenor, the newspapers in São Paulo have started to show him for what he is, the padded bills when he was mayor, or Secretary of Public Works, or head of the subway system."

"Portella is dropping out."

"Where did you get that from?"

"How much you wanna bet? What do you know about what goes on?"

"I've never heard that."

"Asshole journalist!"

"I'm just starting out."

"Finishing would be more like it."

He may be right, thought Pedro. I don't know why I ever came to that newspaper, it's not what I want to do. But this isn't the time to trot out existential questions, not on this Sunday, in this place, with the crippled woman bringing another cold beer and carting the chair around. The other one doesn't even look, just sits down and the chair better be there. I never expected to find such good beer here.

"Do something for me! Find out how Manuela died and come back and tell me. You don't know, nobody knows. You may even be right! Listen to what I'm saying, I know this city well, its people, I know Antenor."

He admitted it. I have to write this down, thought Pedro Quimera.

"Yeah, I know everybody, all the scum that lives here, and not a one of them's worth saving. It takes a lowlife to know a lowlife.

Pay attention, listen to what I'm gonna tell you about the death of poor Manuela."

3

The Godfather, excited, looked out the window at the bustle around the Old Market, with its stops for unlicensed buses and its business of trading secondhand shoes. When he turned toward the counter, Pedro Quimera caught the glassy gaze of Lindorley accompanying the Godfather's movements. She tracked him like a camera in love.

"Write this down. Where's your pad?"

He had a sarcastic expression, as if he didn't believe in Pedro and was making fun of him. Quimera, confused before the Godfather, took out his pencil—he liked writing with a Johann Faber no. 2—and its thick point scratching the surface of the paper. At *O Expresso*, everyone else used a tape recorder, some carried a laptop. Pedro still hadn't adapted; he confused files and windows, didn't know how to edit, and would inadvertently delete entire pages ready to print.

"No one, brother! No one. No one is going to find out how Manuela died. They're going to cover everything up."

"It's too late! The news is already out!"

"And since when do they worry about the news? What do they pay attention to? What became of all the denunciations, the investigations? Doesn't everybody know about the phony accounts?"

"It's not like that anymore. Things are changing, since President Collor's impeachment."

"Impeachment, my foot! It'll still take a long time to strip the firepower from those people. They come back, they revive."

"You're out of touch, living here in the Snooker."

Until then, the Godfather had had his back to Pedro. And then he turned, sprightly, his body rigid, extended, ready to explode; frightening. Pedro drew back. Why is my tongue faster than my good sense? Just like Luisão says. The Godfather, with a dramatic air, raised his arms like Charlton Heston-Moses facing the Red Sea in *The Ten Commandments*, the film he was watching when the newsroom called him, the night before.

"Not in a thousand years! Not in a thousand years will you know what I know!"

A cunning expression fleetingly crossed his face, like a snake scurrying to its den.

"He's evil! Go away! He's evil. What did you come for?"

Lindorley, agitated, dashed from one end of the counter to the other, squealing, shaking the cleaning rag, spilling dirty water everywhere.

"Go away, go away! When he gets all worked up, the world seems like it's coming to an end."

"Shut up, fat ass."

"Don't do nothing to the boy. Don't do it!"

"Who says I'm gonna do anything?"

"I've seen the way you look! Seen it lots of times. When you get like that, there's no stopping you."

"What're you talking about? You want the Floral Mansion, is that it?"

Immediately she calmed down, went to a corner of the room and sat on a small stool, her image reflected in the cloudy mirror.

She had taken the bucket with her and was weeping softly. What a day! thought Pedro Quimera. What had he gotten himself into? Everything in the city was strange, the atmosphere was heavy, like in the worst days, when all forty juice factories launched the thousand smells of acidic fruits into the air and a thick haze enveloped the buildings like old London fog. He was spellbound. The Godfather placed both hands on his shoulders. They were heavy.

"I should've died a long time ago. So I wouldn't see this day."

Pedro guessed, "Manuela's death?"

"Damn this day! Damn Antenor!"

"You hate him, don't you? Why don't you tell me about it?"

"Shoeshine Man came by here early this morning."

He stopped talking. For a moment, Pedro was sure he was looking at an actor who knew very well how to deliver his lines. Sentence by sentence, awaiting the result, probing the effect. What about that cleaning woman? What was she saying?

"And why did he disappear?"

"Because he's going to die, after what he saw."

"And just what was it he saw?"

"Antenor getting out of the car."

"But he was at the lecture. He was seen at the Whale, at the airport, in the hotel restaurant."

Even in his confusion, Quimera noticed a subtle hesitation, a cunning gleam in the Godfather's eye. A momentary flash, as if he were pleased to pass along this information. False, or accurate?

"He was seen getting out of the car."

"What was Shoeshine Man doing at the pharmacy? It'll be his word against that of all the powerful people."

"The Shoeshine Man is a chance for Antenor's enemies. They won't let it slip away. If one side finds the man, he's done for. If it's the other side, he's saved."

"And you, which side are you on?"

"My own!"

"And which one is that?"

"The side of money."

"Would you be capable of selling out the Shoeshine Man to either side?"

"That's a good one! You, through your story, are going to give him up. What's the difference? He's worth a lot. Except that he got away from me. He was scared, real scared."

"Did the weasel have any idea what he'd gotten himself into?"

"There's nothing weaselly about him. You don't know the Shoeshine Man."

"Any idea where he went? Where he lives?"

"Near the bus terminal, next door to that German who makes tin watering cans."

"Hans of the Deluge? The weirdo who broke all the windows at the Crystal Night?"

"No weirdo. He knew what he was doing. The name of the café was a provocation for him. As if what he suffered in Germany wasn't enough, his wife died in the Flood of '59. The river rose and swept away their bed; they floated for miles, at night, and her heart couldn't stand the fear and burst. Why don't you write *those* stories of the city?"

The Godfather disappeared through a door next to the counter. After a time he returned with a teakettle and cups, and ordered the crippled cleaning woman: "Go see if Gullão's open yet, bring sweet rolls, with sugar on them." A good breakfast, admitted Pedro Quimera, famished. The rolls were braided, warm, with a layer of granulated sugar on egg glaze. The butter was melting and getting on their hands. They ate over the billiard table, its felt covered by an irreproachable cloth of embroidered linen. The Godfather had his delicate touches. Lindorley was downing a foaming mug of beer.

"I'll take you. Give me half an hour, then we'll go after him. Come back at ten sharp. I hate getting behind. And don't show up early. I hate getting ahead of myself."

What was he going to do with that half hour? thought Pedro. He left, the sun peeked out from behind the clouds, creating fleeting mirages, as if the asphalt were wet in the distance. Fifteenth of November Street—Quimera had a thing against naming city streets for historical dates, it meant commemorating just about everything—was sunny and deserted. No one went to the old downtown on Sundays. Beggars were sleeping in doorways, under the marquees of banks, they must be plastered to sleep in such heat. On a corner, workers were waiting for a bus, carrying paper bags tied at the top and singing a country music hit. He went to Nina's Belvedere, a construction of pink granite at a bend of the Tietê. He sat down on a bench under willows. One night, from that spot a Siamese cat named Nina, in heat, had thrown herself into the river, a story that moved the city. Since that time, fifteen years ago, her owner sits on the bench, night after night, waiting for the cat to return.

The polluted waters foamed. Quimera was pleased to be on the case. He felt like a detective. Philip Marlowe, Inspector Chafik

J. Chafik, Nero Wolfe, Ellery Queen, Hercule Poirot, Sam Spade. This ought to be a simple case for someone with experience. Antenor killed Manuela and fabricated an alibi. How to discover anything, without knowing how the woman was killed? He had no idea of how to conduct an investigation, interrogate anyone, relate one thing to another, one person with another. Had he seen Manuela in the pharmacy and become fascinated with the beauty of her firm arms,* her tawny skin, smooth as anything? Like a billiard ball? He didn't even find billiard balls pretty.

4

When he returned, the Godfather was at the door. He took Quimera by the arm and they walked in the sunshine. Clouds were dotting the sky, it would rain again in the afternoon. At the Actors' Station, the shiny Vemaguet was parked beneath a tin roof. The people had given the station that name because its rear was the side wall of a large supermarket, a former drive-in. There, the faded faces of actors from the fifties could still be seen, painted by Master Gentil: Maureen O'Hara, Deborah Kerr, James Dean, Tyrone Power, Burt Lancaster, Marlon Brando, Tony Curtis, Anselmo Duarte, Eliane Lage.

"Nice little car, well preserved!"

---

* Sometimes, by accident, Yvonne had almost suffocated him in bed and he had felt enormous pleasure. Nevertheless, he felt ashamed to confess this and ask her to repeat it. It wasn't normal.

"You like cars? Want to see my collection? Have you heard of my museum? I bought that coffee warehouse near the Focal. I have precious things, rarities."

There's a city unknown to me inside this city, thought Pedro. Sunday was turning out better than expected. Yvonne hadn't the slightest idea of what was happening. She was going to stop by the kitchenette, she loved all-you-can-eat barbecue restaurants that smelled of grease, where you spend more time waving away meat on skewers than actually eating. She'd be mad as hell, she got mad as hell over anything and nothing. The car was unbearable. They opened all the windows, but the air coming in was just as hot. The Godfather accelerated, got onto Freeway* 37 at the top speed that the Vemaguet could attain. The Godfather was a good driver, his No. 6 cigar centered in his mouth, clamped between his teeth. They went up by Coriander Hill, where immigrants from Espírito Santo had created a ring of gardens, and entered a small side street. The car turned right, left, left, right, then ahead. As if someone was being kidnapped and it was necessary to disorient him.

"It wasn't Antenor who killed Manuela."

"Then who did?"

Pedro Quimera was apprehensive. He had a scoop on his hands. Transformed into a hero, the talk of every circle, pointed out by customers at the Crystal Night. The café could be a bit cheaper, so he could afford to go there with Yvonne. If he discovered the plot behind Manuela's death, she would stop considering him lazy

---

* Freeway. The idea of a councilman who went to the United States, visited Disneyland, and loved the term *freeway*. He traveled at public expense? Public? Ours!

and a failure. They would argue about it, and she would throw in his face the fact that by the age of thirty many Americans had already made millions. In one of those arguments, which were beginning to irritate him, Yvonne had said, "You don't have to go that far! When Antenor came to town, he came with money. You know how he got started, when he was a student in Rio de Janeiro? He carried cans of fresh water to the beach and bathed the people, taking off the sand and salt. He used a small brush to clean the feet of the women who were about to get into cars. That's how he made money." Pedro replied, "Everybody knows he made his money denouncing people in the '64 coup." There was an organization of businessmen who paid for each one imprisoned or killed. Things were whispered but never shown. Nothing was proved. There were prisoners who later, in the Opening in the eighties, filed lawsuits, but Antenor wiggled out of it and countersued. One of them, Adriano Portella, a descendant of Spaniards, owner of the used-car monopoly in the region and the largest employer of illegal Koreans, appealed and won. And he again sued Antenor, who had a well-equipped set of advisers who greased politicians' palms, compiled dossiers on enemies, and had infiltrators in various administrations—state secretaries who owed them favors. Manuela was included in one of those favors, it was said.

Adriano, in his second term as federal representative, wanted to run for the senate or for governor. He extended his political base throughout the interior. He had become enemies with Antenor by dominating city hall and half the city council. Now he was fighting for the other half. In public, they were enemies to the death.

Behind the scenes, they got along well, dividing up territories. Or was it the other way around?

Pedro Quimera had the habit of letting his thoughts wander. They would take flight and hasten away, and Yvonne would have to pinch him to bring him back.

"I don't know, I don't know . . ."

The Godfather shouted, Pedro recovered, startled. What if he'd been driving? They could crash, cause a bad accident. Luckily, he didn't know how to drive, always leaving it for tomorrow. Why learn to drive if he didn't have a car?

"What don't you know?" asked Pedro.

"Who killed Manuela."

"And why are you so sure it wasn't Antenor?"

"Because the son of a bitch was too madly in love with her."

"Who told you that?"

"You're a journalist. Reveal my sources? Let's just say I know!"

"It's only your word. Why should I believe you?"

"Who asked you to believe? You asked, I answered. If you want to believe, that's your problem. I don't know you, I'm not interested in newspapers. You asked!"

"People talked about the two of them."

"People talk about you, about me, about the priest, the pope, the dog. The best product of this city is talk. If I could export it, like juice, soy, beer, the heavy equipment they're manufacturing, it'd be the biggest GDP in Brazil. They live for one another. It'd be a shame if others didn't exist. It's others who give us our identity."

Jeez, he's talking about identity. Can it be I'm in the bar with Yvonne's crowd? It seems the Godfather has read Sartre, thought

Pedro, who had recently discovered *Nausea* and *The Wall*. "Behind the times in life, behind the times in reading," commented his girlfriend. "Those people were read in the sixties. All that's missing is for you to drop acid and do psychedelic drawings."

"Nobody knows what went on inside that immense house. The house was always closed. Just the two of them lived there. Closed ever since their son died. A tragedy."

"You speak as if you were an intimate of theirs."

"Everything finds its way to me at the Snooker."

"She frequented the Cue for a time. The whole town knows that, there are people who played with her."

"Get back to the subject. Go interview those people."

"Did you play much with her, those afternoons?"

The Godfather didn't answer. He went on driving. They had to make a large detour. On one street was an outdoor market with the smell of fish in the air. An avenue closed off for recreation, full of people dancing, skating, skateboarding, vendors selling hot dogs and junk of every type. A street fair of antiques, piles of second- and third-hand furniture, kitchen appliances from the fifties, and heavy overcoats. Where do those overcoats come from, thought Pedro, when this city's so hot and we've never had a real winter? The Godfather's hands on the steering wheel betrayed his tension.

"Antenor was taken to the Whale yesterday by Manuela. There were five hundred people at the door when they arrived in their unmistakable turquoise-blue car. It was raining lightly but even so, Manuela got out to greet friends. They insisted that Manuela stay, it would be fun. She laughed, said that it was enough that Antenor liked money so much. She preferred other things. They laughed, and the people around her wondered what those things might be."

"Too much detail."

"I was there. I went to the lecture. When Manuela got out of the car, I was next to it. Antenor went in ahead of me. She left, her car was blocking traffic, and a guard came over and asked her to at least pull it over to the side."

"Did you attend the lecture on Profitable Knowledge?"

"You think I'm an ignoramus? Dumb? Maybe I am, but I had a very good time. I admit I didn't stay till the end. Do you believe in angels, my friend? In magi?"

The Vemaguet went around the bus terminal, crossed the tracks of the disused railroad, entered a narrow street of irregular paving blocks. The Godfather grumbled, "It's gonna throw out the car's alignment." They came to a gate with plastic jambs. In the back-yard of the tiny house a group was singing and reading the Bible, the men sweating in coats and ties, the women with hair down to their waist. The Godfather pushed open the gate. There was a side path full of undergrowth, an open faucet, a puddle of mud. A dog tied to a rope was dead, a bloodstain. "He barked at the wrong person," said the Godfather. The house was closed. They went around it, and from inside came the sound of a television set. The announcer was explaining how to scrape the hooves of diseased cattle.

"Closed. The Shoeshine Man wouldn't come here. He only *seems* goofy!"

The Godfather and Quimera tried doors and windows. Locked. That was when they saw the feet of a man sticking out of a patch of balm at the far end of the plot of land. A large patch, old, with yellowed leaves. It was an area over twenty yards deep, and the patch was in one corner, beside a pile of blackened bricks covered with bushes and weeds.

Pedro wasn't expecting to stumble upon a corpse; that wasn't in the plan. He felt light-headed, maybe it was the sun. He breathed a little as they passed underneath a plum tree full of blossoms and bees. On one of the branches was a shoeshine box, old and rotted.

"You think they caught him?"

"You go first!" Pedro said.

"What's the matter, you piece of crap? It's a guy lying down. You don't even know if he's dead. A live man's worse, don't you know the saying?"

In the next door backyard, everyone was singing in squeaky voices, pouring forth hallelujahs and thanks to the Lord. Praise God. May He grant us eternal salvation!

"How can a chickenshit like you investigate? Wanting to find out about a crime and being afraid? You don't have any idea what you're getting into."

Either he knows a lot, knows everything, which I can't imagine how, or it's a fantasy, and he's a bamboozler amusing himself. Pedro took a deep breath and feared he would vomit. It was necessary to carefully push aside the leaves of the balm. They cut like razor blades. The man was lying face up, his clouded eyes open. In his chest, holes. Quimera couldn't tell whether they were from a knife or bullets. He'd never seen the corpse of a murdered man. Only in films.

"Who would've thought it? The city's gonna boil even more. Just take a look!"

"Is he anyone well-known?"

"Look closely! Of course he's well-known. He's been in your paper a lot."

Pedro, calmer now, circled and saw the face from the front. Of course he was well-known.

THE GENERAL LEFT SIX
MINUTES INTO THE WALTZ

Death changes what people look like. Pedro Quimera remembered that, at his father's wake, he hadn't recognized him in the coffin, his yellowed face. He was another person, with vaguely familiar features. Until the day when, waking up with a violent hangover, he saw a distorted face in the mirror. It was his; it was his father's. The same face as in the coffin.

"Dr. Maciel!"

The chants had ended in the neighboring yard. A man's metallic voice sounded: "A wicked man taketh a gift out of the bosom to pervert the ways of judgment."

"The Proverbs of Solomon," explained the Godfather.

"You're familiar with the Bible?"

"Write it down: it's pure Solomon. If I'm wrong, I'll give you two bottles of whiskey. Knockando. Single malt scotch."

Flies were buzzing around Maciel. A dog came through the fence and began to lick the blood from the larger wound, near the stomach. It was coagulated; the animal didn't have much success. He got a kick from the Godfather and ran away yelping. From the other side was heard, "Amen, Jesus."

"However bad he was, Maciel didn't deserve to have some mongrel licking his blood."

What could the doctor be doing here? wondered Pedro. The man had given up his practice many years ago, and no one knew how he lived. He would disappear for a time, then return with his clothes threadbare. Still, he never stopped wearing a tie and many a night was seen in his medical jacket at Lombardi's Beer Hall, famous for a ninety-five-foot coil spiraling behind blocks of ice. For many years, after he lost his license, Dr. Maciel would prowl around the elegant two-story building, surrounded by gardens, where he once had the best medical office in the city. Today, a computer business, the first to bring computers to the city, part of Antenor's group. One afternoon, drunk, Maciel had gone up to the second floor and entered the room that had been his. There, where he once received the best clients in the city, was a climate-controlled showroom. Maciel threw extremely delicate equipment to the floor until overpowered by security guards. Antenor got him out of jail, and no complaint was ever lodged.

He had been the greatest dancer. The women at the Regattas, the Tennis Club, and even the Getúlio Vargas loved to dance with him.

He would dance with all of them, even those with their husbands. The men allowed it, knowing that the women would be happy at having been chosen—Maciel only invited those who danced very well. Not only for waltzes. Sambas, boleros, congas, swing, fox-trot, *baião*, rumba, mambo. He would conduct to the dance floor the daughters of friends, adolescents of sixteen, young women of twenty, and would do rock, the cha-cha, and the twist, all with the agility of a Fred Astaire. His feet didn't touch the ground, not a single misstep in his moves. It was easy to follow him; any partner was transformed into Margot Fonteyn. Any error in rhythm was compensated for without anyone noticing, such was his subtlety.

The older women remembered the Good Spirits Ball in 1975, in which the fifteen-year-old girls debuted. The largest and next-to-last of the dances of the Hunters Club. That night, the president of the nation, a general, was present, invited by the Hatters Association, and the décor was original, the ballroom adorned with every type of hat known to man. The invitation had been printed on the brim of an actual Panama. The general stayed only twenty minutes at the ball, in the mayor's box. The club held its gathering in an ancient restored theater built at the end of nineteenth century by Italian anarchists for staging operas and political demonstrations.

The general, fourth in a dynastic line of military dictators, was known for his Prussian intransigence and for being in favor of loosening the hold over institutions, as long as it was "reasonable and orderly," whatever that meant. In order to avoid unpleasantness, the mayor had imposed rigid control. Beggars, bums, suspected leftists, avowed leftists—an endangered species at the time—malcontents, troublemakers, provocateurs, union leaders and students, transvestites,* and probable agitators were detained. As they were demanding their rights,** the general was entering the club surrounded by a massive contingent of security forces, to the sound of the city's municipal anthem.

Dr. Maciel was to launch the dance with his daughter. Not only because he was *the* dancer, the star who impressed the public and the general-president, but also because his daughter's name began with the letter A: Anna Karenina. An homage to Tolstoy, a favorite of Maciel, who liked to read. He had an account at all the bookstores and subscribed to the Readers Club and the Book Circle. He would donate the fiction to public libraries and schools. A brilliant conversationalist, he seduced women by turning them into characters. For a few moments, in the doctor's bed, provincial ladies would be transformed into Emma Bovary, the Princesse de Guermantes, Julia, Tatiana, Sonya, Catherine Earnshaw, Gabriela, Capitu, the Girl from Ipanema, Scarlett O'Hara, Nicole Diver, Lolita.

The master of ceremonies announced:

"Anna Karenina."

And she walked proudly, hand in hand with her father, to the center of the room. Both were tall. Anna had the body of Audrey

---

* Attracted by Arealva's reputation for wealth, hundreds of female impersonators openly engaged in prostitution in the city (source: Armando Torres, *Sociologia da Nova Burguesia Interiorana de São Paulo*, 1985). Iramar Alcifes railed against them on a daily basis, accusing them of spreading AIDS among the working class and adolescents. I can add that Iramar, in the future, fired by the media, will become a transvestite, buying a post near the Actors' Station.
** Many of those arrested that night have taken part in an industry that has proved profitable: beginning in mid-1995, they applied for retirement benefits from Social Security, alleging persecution by the dictatorship.

Hepburn, svelte and elegant. Maciel and his daughter bowed to each other, discreet and graceful, and the setting, despite its nostalgic and antiquated air, displaced in time, was fascinating. For a month, father and daughter had rehearsed at Madame Poças Leitão's dance studio in São Paulo. They had a sense of spectacle and knew they were attractive. He was starting to gray and had, for the mothers, the exuberant look of Cesar Romero. The young women thought him a fortyish guy who was from another generation. The doctor took his daughter in his arms and Silvio Mazzuca's orchestra began playing Johann Strauss, Jr.'s *Roses from the South*. A waltz that begins slowly, with rhythmic movements that allow the dancers to smoothly adjust their steps. Maciel and Anna floated over the floor in a harmonious balance, accompanied by the spotlight, in such a way that the MC, enthralled like the entire room, forgot to call the second couple. No one noticed, and not even the girl who was supposed to enter next and was feeling anxious, was bothered. She preferred to wait, fearful of the competition with those two out of an American musical or some old Viennese film. The general-president appeared magnetized, his Germanic descent taking him back to a Prussia he had never visited, to the dances of Frederick the Great at Sanssouci, Potsdam.

Six minutes of waltz had gone by—the complete score is ten minutes long, but the orchestra can extend it if it wishes—when muffled sounds were heard in the mayor's box. An adviser leaned over and whispered something in the president's ear. The general rose, held out his hand to the mayor, said a few words, and left for the parking area, a park full of trees, a cool and pleasant place now transformed into a shopping center. In eight minutes the Air Force jet would take the general back to Brasilia. The dance went on, without the majority having been aware. Actually, few care about the presence of politicians. Only the next day did they learn that a journalist had died in a police precinct in São Paulo. As he was little known to the larger public, no one seemed affected by the news; reaction would come later—the dead man's name was Herzog.

Many intellectuals* who were at the ball compared Maciel and Anna Karenina's dance to that of Prince Salina (Burt Lancaster) and Angelica (Claudia Cardinale) in Luchino Visconti's film *The Leopard*. The latter, a classic cinematic scene; the former, a classic in the life of the city. Especially because what happened in the parking area, at the end of the night, profoundly affected Maciel and shook Arealva, still a medium-sized city. Everyone swears that the doctor never recovered, sliding gradually into madness. Even though most will admit that Maciel showed no signs of insanity, they were aware of what he was doing, merely using the parking lot tragedy to justify the acts that virtually plunged the city into a state of shock.

The facts are part of a disjointed series of stories with Maciel as character, and Pedro Quimera, looking at the face that was beginning to decompose in the sun, tried to reconstruct or fit together pieces of a jigsaw puzzle without an illustration to guide him. He imagined the shake-up the news would cause in the Crystal Night. Why hadn't he brought a photographer?

---

* As unbelievable as it seems, there were intellectuals in Arealva, and very intelligent ones at that, one of whom was the author of a work on Wittgenstein. A thesis defended by an academician from Arealva, because of its broad interest, had worldwide impact: *Is the Term Grzn in Ugaritic Related to Hrsn in Hebrew?*

"The doctor's in really bad shape."

"It's no wonder."

"I ran into him, some months ago, trying to get money from an ATM. He couldn't get the password right, and the machine swallowed his card. I tried to help, and he almost attacked me."

"He must've stolen the card, he was living off that. And mugging old people."

"And what was he doing here?"

"What everybody came here to do."

They heard footsteps, an angry exclamation of rage. They saw Antenor coming down the muddy path, and he had sunk his German-leather shoes in the puddle beside the faucet.

"Godfather?"

His listener was surprised. "What are you doing here?"

Antenor didn't reply. He looked at Quimera.

"Who's this?"

"Pedro Quimera, a reporter from *O Expresso*."

"Reporters are everywhere in the city. Don't talk to me. Don't ask me any questions!"

Authoritarian and arrogant, out of place in those clothes on a hot, sunny Sunday, thought Pedro, intrigued by Antenor's presence. Why was he there? Had someone alerted him?

HONEST CHEATS PLAY DIRTY GAMES CLEAN

1

Let's go back to the night before, since Pedro Quimera doesn't make things happen and, given the way they're coming to him, we don't know what's real and what's not. He doesn't provoke, doesn't lead, perhaps he's out of touch. Pedro is unaware that some time after Antenor dropped the Great Leader of Profitable Knowledge at the airport with an envelope stuffed with dollars, which the man kissed the way you kiss the feet of St. Fatima on a pilgrimage, the doorman at the Hotel Nove de Julho approached.

The smell of ether from an aerosol can* hung heavy in the air.

"Mr. Antenor, sir, excuse the interruption. The man has been at the reception area for an hour and said he won't leave until you see him."

"What man?"

Antenor took a hit from the aerosol can, felt his heart race, his head buzz. The world plunged into an enormous silence, then came the thump-thump-thump, like African drums** echoing off the walls of his brain. He slowly recovered his senses and saw the doorman standing before him.

"Dr. Maciel."

"Maciel?"

"He said he won't go without talking to you. It'd be better to leave, Mr. Antenor. The man is crazy, and he's armed."

"Armed?"

Surprised. The effect of the ether was disappearing. What did Maciel want, armed, in the hotel lobby?

"A real cannon! He swore he's not going away. I called the 27th precinct, they said they're too busy to bother with brawlers. Some guy just killed himself in the Whale square."

"The black quarters are hot today!"

Antenor leaned over to his lawyer, Bradío.

"You got your Beretta there?"

---

* Imported from Argentina. They replace, though lacking the same excellent quality, the old Rodouro and Colombina brands, whose manufacture in Brazil was outlawed by the baleful Jânio Quadros administration in 1961. A decree that should be rescinded by now.

** In primitive Africa, that is, in the continent depicted in the Tarzan films. I don't want to come across as prejudiced.

"Of course. Did you ever see me without it?"

"Lend it to me!"

"What're you going to do?"

"There's this guy . . . Maciel . . . You know who he is . . . Wants to talk to me at the reception area. He's armed."

Whiskey, many lines of coke, hits from the aerosol can. The two men left, staggering. That's how they started to get high. The women would arrive afterwards, late at night. A first-class selection, brought from the Portfolio* nightclub in Ribeirão Preto, which specialized in supplying plantation owners, businessmen, and cowhands.

Maciel was dozing in a worn leather armchair, a remnant of the grandeur of a hotel that had once received Santos-Dumont, Getúlio Vargas, Marta Rocha, Adhemar de Barros, Cléia Honain, the coffee queen of Brazil, Eliana Macedo, the queen of Atlântida film comedies, and Cyl Farney. And showgirls from the review theater of Walter Pinto, who in the fifties would spend a week in the city every May, the month of Our Lady. Dazzling** women who pretended to bathe in waterfalls made of silvery cellophane, wearing tiny bikinis. Nude showgirls—a daring display that shocked families—would line up on golden staircases, motionless.*** The Hotel Nove de Julho stubbornly clung to its dignity and, strangely, was frequented by people who mattered. "Men like to live among

---

* Address: 5768 Rua Almirante Amaral. Telephone: 856-8789. They are very pricey women.

** From Luisão's vocabulary. I borrowed it.

*** Nude women were not allowed to move, a restriction imposed by censorship. In those days the word *showgirl* had a powerfully sensual connotation for young men.

decadence, and take pleasure in seeing things rot and deteriorate," declared Dorian Jorge Freire, the most cynical Catholic ever.

"What is it, Maciel? I'm in a meeting!"

"Sure, an orgy's a meeting . . . At your office you fuck the competition. Here it's women!"

"Is that all you came to say?"

"No, there's something else. It can be fast. You're the king of fast negotiations. Mr. Speedy. Did you have a quickie with Manuela too?"

Bradío looked at Antenor, who didn't move a muscle, took the blow and let it pass. The lawyer was surprised. Why didn't Antenor react?

"Let's hear it!"

"When you get high, you can't go five minutes without a little snort?"

"Ciao, Maciel! Look me up at the office."

"I'm not going to cross that wall of security guards and sycophants. You've got so many ass-kissers in this town! What's with the midget? Why'd you bring him?"

"My lawyer."

"I know he's your lawyer. Bradío once tried to throw me in jail. When your son died. One huge farce. I was the scapegoat. They set me up real good. I was in jail for two months. Portella bailed me out."

"If that's what you're here to talk about—"

"It's not about that. It's about mother's love."

"Are you high?"

"Whaddya mean high? The subject is of interest to anyone who's going to run for governor or senator. Or any other shitty place where he can be even more of a lowlife. I have something that can either help or hinder."

"I think I should stay, Antenor," said Bradío.

"Without him, Antenor! Just you and me."

Antenor made a gesture of consent. Bradío handed him the Beretta, infuriating Maciel.

"You don't need that. It's only to talk. Besides, just look at the size of mine!"

He showed an automatic pistol used by the army. You could buy one for two thousand dollars from the gun dealer who frequented the Regattas, a fat ex-radiologist famous for having had three hearts attacks while on top of women he was screwing.

"Leave it to me, Bradío."

"Be careful, that guy there is batty!"

"What's your problem, ambulance chaser? If it weren't for Antenor you'd be selling habeas corpuses to faggots."

There were still in Maciel traces of the well-favored person he had once been. He displayed the caricature of an elegant man, his gestures affected by drugs and alcohol, his head swaying from one side to the other like a chained circus elephant. His right eye hidden by a hematoma, which might have seen a punch or a fall. He was wearing blue sneakers, one of which was missing its shoelace. Facing someone who sported custom-made Clarks, Scatamacchias, Spinellis, who brought from Paris products by Lorenzo Banfi, Cole Haan, Giorgio Brutini, Dingo. In the period when it was trying to establish itself economically, far from its original ideology, *A Lista* published a list, drawn up by Iramar Alcifes, of the wardrobes of the Beautiful People in the city. Iramar bought an apartment with what he got from organizing such articles, because he collected money from the elites and businessmen cited. Maciel's two hundred pairs of shoes had a prominent place in the write-up, and from then on, when he went by, everyone would look at his feet.

"Let's go to 316. We can talk there."

"No! It must be bugged."

"You think you're in some movie? Just why would I bug an apartment where I take whores? It's a three-ring circus. If you knew who I've screwed there . . ."

He laughed ironically. He was referring to Valéria, the doctor's ex-wife. Maciel, pretending not to understand, went upstairs suspiciously. The apartments preserved the decoration of forty years earlier, and smelled of damp, mustiness, with thick, dusty curtains. Antenor's head ached. What the hell did this guy want?

"Get to the point."

"I have something that concerns you."

"I know. You told me . . . What could you possibly have, Maciel, that would interest me? Blow? Crack? Not even some crappy grass. You've become a sad case."

"Maybe I'll be less of one after we've negotiated."

He had a triumphant air as he took from his pocket a brown envelope, from which he removed a smaller one, blue with a worn gilded initial.

"Recognize this?"

"Say what it is, I'm drunk and need a snort."

"A letter."

"It doesn't look like shit . . . A letter, so what?"

"Don't you want to know who it's from?"

Antenor wanted to get out of there. He had recognized the envelope.

"Yes."

"Then ask me who it's from."

Antenor was afraid to let it be seen that he knew. The envelope was familiar; it had passed through his hands many years before. They arrived every week for ten years. How had Maciel gotten hold of it? Did he have others? They were wrapped in brown paper, in the cellar where the gear for the boats was stored. Locked, no one went there, they were horrified by boats and water ever since his son had drowned in the swimming pool. It was an innocuous package, tied with common string, like a bundle of stale bread ready to be ground into bread crumbs. Why was he thinking about bread crumbs? Could it be the beef Milanese served on Sundays at the Botafogo Boardinghouse on Rua Voluntários da Pátria, in Rio? The cook was the flag bearer for the Salgueiro samba school and had monumental thighs and would dance the samba in the kitchen wearing tight Bermudas, coating the meat with egg and bread crumbs before tossing it into the frying pan.

"Recognize it?"

Maciel was insistent. Antenor actually liked the man. He had a horror of people who go around preaching virtue, shouting about morality while cheating, swindling, and disobeying the ethics of the illicit. Those are the really dangerous people. They don't know how to play the game and end up resentful. Maciel was an honest

111

cheat. He played clean, in accord with the norms. He had gotten hold of a good product and wanted to deal. How was it that he had the letters?

"No. Who are they from?"

"Your mother."

"My mother's dead, Maciel."

"What if I take you to her?"

"Huh?"

"What if I take you—or better yet if I show your mother on a TV program? How much would Portella or Iramar pay?"

"Sell to Iramar and I'll buy Iramar. Anyone can buy that mad mongrel."

Maciel realized, in the fog in which his mind dwelled, that he was holding a pair of aces: the letters and the possibility of taking Antenor to his mother. He saw the terror in the other man's eyes. He had to be careful. He couldn't let his guard down; Antenor was a man who took things to the end. There were so many unexplained cases. Where was the watchman from the parking lot the night of the Good Spirits Ball? And who left Cyro's son, from the flour mills, in a coma?

"Explain."

"I'm not explaining anything. I have more than 1,079 letters with this same envelope. I counted. I read them, one by one. It took a long time, the handwriting is terrible. In them, everything becomes quite clear. Who your mother is. How you went to Rio. Why you stayed away. Who your father is. His shady deals. Meticulously worded letters from a mother to her only son. Getting things off her chest. Your mother could write a novel, Antenor. She could be this city's Dostoyevsky, if she weren't semi-illiterate. But she saw things, she was shrewd, she recorded everything. Also, doing what she was doing. Handy information for enemies of a would-be candidate. Remember the presidential campaign of '89? That television program where Lula was defeated? Because of his daughter, his ex-wife who sold out, the secret briefcase, the stereo equipment? Well, this is going to have the same effect."

"And . . . ?"

"You're going to pay me for these letters. And pay well!"

"How much is pay well for a nobody like you? At the end of the line. A line of cocaine . . . Ha ha ha! You've become a blackmailer. A thousand dollars?"

"The nobody, with what he has, is worth five hundred thousand dollars."

Antenor guffawed, nervously, without conviction.

"Five hundred grand. Do you know what five hundred thousand is?"

"And I want it in U.S. currency. And don't come to me with any of those brand-new notes you and your bunch bought in Panama and dumped on the market. They were worth as much as your word."

"You poor devil, you drunk!"

"Five hundred thousand, Antenor!"

"Limp-dick blackmailer!"

"Five hundred thousand. And you're going to hand it to me personally."

"Cuckold! What proof is there that you have the letters? Where did you get them?"

"See? You know I have them. If you knew how I got them, you'd kill people! You have two days, Antenor, to make certain the letters are in my possession. Then show up with the money."

"You've planned poorly, Maciel. You're an amateur. When you leave here you'll be followed. They're gonna beat the shit out of you and take those letters."

"Like in a movie. 'Follow that taxi.'"

"I'm gonna put a hundred guys on you and get those letters, one by one. You know I can do it! I've been wanting to get you for a long time. Because of what you did to Manuela. Because of all the drugs you gave her, because of that afternoon at the pool. I'm gonna put an end to you."

"You think I'm stupid? I'm not! Or an amateur! I'm not in this alone. The letters are on diskettes. We bought the diskettes at your store. Ironic, isn't it?"

"You're bluffing, Maciel. How could you type anything, with that tremor of yours?"

"I didn't type a thing. You sell them but you don't understand the first thing about computers. The letters were scanned."

"I'll believe that when I see it."

"Believe it. Don't you come from a family of gamblers? How many people fucked up their lives in your father's casino?"

"What father?"

"You know which one. I read the letters, Antenor. You're an idiot, the drugs have shorted out your neurons."

"You're the professional when it comes to that. Drugs and shorted-out neurons. There was a fire inside your head."

"If you want to kill me, go ahead. There are others in this deal who can send the diskettes to the right people."

Antenor heard only the sound of a steak in the frying pan. He smelled the sweaty scent of the flag bearer's thighs. His mouth watered with excitement.

2

Maciel and Antenor left 316. Bradío had his ear glued to the door, more curious than apprehensive.

"Did you hear it all, you jailhouse midget? You're like a whorehouse cleaning lady!"

"I'll break you in half, you asshole junkie!"

"You'll need a security guard."

Bradío's problem was his height. Minimum, not even five feet. Compensated by singular shrewdness and cunning knowledge of how to get around laws, placed at the service of whoever was paying. A large part of his income derived from ready-made rulings delivered to bribed judges. Sniffing out the illicit, he circulated along the tortuous paths of the criminal and civil codes with the patience of a bee seeking pollen. If Bradío could earn a million dollars by legal means, he preferred four hundred thousand by illegal means, for the pleasure of beating the system, to feel the adrenaline rush. He was born to swindle, it was his sublimation against his short stature. Thus the perfect alliance with Antenor: valve and piston, well greased.

Maciel didn't wait for the elevator but took the stairs, bursting with energy. The hope of getting his hands on a bundle of money rejuvenated him, as if he had just come from a geriatric clinic. Antenor would try to negotiate, he'd make a counteroffer, his temperament was not to yield in the opening round. He would squirm, trying to win something. A reduction in price and it'd be a done deal, if Bradío didn't butt in, pointing out pitfalls. Bradío couldn't stand him; he was jealous of his relationship with Manuela. The lawyer didn't know anything, but he had a hunch. Maciel reflected: even if he got a hundred thousand dollars, it would be enough to disappear from Arealva, bury the memories, run away from the vision of the parking lot that tortured him. But, taking Manuela with him would be the final incentive, the coup the city didn't expect.

Antenor asked Bradío to make an excuse to the group in the restaurant and say he'd be back in half an hour. In the corridor he called home on his cell phone. He let it ring, then tried the call again; maybe he'd dialed wrong, cell phones worked poorly in the city—Portella's fault for contracting shitty service providers. He gave up, left through the rear of the hotel, once a large orchard, today a deposit area for used tires. He went through the small gate cautiously, caught sight of Ruy Banguela in the bar across the way. He wasn't sure if the crooked photographer had recognized him. It would be simple to make him forget everything; he accepted money of any kind, working together with Iramar Alcifes.

There was movement in the streets, a lot of filth, shattered glass, broken roofing tiles, burst bags of garbage, damaged signs, lamp-posts on the ground, live wires thrashing on sidewalks like snakes pouncing futilely in the void. Traffic lights weren't working, so he dashed across intersections at full speed, unconcerned. He passed by the Crystal Night, en route to Hydrangea Gardens (yes, with an *s*). Efrahim had chosen a good spot for his café. He double-parked, got out without removing the key. The security guard greeted him with a wave.

"Is Manuela there?"

"She was, she didn't stay long."

"What about Efrahim?"

"In the Venetian blind room."

The Count was in his office, from which he could observe what went on in the café through Venetian blinds inspired by the film *Gilda*, one of his favorites. His daughter was named Rita, in honor of Hayworth. Every night, the café was opened to the strains of "Amado Mío." He had wanted to call the Café Gilda, but there was already a chain of popular stores with that name that sold panties and bras.

"Antenor? *Non ci credo* . . . Here? A hurricane produces miracles."

"I want to know about Manuela."

"You're the one who should know, you're the husband."

"Did she come here tonight?"

"She always comes here, has some sherry, and leaves. You know, table nine was reserved for her until ten o'clock."

"Do you know where she went?"

"Ask Evandro the pharmacist. As soon as she leaves here, she heads straight to the pharmacy. That's nothing new either."

"The pharmacy? What she's going to do at that den of gossip?"

"Ask her. What's up? After twelve years of marriage Antenor decides to investigate?"

"What time did she arrive? Was she with Maciel?"

"Ask the doorman. Ask in the main room. Want me to announce over the PA: 'Anyone who knows of Manuela, please come to the manager's office?' You'll see how it'll swarm with people."

"Asshole sonofabitch! One of these days I'll bulldoze this and put an avenue over it. I'll see you in jail, you and your Nighttime Shoeshine Man."

"Just like your father. One sets fires, the other sends in tractors."

"Father? What father? You're hallucinating, the Shoeshine Man's got you high on blow."

Antenor was paralyzed, cold. As if his skin encased a block of ice that, as it melted in the heat of evening, would leave him nothing but an empty sack. What did Efrahim know? Could he be in league with Maciel? But there were things Maciel couldn't tell without risking his life, he knew that. What stupidity to have thrown in with Efrahim, the wop. It took a lot of whiskey and ether for him to imagine that the Count could help him. Back on the sidewalk, he called home again; no answer. He called the Shoeshine Man's cell phone, which the man carried inside his shoe-polish box. Busy. He got the number of the How Come Pharmacy from Information and a woman by the name of Idalina answered. "No, Evandro isn't here, you can leave a message. I'm waiting to hear from him myself, I need an injection. Could you maybe give me an injection?"

"Excuse me, sir. Your wife left, then came back, before the storm. She stopped by for a minute and spoke to the Shoeshine Man."

"The Shoeshine Man? Are you sure?

"I know the man, don't I?"

"If he shows up again, tell him I want to speak to him. I need to!"

"You need some product? I've got some here, he leaves it with me."

"No! I need him."

Antenor's house was in a condominium under construction, Hydrangea Gardens, surrounded by a stone wall, a reproduction of the Walls of Ávila in Spain, with watchtowers every five hundred feet. A corporation belonging to the Spaniards who had given up the scrap metal business for civil construction when it became the hot enterprise of the seventies. Guards, cameras, and spotlights reinforced the sense of border security at the entrance gate.

Every two weeks, an agency would bring in tourists to take a look at the houses, familiar through home décor magazines or such popular television programs as *Residential Status*, *Homes of Those in Command*, and *You Too Can Be a Success*. Between the pleasure of showing off, fear of being scrutinized by Internal Revenue for obvious indications of wealth, and terror of robbery and kidnapping, the predominant emotion was the arrogance of flaunting their possessions and the orgasm of ostentation. Because showing off is a form of dominance, a way of leaving others suffocating from so much power.

"The public is left breathless and loses its reason at the massive number of paintings, lamps, candlesticks, consoles, statuettes, vases, small desks, armchairs, platters, luminaires, curtains, tables large and small, sinks, hundreds of objects of indefinable function, wooden or marble columns, all arranged in an excess that brings transparency to discussion of taste in contemporary society through the art of fine living." Commentaries by Dorian Jorge Freire, who loved to waste time leafing through such magazines, where he discovered a humorous side. "They're sociological photos, with as much value as texts by Horace, Titus Livius, Juvenal, Plinius, or Petronius. Through them we can study the soul of an elite that reeks of the suburbs but takes on aristocratic airs by exhibiting its *domus aurea*." Born in Mossoró, Dorian was a professor of philosophy defined by Luisão as a cynic, which irritated him: "I'm not a cynic either in the philosophic sense of the word or in the traditional popular sense. I'm a furious person, a radical, a fundamentalist, because I lack a *sens de l'humour*."

When Dorian visited the *O Expresso* newsroom to hand in his widely read column, which was called "Newspaper Review"—where he distilled verve and criticism, laying bare the ignorance of the local press—Pedro Quimera liked to draw near to listen to him. A short man, with a large head and a lively look behind his glasses, his nervous hands constantly holding a newspaper or magazine—he read French and Latin—and his fingers rubbing against one another. He was successful with women; the girls in the newsroom adored listening to him, and they could go on all night. Dorian liked spicy soups served in bars by women: "I'm a philosopher and a Catholic, never a Catholic writer, philosopher or theologian. I'm constantly at odds with my church, even though I am accompanied by the Spirit of the Paraclete. So much so that an old and saintly priest in Santa Catarina tells me: 'You're a problem from God.' Verbatim. Dorian is a problem from God. I don't yield, I don't forgive or pardon sin, I don't accept abortion or second marriages if the first spouse is still alive, I don't accept condoms or IUDs. If you don't want to get pregnant, don't do the deed."

Pedro Quimera, surprised at such determination and fury, tried unsuccessfully to find out what the Spirit of the Paraclete meant. Dorian was feared because he was controversial, cultured, erudite, and possessed a devastating ability with language. But he admired Manuela and once wrote about her the longest profile ever published in *O Expresso*. Pedro considered Dorian a paradigm. The man never bowed down, always maintaining his stance within a gelatinous society. He didn't tolerate bores and felt nostalgia only for his permanent table at Gonzaga's bar and bookstore, in Natal, in the state of Rio Grande do Norte. He spoke all the time of Gonzaga and the vodka-and-passion-fruit cocktails he would make.

To visit the condominium, the tourist had to submit to a complex procedure of verification of identity, criminal background check, letters of reference, all of it analyzed by a computerized system with passwords and codes that changed weekly. Visitors felt it was worth the sacrifice and the wait. It was magic to penetrate the redoubt of people spoken of in the media or those known of but never seen. Mythological characters: entrepreneurs, bank presidents, politicians, owners of nightclubs and restaurants, currency exchange executives, financial investors, TV actors—they would come on weekends or during breaks in filming—two Brazilian authors of self-help best sellers (an effort was made to sell the Great Leader of Profitable Knowledge a site, but he refused; all his investments were in Miami), *marchands*, smugglers who brought in their merchandise from Paraguay in freight containers, owners of supermarkets, computer stores, pizzerias, meals priced by weight—a success that saved a lot of people in the recession of the nineties—lobbyists, treasurers of political campaigns, men who ran clandestine casinos. Casinos that descended from the Imperial Palace maintained by the Godfather on the banks of the Tietê until shut down by President Dutra's administration in

1946. The arm of land that penetrated into the lake was called the Peninsula of the Ministers of God. The multimillionaires of the new religions.

In the condominium, each villa* has a name and nobiliary titles have been exhausted by the use of kings, counts, marquises, viscounts, dauphins, not to mention places considered ultrachic like Central Park, Plaza Athenée, Vendôme, Aspen, Martha's Vineyard, Fifth Avenue, Place des Vosges. There one can contemplate the extent of human fantasy and invention, the pride of Arealva, the Brazilian Carmel, Scarsdale, Saint-Tropez, California, Boulevard Haussmann. Columnists ran out of nicknames. Antenor felt safe when he entered his territory. The avenue made a winding curve, the trees were new, many of them damaged by the cars of the youths who came there for pick-up soccer games on the weekends. The guards approached, weapon in hand, with a camera—the established procedure. They took Polaroid photos, jotted down the license plate number and time on a notepad, and raised the barrier. Antenor pressed down on the accelerator. Eight hundred and seventy-five yards to his house, beside the large lake whose waters connect with the Regattas and Navigators. The houses brightly lit, massive sound systems could be heard, many people with glasses in their hands on the lawns,** the parties merged into one another, it was considered classy to have guests over on Saturdays. Couples kissed beneath the willows*** which gave the atmosphere the appearance of an American movie. He thought about Manuela, the

---

* Villa is more chic than mansion, advised the decorators.

** Lawns were mandatory.

*** The landscaper was obsessed with Josh Logan's *Picnic*, featuring Kim Novak at the height of her beauty.

early days of their romance, when they would run off to motels.[*]
They would ask for the best suite, watch porn films while lying on
water beds, take bubble baths, amuse themselves with the pyro-
technics of lights. That was all; she wouldn't yield. She loved to be
embraced, nude, wouldn't allow the air-conditioning to be turned
on. She wanted to sweat, their bodies to stick together. It drove
Antenor crazy. Once he tried to force her, and the result was bru-
tal. She was strong and almost knocked him out—mostly because
it was unexpected—and left the motel, taking the car, making him
walk back. She disappeared for two weeks, going back to hanging
out at the Crystal Cue. She would spend the afternoons behind
curtained windows, playing with the lights on, not allowing Antenor to approach her, counting on the old man's complicity.

Antenor went around the house to the boat moorings. The
guards saw him, dogs barked along the edge of the lake. The waters were dark, the warm, humid days had returned. He ran to the
old, now disused boathouse. On nights like that, Manuela would
take the small launch out for long cruises, making her way as far
as the river. Now and then, if she was in a good mood, she would
amuse herself by watching Antenor looking for her in a game of
hide-and-seek. She would even let him catch her, without, however, yielding to him, which made it more exciting.

The door to the boathouse was closed. He pushed against it with
his foot and the door opened, enveloping him in a smell of aban-
donment. Choking, he drew back. The light still worked. Everything in order, the large boat was covered, the two launches, the Jet

---

[*]   When they first came into existence in the seventies, motels were the object
of a violent campaign by the Church.

Skis, the cabinets with fishing gear, boots, toolboxes. He searched for the package wrapped in waxed paper, waterproof. Sweating, he descended seven steps, noticing infiltration of water, two rat skeletons. The box was there, but missing its lock. He opened it. Empty. Manuela. It could only have been her. The old feeling, familiar and indomitable, began to be reborn in him. Which Antenor refused to admit, but it was hatred. And it was good to harbor that hatred, for it swelled his chest, made his mouth throb.

The same hatred he felt when, with a toothbrush, he used to remove sand from the feet of the women in Copacabana so they could get into their cars nice and clean, while he would return to his shack in Engenho de Dentro, well before he moved to that boardinghouse in Botafogo. Hatred when he found out who was his father, who had money and had kept him far away for some reason. Hatred when he would receive letters from his mother and found himself blocked from returning—but what was it that held him back? How many times had he bought the ticket only to turn back, standing on the platform? Hatred for his father when he got the letter informing him that his mother had died. But how, then, had he received several letters from her afterward?

Why had Manuela given Maciel the letters? If she was the one who did. Where was the damned woman now? He returned home, went through the house room by room, most of them closed up—they used only a small part of the villa, as for some time now they had planned on moving to a penthouse. He went around flipping on switches, spotlights that hadn't been turned on for years lit up the gardens and lawns, everything illuminated like in the days of the parties that Manuela had commanded. The press and their friends complained that they had withdrawn and the social life of the city had lost its spark. "One of these days they'll hang a ham at the door and everyone will come back," explained Dorian Jorge Freire. Where the pool had been was now a greenhouse with plants. Can it be true that the soul of a dead child stays on in the place where it died? Antenor got the car. Security guards appeared with their ferocious police dogs.

"Anything wrong, sir?"

"No, and don't turn off the lights."

He drove away, seeing the image of the house in the rearview mirror, as if it were a laser projection. The best thing was to go back to the hotel, shove some powder up his nose, inhale all the ether on hand, and tomorrow think about what to do. He wanted to screw ten girls, line them up and have at it.

Few had noted his absence, they were all unclothed. Bradío approached, a grotesque naked dwarf with a prominent belly, leading a black woman twice his size. He was crazy about black women, and this one had bleached her hairs, an exotic bronze above the skin.

"Well?"

"The letters have disappeared."

"Shit, what letters?"

"From my mother. Maciel has them."

"Letters from your mother? Whose mother? What's the story?"

"Maciel wants to blackmail me! He has letters from my mother. I'm not going to explain now!"

"Have the squeeze put on him, the old bastard will hand everything over. He's a chickenshit! Know something? Kill the guy. Kill him. He's sick, nobody will care, they won't even notice he's dead."

"Somebody else has the letters and copies of the diskettes."

"Fuck the letters, no one these days cares about letters. Most people don't even know how to read. And the public loves scandals, they'll all vote for you. Especially if it's a sex scandal. Women adore machos!"

"I don't know, I don't know."

"Antenor, you're a pain! A goddamn pain! Scared shitless, and you want to be a politician. You won't even make it to alderman. Nowhere. You need to grow some balls first. Don't give a shit about the others. Look around you! So many women! Lots of pussy, a shitload of blow. Get with it, and do your thinking tomorrow."

That was when the doorman said, "Mr. Antenor, there's two policeman waiting for you. Something has happened to Dona Manuela."

THE JAPANESE CORONER
FONDLES MANUELA'S BREASTS

1

"Antenor! You shouldn't be here!"

"I couldn't stand being at the morgue. The doctor began the autopsy, I managed to stay a short time, then I ran out. I left Bradío there!"

7:15 Sunday morning at the Crystal Cue. The Godfather offered Antenor a beer. At the first sip, they both had their lips covered in thick foam, a strong taste of yeast. On an old settee lined with gilded cloth, Lindorley was asleep, snoring, her entire body shaking, beset by nightmares. The sun penetrated, reflected off the glass, caught in the stained mirrors, the Snooker was transformed into a greenhouse. The fans with their large blades were motionless—the miserly Godfather saving energy. From the Old Market came the sickly smell of barbecued cat, roasted in braziers made from cans of cooking oil.

"You could've stopped the autopsy! Manuela didn't deserve that! Being sliced up by those butchers."

"The lawyers tried, you know! Portella's got the police in his pocket. He managed to get more people on the council than me. Besides that, I didn't have the strength to fight."

"They're going to use that! Your disappearance. It's time to show that you're unflappable. In control of everything!"

"Father! How was I supposed to stand it? When Morimoto, who detests me, picked up the scalpel and opened Manuela from neck to belly, I thought I'd die. Not a drop of blood came out. The sadist looked at me and smoked. On top of everything else, that cigar. The smoke, the smell of formaldehyde, I nearly fainted. The guy touched Manuela's breasts. They didn't even seem like her breasts anymore. Whitened, bluish. He did it on purpose, because I was there. He did it to provoke me. He fondled them and I was paralyzed. I didn't react, I left."

The two men went to the draft machine. Antenor filled two mugs. He pulled skillfully, practiced.

"How long has it been since we had a beer together?"

"The Sunday ones were the best. The only time we could meet, without pretending, free."

"Was it you?"

"Me what?"

"Who killed Manuela?"

"Are you insane?"

"I know what you're capable of! You can tell me. I'm the only person in this city who's not going to betray you, whatever you do."

"You had to see Morimoto's face looking at Manuela naked!"

"I thought about that. Did he discover everything?"

"We have to do something, I'll leave it up to you."

"The dirty work always ends up in my hands! Morimoto's smart. He'll do business. How was she killed?"

"Strangled."

"The Good-Bye Angel?"

"She didn't have the prayer card or any mutilation."

"Why the autopsy?"

"They want to know if drugs or alcohol's involved."

"You're losing your power, son. What about her car?"

"I don't know, Bradío's looking into those things. Who was it? Why? And to Manuela of all people? Spite, revenge? Maciel? Portella?"

"Manuela was acting strange."

"After the boy's death Manuela changed. Slowly, very slowly. Her mind was falling apart. I even thought about Alzheimer's, but the tests in Cleveland were negative."

"So it was her? They said you'd gone there for a heart operation. Why didn't you tell me? Why did you abandon our Sunday beers?"

From the parking lot in the Old Market came the sound of steel wheels of skateboards scraping the asphalt, the cries of boys. Lindorley changed positions, stopped snoring.

"Put the squeeze on the pharmacist. Manuela practically lived there."

"I need the Shoeshine Man, father! He said he saw me! A group of people leaving the Crystal Night heard him. Efrahim's hidden the guy."

"They didn't speak about you, they said it was about me. Talk about me. A cab driver told me that he picked up Efrahim last night. We need to squeeze him."

"The Count is a piece of shit," the Godfather said.

"But he's never forgiven you! You yourself said that he might come after you at any time."

"It's so long ago. It's like nobody ever forgets anything, always living in the past . . . You left the dinner at the hotel and disappeared. You're going to have to explain. The complication is that the photographer from *A Lista*, that Ruy Banguela guy, went looking for you and they made some excuse. No one had noticed that you'd left, they thought you were in the bathroom. The people there are your friends, they stood up for you."

"I went downstairs to the lobby and ran into a guy. We went to 316, I needed to talk to him."

"So the doorman can testify to that!"

"The man who came to talk to me at the hotel was Maciel."

"Maciel?"

"He was blackmailing me."

"Because of the boy? That's an old story, forgotten. It was an accident, that's been proven. The case is closed."

"It wasn't because of my boy. It was because of his daughter, Anna. And he wants a lot of money."

"I understand, I understand. Anna. And better, much better, if I know the people. It's not the money. Maciel is getting even, he's spent his life thinking about it. Avenging Anna Karenina."

"How does she figure in this? Everything was arranged. She left twenty years ago and is living with her mother in Araraquara. She became a dyke and hates men."

Their heads were beginning to grow foggy from the beer and their tongues were loosening. The Godfather went to the refrigerator and returned with a frosty bottle of Steinhäger. He drank two doses from a small festive beer mug depicting a white whale: "One of these goes down well, and it's pure." The beer kept coming, and both men were nodding.

"I haven't forgotten. I'm drunk but I haven't forgotten. What happened with Maciel? What went on with his daughter?"

"It was that night, in the parking lot. He caught me getting it on with Anna Karenina. He went wild."

"Anna. But she was fifteen. She had her debut that night."

"We were crazy about each other."

"You were much older. Almost her father's age!"

"Not that much."

"Not that much? You were thirty-one years old. You were born a year before the war ended. I remember, we went on a long trip, tiring, with your mother afraid you'd be born on the road. We went to Aparecida. After what they did to your mother at the hospital here, I wanted you to be born far away from this place. She offered you to Our Lady of the Conception."

"The hospital?"

"When I went to reserve the room, they refused to accept your mother. They claimed we weren't married. The priest in charge said there weren't any vacancies. That's another story. What about Anna Karenina?"

"We were seeing each other. She liked it because I was older, she considered people her own age assholes. Of course, all of it behind Maciel's back. He wouldn't let anyone near her. He was jealous. He guarded his daughter like a holy relic. Her mother liked me and protected me. He wanted to catch me, thinking I was having an affair with his wife, Valéria. He didn't know I was in love with his daughter."

"Valéria! A lot of fun. And Maciel? Bad temper, though a good doctor. He screwed other men's wives but they couldn't screw his!"

"Valéria was in love with the trapeze artist in the Orlando Orfei circus. Wherever the circus went, they would take Valéria. In that old Vemaguet station wagon you like so much. We'd wait in the car, cuddling, while Valéria was balling in the trailers at the far end of the circus. The trapeze artist died one night. He got out of bed and went directly to the ring, without concentrating, and fell outside the net. Anna and her mother were very much alike. Fun, debauched, scheming. Anna considered it all an adventure. She didn't like her father, Maciel was possessive. Hard line. A real prick, controlling everyone. What happened, happened. One day he caught us kissing, her with her blouse unbuttoned, and he beat me. He swore he'd kill me!"

"So, didn't you fall apart and end up on the scrap heap? Why didn't you tell me?"

"I couldn't. If I did, you'd want to settle scores with him. And people couldn't know you're my father. You didn't want them to! I've never understood it."

"Don't play the innocent now. It was a good arrangement. You agreed. You were ashamed of me, scared to death they'd find out I was your father. Who was I? The owner of a pool hall who bankrolled card games in illegal casinos, a loan shark with lots of charges against me, assault, accusations of rape—all false—on parole, a man of bordellos and illegal lotteries. A criminal, a sonofabitch to most, a scapegoat to the police. Who wanted that for a father? Often, alone here on a Sunday, I thought you never should have returned. Stayed in Rio, made a career, studied at the university. You had the money every month. Why'd you come back?"

"I came back. Did I do the wrong thing? With all I have now? It was Mom's letters."

"What letters?"

"She wrote me. Every week when I was living elsewhere. One thousand and eighty letters. The same envelope with no return address."

"Damn. A stubborn woman. Damn her a thousand times. She broke the agreement."

"Agreement?"

"I thought she was a rock. She was just a mother like all the rest. I was wrong, she couldn't take it."

"She's alive, isn't she? Somewhere, and you know where."

The doorbell rang, four, five times. Antenor and the Godfather looked at each other. The crippled cleaning woman awoke with a start, jumped up, and staggered to the stairs, pulled on a small rope, and the door downstairs opened. She saw a tall dark man, some thirty years old, coming up the stairs. She looked at the Godfather and Antenor and descended a few steps.

"Hey, hold it right there. Who are you and whaddya want?"

"I'm Pedro Quimera, a reporter, I want to talk to the Godfather."

"Stay here. I'll be right back."

She went up, limping and farting.

"There's a reporter here, Godfather."

Antenor leapt from his chair.

"Don't let him in, don't let him in. What does he want? How'd he find me? I did everything possible to throw them off the trail."

"Take it easy! Relax! You don't know if it's about you. Leave it to me! Go in there. It's the room you used to like when you were a child. The castle."

Antenor disappeared behind a faded mirror. Pedro Quimera came up.

"What do you want, boy?"

He looks gullible, I'll have no trouble stringing him along, thought the Godfather. It'll be fun, this Sunday's going to be a lot of fun. It's time to stir things up, go all out, change everything around a little, Arealva's getting to be monotonous. *Woe to thee, bloody city*, as Father Gaetano would say.

2

Antenor was uneasy, feeling himself a prisoner in the Godfather's office, unable to hear the conversation that seemed longer than it actually was. Finally, Pedro Quimera was sent on his way. The Godfather waited for the door to close, then looked down the stairs. The journalist had indeed left. That old suspiciousness.

He crossed the room, pushed against the mirror behind which Antenor had entered, crossed a short hallway and arrived at the office.

It looked like a disorganized person's storeroom. A museum awaiting a cataloguer. Shelves overflowing with papers, magazines, glass containers in which floated indefinable creatures, liquor bottles, billiard and bocce balls, boxes of playing cards, inkwells, blotters, floor tiles, stuffed birds, rolled-up tobacco leaves, wire, springs, tools, a printer, telephones, dolls, packages. There wasn't a single particle of dust; everything was impeccable, the floor lustrous. Lindorley took great care.

Photographs covered the walls, each one with a name and date written in ink. In some, a muscular youth in boxing gloves; in others, the same man in the ring, standing over a fallen opponent; framed newspaper clippings. The Godfather, champion of the middleweights, possessed a furious left. Antenor, intrigued, looked at a photo in which a brunette with curly hair and enormous earrings smiled at the camera, in front of a pair of cardboard swans. The Godfather contemplated the photo for a second. He gave the impression of a puppet with its strings down, with no one in command, loose in a bookcase. His eyes were dead.

"You're a liar, Antenor!"

"How can you say that, Father?"

"You're not worth a cent of what we spent on you, your mother and I. Her life gone, she lost her son, to make something of you. And you turned out to be a worm!"

"Godfather, I'm going to have you committed. You're becoming senile . . ."

"I was steering the conversation to see how far you'd go. How can you lie to your last ally?"

"I misunderstood."

"You say that night in the parking lot, after the Good Spirits dance, Maciel tried to kill you. Why didn't you kill each other? You deserved it."

"I told you the absolute truth."

"The truth? I know the truth! I got rid of the watchman who saw it all. No-goods, you and Maciel both. Letting yourselves be seen in the middle of the street. How do you think I've gotten out of all the charges they've brought against me? No proof, no witnesses, no trail. I was ashamed of your stupidity that night."

"Who are you to give lessons?"

"You killed Manuela! The only honest thing in your life."

"You, talking about honesty?"

"So, Anna went to Araraquara and became a dyke? You believed it? Then it's time to know the truth. Who killed the girl in the parking lot? I know about that mysterious crime! Does your memory wipe out whatever doesn't concern you?"

Antenor became suddenly sober. Completely, as if he hadn't had a drop of alcohol. He had a frightful tolerance and could drink opponents under the table. He would sit down, the others would get stinking drunk, open their mouths, while he remained quiet, intact.

"I didn't wipe out anything. What I know, what happened afterward, you told me. I fainted, and when I came to, I found myself stretched out on a pool table. And you, over there. It's your memory that's changed. You're full of games, Godfather."

"Why do you call me Godfather?"

"From time to time I can't recognize you as my father. My whole life has been one of lies, that's what I've learned. I grew up abandoned!"

"Abandoned? I taught you how to survive in life, I taught you all the tricks. Who supported you in Rio all those years?"

"Who was it told me everybody was no good and that in this world you have to be no good too, and lie?"

"And that's really the way it is. I don't believe in anybody, nobody believes in me. That's how you become a man."

"That night, Maciel shot me. At least that's what I've been carrying around inside me for twenty years. Or was it him? Then, Anna was killed. I was in love with the girl, she would've changed my life."

"Changed? What did you want to be? Some poor bastard with a profession? A shyster lawyer? A teacher? Accountant? A clerk with a bunch of kids, struggling to pay for their schooling, sweating out the rent or the mortgage on the house? Who are you putting on an act for? You inherited my underhandedness, went far, got involved in everything. There's no turning back."

"Didn't you ever notice how Manuela looked a lot like Anna Karenina? When I went into the Snooker and saw Manuela playing, I was shocked. She was Anna! The same height, same manner, same bold look."

"Romantic . . . It's not your style . . . Today's the day of psychology, that reporter out there wanted to figure out things."

"I looked for Anna Karenina everywhere. I followed the leads people gave me. Now I see. You were the one who planted them, and I went along. It led nowhere. At least tell me where she's buried."

"I don't know. I didn't go to the funeral!"

"Then what happened that night? Who told you what?"

"The watchman. He was a ticket collector for me, he'd pick up betting slips for the underground lottery. He and the Nighttime Shoeshine Man knew what was going on in Maciel's car. The Shoeshine Man always loved watching couples humping in cars, he was an expert in peeking through windows to see naked women."

From the home of the piano-playing twins came the loud sound of "Valsinha," by Vinicius de Moraes and Chico Buarque. *One day he arrived so different / unlike most days, he looked at her much more heatedly / than the customary way he would look at her.* Antenor's gaze was distant, obscure.

"You went after Anna. You hadn't even danced together a single time. Maciel gave no quarter and wouldn't let you get close. He detested you, knew about your complicity with Valéria, who was cuckolding him. You would spend the entire dance circling each other, watching each other from a distance. Until the moment Anna went out for some fresh air, escorted by one of Maciel's assistants, who disappeared, probably to do a few lines. The general had already left, the coast was clear, without the security guards hampered by their tuxedos. It was cold, you searched all over the ballroom, went out, looked for Maciel's car, didn't find it outside the club, went to the large piece of land that had been rented for parking that night. Some intuition, some animal instinct led you to her, attracted by the scent, your heightened sense of smell. Both of us always had a nose for women, my son. We're good at it, first-class hunters. That was when you heard the muffled moans. In those days, Maciel had a blue Impala convertible, the hit of the city. New, shiny, imported, God knows how—he was always a man for maneuvering. It was the moan of your woman, son, and you recognized it, the way the male must. You sensed danger, menace was in the air. You walked up to the Impala. But you were cautious. That was always one of your qualities—caution. You never subjected yourself to risk by leaving your flank exposed. Even in business matters you act that way, especially in business matters. That's why they've never laid a glove on you. Sly, suspicious, you circle around, from afar, before you come close. That's what you did at the parking lot, even though you were excited. What could be happening to Anna Karenina? You went up to the car and saw the doctor on top of his daughter, covering her mouth with one hand."

No, no, that's horrible, poppa, no! For the love of God, no, poppa, oh my sweet mother!

Your mother's not going to help you, that cow's in hell, and you're just like her!

You're crazy, poppa, why, why?

"I don't forget, Antenor. Not a word of what you told me. Just the way you told it while you were delirious on the snooker table. I brought the doctor, he removed the bullet, it was a light wound, but it wasn't the wound that threw you into that fever. A hundred years from now I'll be able to repeat everything, just the way you told it to me. Anna's perfume filled the air, a smell of lime and lavender, mingled with the perfume of the germander—there were over two hundred trees around the club. You opened the door and, before Maciel could turn around, you kicked him in the tailbone, which hurts like the devil. He howled, shot backwards as if hurled by a catapult. He pushed the button that controlled the top, and it opened. Anna started screaming, Maciel got the revolver from the glove box, all very fast, there wasn't even time to clearly see what was going on. You didn't know whether to help Anna or jump on the doctor. He got off one shot from a snub-nosed .38 and then you were all over him, howling, punching, you always were strong. Maciel was a weakened man. Then the second shot, then another. The sound from the orchestras was loud, both* of them playing at the same time, the high point of the ball. People looked for Maciel and his daughter, wanting them to dance again, they were such a pleasure to watch. You pushed his head under the steering wheel, there was no way he could move, he took one on the chin and passed out. Then you saw Anna stretched out on the rear seat, the hole in her chest, her white dress stained with blood. The instinct to survive took hold of you. You looked around. No one. The car in the middle of the parking lot, one among hundreds, from all over the region. You didn't notice, you were terrified, you couldn't have noticed the hidden watchman. You tried to get out of the car and realized you were wounded. The blood frightened you, and you saw you couldn't walk, you'd been shot in the leg. It was then that another shot rang out, and the police later said it was this shot, from an automatic pistol, that killed Anna Karenina. You went into a state of shock. It wasn't fear but confusion, your head swimming, the horror of seeing Anna like that, an immense pain that didn't burst into sobbing as a release. We're two of a kind,

---

* They were the Tabajara and Silvio Mazzuca orchestras, the best in Brazil.

son, we can't cry. We try but not a single tear comes out. We can be devastated and we remain dry-eyed, which makes people think we're emotionless. But it's good for them to think we're insensitive. They leave us to ourselves and don't mess with us. They're afraid, people here are afraid of us. None can predict what we're thinking, or what we're capable of. I keep imagining what a full plate it'd be if Adriano found out we're father and son. What he'd do with it. Him and that shitass newspaper O Expresso. A big explosion that'd leave no stone standing."

Antenor was astonished. The Godfather had fired, like a rotating machine gun. Something repressed that only now exploded. Anna was dead. But who had fired the shot—him or her father? Everything had been covered up in some way he didn't know. The Godfather had sent him far away, to a hospital in Curitiba. His wound wasn't serious, but the doctors were psychiatrists and therapists and he was there for a long time, eight months away from Arealva. When he returned, he learned that Maciel had lost his medical license; women had come forth accusing him of rape, and his office was shut down. The doctor was said to have gone to Europe. Valéria had been in Araraquara for some time, where she gave classes in ikebana, bleached her hair, had plastic surgery done, and lived with the administrator of a hosiery factory.

"Who fired the shot? Him or me?"

"At this juncture, who can tell? The mystery is that last shot."

They looked at each other fiercely. Staring at the Godfather, Antenor felt ill. His father's eyes were locked on him in rage.

"Why was Maciel blackmailing you?"

"He says he has the letters from my mother."

"All of them? Over a thousand?"

"One thousand and eighty. On diskettes. And someone has copies of those diskettes."

"Efrahim? The Shoeshine Man?"

"One of them's an odd bird, you never know what side he's on. The other's a poor devil."

"The Shoeshine Man was never a poor devil. He pretends, because it's better that way. The only reason the police don't haul him in is because he's protected, big time. If he's brought down, the roof caves in, and nobody wants that. If you feed the lion well, he's tame, and the police in Arealva are the best fed in the world."

"Efrahim doesn't have a motive."

"Maybe he does, maybe he does, if it's what I'm thinking."

"Except you never know, never did know, never will know what he's thinking. And what he's going to do. Or how."

The Godfather stared at Antenor, absorbed. Nothing seemed to faze him.

"She's alive, isn't she?"

"Who's alive, Anna Karenina?"

"My mother. Maciel swore it."

"Maciel, Maciel, Maciel. Two hundred thousand people in this town, and I come up against the pits, the garbage. Fart dust. He's bluffing. He doesn't have the letters, that diskette is blank. At the card table at the Crystal Cue he would bluff, bluff so much that he was forbidden to play. Nobody would sit down at the table with him. He enjoyed bluffing. Even when he held good cards, he would pretend to bluff."

"I went home. The letters have disappeared."

"The asshole!"

The Godfather was talking to himself.

"What a habit your mother had. Rather, it wasn't her but that asshole at the School of Commerce. He was in love with her."

"In love?"

"Him and the others."

"Others? And you didn't do anything?"

"I couldn't, and I'm not going to explain, because it hurts me and it'll hurt you."

"I'm a big boy now, I'm grown up."

"But you won't like it, and I'm not going to tell, it's irrelevant. Now let's take a break here, I'm going with that reporter to the Shoeshine Man's house. I can make use of the creep, give him some red herrings."

"I'll go with you."

"Not with me! You can show up later."

EVERY CORPSE CONCEALS A TELEPHONE NUMBER

1

We return to the following day, to the backyard of the Nighttime Shoeshine Man where Maciel was found dead. Let's accompany Pedro Quimera to find out if he's doing any better.

Antenor was wearing a strong, sweetish cologne that Pedro couldn't identify. He knew little about such things other than what he read in the society columns. On a certain occasion one of them had profiled Antenor through his habits and customs. The clothes he wore, the tie, socks, shoes, the toothpaste, a brand Pedro had never heard of, it must have come back in their suitcases when the couple returned from Europe or Bangkok. Why did they go to Bangkok so often? Wouldn't that be something to investigate? Tourism or something else? A tax haven? Luisão could send him on an international fact-finding assignment.

Antenor was wearing a suit made of opaque acetate weave, beige, with his inevitable garish tie, red and yellow, depicting mandolins and guitars. How did he manage not to sweat in the warm haze? What is it the rich do to always seem at ease, as if just stepping out of the shower? He often asked Yvonne, when she would arrive at the shopping center parking area on a summer afternoon, breathless and sweaty, her blouse stained under the arms, and he would see those women, cool and with soft skin. It was known that Antenor chose the color of his clothes by the horoscope prepared by the seer he'd brought from Passo Fundo, the region that produces the best specialists in Brazil.

"Did they kill the Shoeshine Man?" asked Antenor.

"No. Maciel."

"Maciel? So he finally got what was coming to him."

"And, as a result, you didn't get what was coming to you."

Pedro Quimera glimpsed a dubious expression on Antenor's face. One of amazement, incomprehension.

"I don't know why you say that."

"Yes, you do. You know you escaped."

Antenor, uncomfortable, looked at Pedro Quimera and the Godfather.

"He was going to get you, sooner or later."

"I don't understand."

By now the effort to quiet the Godfather had taken on an air of desperation. He obviously took pleasure in Antenor's anguish, pretending he didn't understand the signals, which were no longer imperceptible. As if Antenor were shouting through a megaphone. What was the connection between the Godfather and Antenor?

"Your luck was that Maciel was a coward. He spent his life making plans to get you. It took a long time, and he got worn out, completely worn out. All over. He fell into the hands of the Nighttime Shoeshine Man. And that was real decadence!"

"Sonofabitch! He deserved every inch of the hole he sank into."

"A hole that began in the parking lot."

The Godfather's eyes were gleaming ironically. He was enjoying needling Antenor. There was no other explanation for the phrases. Pedro Quimera might not be the greatest journalist in the city, but he was connecting the old story of the parking lot to what the Godfather was now saying.

"You never could stand the friendship between Manuela and Maciel. You were always suspicious. Besides, you spent years afraid of the revenge the doctor was preparing. It was an open vendetta. Everybody knew about it! For years the city waited for the big moment, the encounter between Maciel and Antenor."

These are things that happened before I came here, thought Pedro, his ears pricked up. At the same time, he tried to hide it. Obvious eavesdropping could interrupt the conversation.

"He was afraid of me."

"Maciel wasn't afraid of anything. He had exceeded all the limits. He was on a road with no turning back."

"That's crap, Godfather! His head was full of fantasies. If Maciel wanted to get me, he would have. We ran into each other a million times after that night."

"The man followed a particular code of ethics. He wanted to get you in a special way. He wanted to set up a scene that would bring people to admire him again. He was looking to win back the city's respect, he longed for the time when he was envied, idolized. And he blamed you! You were the one responsible for everything."

Pedro was perplexed by the Godfather's speech. He had never imagined him to be intelligent and curious. It would be necessary to live beside him for many years to find out everything, the plots that he was hiding. Suddenly, Quimera found seductive this surreptitious world full of codes. He should have the powers of Alice to go behind the looking glass and see everything from the opposite side. To enter the backwards world. Transform his life. What dazzled him in the Lev Gadelha Museum was a book and a collection of Italian drawings, *Il Mondo alla Rovescia. Ossia il Costume Moderno*. He would spend hours with the volume that Manaia, the curator, had placed in his hands. There was the man on a spit being roasted by a steer, the husband sewing and the woman heading off to work, the rooster laying eggs and the hen crowing, the fish fishing the fisher, the donkey whipping the man pulling a plow, the rabbit hunting the hunter, the student slapping the teacher's palm with a ruler. This upside-down world amused Quimera, who dreamed of blacks becoming white, whites becoming black, women becoming men and men becoming women, gays becoming lesbians, Chinese becoming Japanese, automobiles in the kitchen and ovens out on the street, lightbulbs growing on vines, traffic jams of washing machines.

He came out of his reverie when he heard the Godfather shout (why does he shout such things for no reason?).

"Five people knew what happened in the parking lot, Antenor! You, Maciel, Anna Karenina, and the watchman. Who was the other one, the one who fired the single shot with an automatic? The watchman disappeared the next day. He vanished. No corpse, no crime. Where are his bones? Doesn't the city want to find the whalebones? So why doesn't anyone look for the watchman's bones?"

From the other side of the wall the metallic, tireless voice under the heat of the sun droned on: *Woe unto you, scribes and Pharisees, hypocrites! for ye are like unto whited sepulchres, which indeed appear beautiful outward, but are within full of dead men's bones, and of all uncleanness . . .*

"You're a Pharisee, Antenor!"

"What's a Pharisee?"

"A Pharisee is an ignorant person. You were in your element last night, kneeling at the feet of that imposter, sniffing the gold."

"Hey, Godfather! Anybody listening would think you're St. Teresa."

The worshippers began to leave the neighboring yard. Through the holes in the fence they could see Pedro Quimera, Antenor, and the Godfather. They were approaching to hand out a pamphlet when they saw Dr. Maciel's body.

"Is there a problem, brothers? Can God help?"

"The one who needed him, he abandoned. That one there. He's already on his way to meet the Lord and settle accounts. His good God has a lot to answer for."

Pedro noticed the worshipper restrain himself, anger crossing his face at the Godfather's irony.

"God will receive him well."

"He's going to have a hard time answering why he put him in this world. Maciel's going to nag him till he finds out why he was so abandoned."

"God has his ways . . ."

The worshipper's companion realized the conversation was pointless, the situation there was different.

"If you like, we can call the police."

"Don't get involved, brothers, don't get involved. Stick to your prayers and your hymns, your Pharisees and your psalms."

The men left. They were God-fearing, but they weren't stupid.

"They're going to call the police."

"Let them! We're not leaving here till we get into the Shoeshine Man's house. Who could have killed Maciel?"

"Come on! What do you care? Did you search his pockets?"

"Want to bet? We're going to find a phone number and a name."

Pedro Quimera admired the calm with which the Godfather stuck his hands in the dead man's pockets, turning them inside out. They were empty, and he continued, imperturbable. Like a jealous woman going through her husband's pockets in search of proof of infidelity, a ticket, a lipstick-stained handkerchief. The already rigid body was turned on its back. Quimera closed his eyes, it was sickening, sickening. But alluring, despite all the mischief Maciel had caused.

"Didn't I tell you?"

He wasn't sure, but Pedro had the feeling that the small slip of paper had already been in the Godfather's hands.

"A name? Whose?"

At that moment they heard the sound of a car braking, tires skidding, a collision, shouts, a second collision, an engine accelerating, moving into the distance. They saw the worshippers running, panicked. Antenor went to a spot in the passageway, shielded by a vine that covered an orange tree like a veil.

"A car just ran over the worshippers!"

"The police are on their way. We have to get into the house."

The Godfather unfolded the piece of blue paper.

"Mariúsa."

Pedro Quimera had approached close enough to see the number. Dazzled by the possibility of detective work, he didn't realize that the Godfather left it open long enough for him to memorize it.

"Mariúsa! Mariúsa! What does she have to do with all this? That SOB, what did this guy go and dig up? To me the woman is dead. Dead!"

"The dead come back, Antenor. Maciel could've phoned her last night. Why? What did they talk about?"

"I've had enough of this hellish day! Manuela dead. Maciel murdered. Mariúsa! Why did she have to reappear?"

2

When he realized it, Quimera was standing before Antenor. Why was he speaking so openly about this Mariúsa? How to find out? Investigation was such a pain!

"You! What are you doing here?"

Antenor, bewildered, found the question intrusive. He was known for disdaining reporters after the press had raised suspicions about how he became rich.

"Which paper are you from?"

"*O Expresso.*"

"Ask Luisão to call me."

"The Shoeshine Man saw you getting out of Manuela's car during the storm."*

"He couldn't have seen me, I was in the Nove de Julho, having dinner. I stayed there until the district attorney notified me of the crime. And the Shoeshine Man has disappeared. No one knows, no one saw."

"A businessman who was at the dinner says that you disappeared for half an hour . . ."**

"Who? What businessman?"

It's fun tossing crap into the fan, thought Pedro. He was enjoying himself now. Drops of sweat were running down Antenor's forehead, staining his coat. Quimera would feel more confident without the Godfather, whose presence provoked uneasiness because of everything he seemed to know. Or was that just a ploy? What a disconcerting man, so up on the city's underground.

"Answer, Antenor!"

"What's your game, Godfather?"

"My game. It's mine. Not yours. Or Manuela's anymore."

"Enough! It's over! With Manuela dead, it's over."

---

* It had suddenly occurred to him, and Pedro said what came into his head.
** Another shot in the dark. He knew that in films and books you can say anything.

He was enraged, but his body wouldn't move. His lips were contorted in anger. The Godfather placed his hand on Antenor's head. Antenor drew back and then lunged forward, attempting a head-butt. The Godfather stepped aside agilely. Antenor lost his balance and bumped into the door of the house, which opened, and he fell into the interior of the living room lit by the television set tuned to an ecological program. Thousands of dead fishes along the riverside.*

The Godfather went in, hurriedly. The house was turned upside down. Open drawers, shoe polish cans of every color scattered everywhere, brushes, buffing cloths, shattered boxes, chipped wood, the telephone off the hook. In one corner, covered with a burlap bag, the computer. Quimera was surprised. What was a PC doing there?

"The diskettes. The diskettes. They must have been made here."

Antenor reransacked what was already ransacked, accompanied by the Godfather. Nothing was whole, slashed pillows, a perforated dirty mattress, bedside tables turned upside down, kitchen cabinet with no glass.

"Did they take everything?"

Bewildered, they made their way through the four-room house, looking into the Shoeshine Man's boxes. There were several, each of a different kind of wood.

"Nothing's left. Who could it have been?"

"He received a shipment when? Day before yesterday. He stopped by the Snooker, but all he managed to sell was a little crack. The guys there are tough. When he saw you at the square, it was undoubtedly because he was bringing you an order."

---

* A politically correct instant.

"No one saw me! And I wasn't doing business with the Shoe-shine Man."

"What are you doing here?" asked Pedro.

"I heard you talking at the Snooker and followed you."

Had he heard? So, he was at the Snooker? Doing what? Shit, this business is getting me screwed up! Quimera was upset.

"Let's go now, in a little while this place is going to be crawling with people and the news will spread. I don't even know how you got here, the dinner at the hotel was big-time. And you didn't take good care of Ruy Banguela. He saw you leave out the back and tried to sell me the information. You can be sure he went to Iramar."

"Let him go to Portella. Find the guy."

"Now I see Ruy was right. But I thought you hadn't left the hotel."

Pedro was pleased. His shot in the dark had hit home. Antenor had left the hotel.

"Just cut off my head and hand it to the kid on a platter. Deliver it to Portella, take it to the papers. You're not hearing anything, fat man! He's senile! Decrepit!"

Decrepit, thought Pedro. Where does the man find those words? Why is he so careful when he attacks the Godfather? What's going on between the two of them? I haven't advanced an inch, I'm a failure, I don't know where to look next. Even that blind detective, Max Carrados, saw more than I do. Quimera had discovered Carrados in the basement of the municipal library, where there were piles of dusty books. He amused himself more with Ellery Queen than with Hegel, whom Yvonne so adored.

"Whoever was here did a good job. Let's go."

"What about Maciel?"

"Finito! To hell with him!"

"The neighbors saw us. And the evangelicals. They're curious, and they know you. They're going to talk. The rabble love gossip, and you're a hot item. The police must be on their way because of the traffic accident."

Fifteen minutes later, police vehicles pulled up. One of the policemen came straight to Antenor.

"Good afternoon, sir! What's the problem?"

"With me, nothing. But Maciel had one. He's dead!"

"Dr. Maciel! So they finally got the pussy hound."

The cop went to the lemon verbena, crouched down, prodded Maciel's chest.

"Gunshots and stab wounds!"

He ordered the other policemen to search for the weapons.

"What a day, sir! You must be on your last legs."

Man, observed Pedro. If there was anyone who didn't seem on his last legs or shook up, it was Antenor. In reality, it didn't seem that his wife was dead. And why didn't the cop ask what the man was doing there? He wasn't ever going to ask. You could see that by his servile attitude.

"The worst day of my life . . . What's your name?"

"Dosualdo."

"I'll remember it! The police have been very kind!"

Why doesn't he go home? How could he leave his dead wife and come to this hole? Pedro was unresigned, bothered by the heat. The sun had disappeared. Heavy clouds, the sultriness was stifling, the city was like a greenhouse, a shortage of air. Vehicles with forensic personnel arrived, along with photographers.

"Aren't you going to give me an interview?" Pedro asked.

"You haven't seen me and you're not going to say anything. Keep quiet, you're my friend, and I like my friends very much."

"What's that supposed to mean?"

"That I'm making a new friend. I like you, you're a clever young man! Don't let yourself get caught and don't write what you shouldn't."

Antenor said good-bye, made his way through the gathering that filled the street, and got into the turquoise-blue Honda Civic, accompanied by the Godfather, who clapped Pedro on the shoulders.

"If you liked Lindorley's drafts, drop by and we'll have one together!"

"What about the interview?"

"I never gave one. And nobody's going to believe me anyway. And in any case, I was only going to lie, say whatever suited me. Just like everyone else."

At that moment, beyond the crowd of people, Pedro saw Efrahim trying to look past the shoulders of two fat women who were blocking the way. He seemed anxious. Him too? The Shoeshine Man was more popular than he could have imagined. He wanted to see if he could reach Efrahim. But the café owner slipped away up a side street, protected by an umbrella and carrying a package wrapped in pink paper. Intrigued, he decided to follow the café owner. He was killing time. The narrow street passed under a small bridge, an old branch of the railroad, a future avenue to be constructed by Portella's firm, and led to a working-class neighborhood. A housing project dating back to the 1940s and built by the hat factory, transformed into a tenement occupied by the landless, day laborers, idlers, the unemployed, indigents, thieves, juvenile delinquents, street kids, people fleeing the Northeast drought, drunks, junkies, dealers, numbers runners, retirees, street vendors. A refuge that was bursting at the seams with shacks made of wood, plastic, cardboard, tin—every kind of material available. Iramar Alcifes suggested that everything be set on fire, but faced with the violent reaction, he shut up.[*]

Efrahim and Pedro, on his tail, crossed, on the better side of the favela, a street with masonry houses, the majority with their stucco in bad condition. They entered a thicket. Pedro was sweating, his shirt was soaked. Drops of rain. If the promised downpour came, it would be violent. Just ahead, the large wall of Focal, a vast burned-out ruin. Efrahim continued skirting it until he found a hole hidden by the castor-bean plants. What was he doing there? To meet with the ghosts of the locomotive engineers? Along the length of the wall, stubs of colored candles, clay pots, chicken bones, bottles, framed portraits, ceramic objects, body parts reproduced in wax and known as ex-votos, from people who asked favors of those who died in the 1953 fire. Many miracles had come from those flames, and there was an annual pilgrimage. That was when it occurred to Pedro[**] that Manuela's car, the turquoise-blue Honda Civic, was with Antenor.

---

[*]   However, the idea stuck in the minds of many, from time to time when they talk about the matter.
[**]   Quimera is quick at times, very slow at others.

SHEATHE YOUR DICK IF
YOU DON'T WANT TO DIE

1

If Pedro Quimera owned a car or had the newspaper's jeep, he could have followed the Godfather and Antenor. Thus, while he was following Efrahim, guided by intuition—a quality he always possessed, it's important to mention—let us accompany the Honda Civic. Could this be the car the Nighttime Shoeshine Man saw stopping? Was it Manuela's body that came out of its trunk?

"Face it, Antenor. The longer you wait, the worse it gets. You have to confront it, it's time."

"Go home? With that crowd on the avenue? It's a circus, I've become an animal in the zoo."

"Let's go to the Regattas and Navigators. We can get to your house by the lake."

The road to the club was a thoroughfare lined with trees, with their canopies merging to form a kind of tunnel. When they were a mile and a half from the entrance, the weather turned ugly again.

"If it's like yesterday, we're screwed. We'd better hurry."

Eighteen-wheelers, heading for the sugar mill, prevented them from passing. The sky dark, unbearable summer heat. Antenor pulled onto the apron, leaving the trucks behind. The asphalt was covered with bagasse, crushed cane, sticky puddles swarming with flies and bees. At the door of the Regattas and Navigators, the doorman, in a grotesque blue and white maritime uniform as if ready to command a yacht, looked at Antenor in surprise.

"Oh, sir! . . . I heard . . . My . . . condolences . . . And this gentleman?"

If it was something good, no one would know, thought Antenor.

"My guest."

"ID, please."

"Is the number good enough? I don't have—"

"I'll vouch for him," said Antenor, irritated.

The doorman let them in, and Antenor turned to the Godfather.

"You have so many IDs and when you need one, you've got nothing."

To avoid the social area of the club, they went around through the forest that surrounded the lake and arrived at Pier 9. Maybe someone could lend them a boat. A fat, suntanned man was alone at the pier, sitting on a pile of tires. Alencastro, owner of a TV station.

"How sad that business is! Real sad! I don't know what to say! What're you doing here with all this mess?"

"I'm going home. Except that the street is jammed with rabble, the media, they're really pissing me off. The only thing to do is to go this way. Got a boat you can lend me?"

"The *Princess of Mesopotamia* is with my daughter, she went sailing in the east lake. If you want, you can take the launch, the *Zoraide*. It's speedy as can be, but I think it'd be better to wait out the storm."

"I can't wait! I'm not afraid of getting a little wet."

"I'll be right back, I'm going to ask the sailor to get the *Zoraide* ready."

The two men stood there amid the silence. Small waves made a chop-chop sound against the pier. Fear of rain had kept many people away from the lake. Few boats could be seen in the distance.

"Now tell me. About my mother. She's alive, isn't she? What happened? What's this story about men in love? You speak in riddles, and I was always lousy at riddles."

"Those weren't letters from your mother that Maciel had."

"I know the envelopes. I don't know how she managed to get so many all alike."

"I got them for her."

The Godfather was imperturbable. Antenor had always known him to be like that, calm in the face of the worst situations. Tremendous self-control, a poker face that irritated his gambling opponents. And he had seen his father confront unusual, highly charged circumstances, especially when desperate men who had borrowed money and couldn't pay threatened violence. He should have inherited that quality for his political debates. They were his weakness, he would lose his patience, turn over the table, especially with Adriano Portella's provocations. It was said that Portella had learned to endure torture in the days when he was a subversive with his face on Wanted posters. A past that frequently came to the surface, ridiculed by the younger generations; after all, more than thirty years had gone by. However, the Godfather is a singular man who can blow up over nothing, a match that fails to light, coffee spilling from an overly full cup and staining his shirt, a chipped plate, wine or beer in a plastic glass.

"Maciel said you could take me to her!"

"Maciel's dead!"

"That's not the problem, it's what he said."

"What he said is worth about as much as goat shit."

"And the letters? What's this story that you got the envelopes for her? What's going on that I don't know about? What are they hiding from me? *Why* are they hiding it from me?"

"Don't go to the well so often, or it'll dry up . . . I got those envelopes for her. Manufactured by Ferrari, a big guy and a good man. His wife made the best feijoada in the city. Every six months I would go to Araraquara, and Navega at the stationery store would have the package ready. After your mother died, I never went back."

"Except she didn't die, did she?"

From a radio somewhere in the boathouse came the voice of Harry Belafonte singing "Merci Bon Dieu." An old song from the guitarist Frantz Casseus, part of the *Suite Haitiana*. The Godfather was silent, his eyes lowered.

"The first time Heloísa showed up at the Snooker, we were refurbishing the tables."

"Heloísa?"

"Your mother. For years and years she would come through the door and stand there looking at the stairs. She never found the courage to come up. That afternoon, she slowly climbed the sixty-five steps. That was going to be the name of the Snooker, 65 Steps, until the day the hunchback who cleaned the church and played very good pool told me, after a game: Your cue seems like it's crystal, Godfather. I found that glorious, Crystal Cue. When Heloísa began coming up, the blind woman in the pink house opposite the Old Market put on the record with that song. She would play it all day."

"Weren't you going to call it the Broken Cue?"

"That wasn't commercial, just a recollection of mine. I rejected it as soon as I thought of it."

"I want to know about my mother!"

"I'm talking about her. Heloísa hated that place, maybe because I liked it so much. It was a passion, I'd spend all my time there. The green felt, the pockets, the shiny colored balls, the wooden triangle, the first stroke, the balls scattering, each one seeking its position. The balls get to know you, to love you or hate you, they realize whether you like them or not, whether you're good at your craft, and then they help you or defeat you, they place themselves in friendly or inaccessible positions, roll easily or stop, turn aside or happily find a pocket."

"It's raining! Let's get inside!"

The Godfather didn't move. His eyes were bulging out of their sockets. He's pickled, thought Antenor, what did he have to drink? When the downpour became constant, he felt the entire weight of his fatigue and the image of Manuela's nude body on the Formica table at the morgue reappeared. He shuddered with pleasure. He wanted to see the body sliced up by Morimoto. Never had he felt as much desire for Manuela as now.

"Three hundred and sixteen matches with that cue. In a row, without a loss. I never lost, nobody wanted to play me. I cleaned out everybody and bought the bar at the station. That's where I saw Heloísa for the first time. She was arriving from Lins, about to change trains, four fifteen in the morning. She ordered malzebier, I didn't have any, so I ran to the bar at the Nove de Julho. She drank it and the foam made a ring around her lips, which she removed with her tongue. I felt like drinking beer licking that tongue."

"May I sit down?" I asked.

"It's your bar, your table, your chair."

"But when a customer sits down, the table becomes his home and it's the other one who needs to ask permission."

We went on talking foolishness like that to each other until she took the last swig and looked me in the eye.

"If you want," she said, very serious and professional, "if you want, I'm waiting for the train, but I can earn a bit, I don't like wasting time."

I was speechless, but I'm the practical type. I closed both doors to the bar, pushed the tables aside, and she saw that I had two crystal cues, one at the Snooker, one on me. That's how it was. The train came and went, people knocked at the door, I didn't open the bar till the next afternoon. We were aching—shit, what stupidity to screw on a cold granite table, I threw out my back. And you know what she did? She told me:

"We did it this many times at so much per time, you owe me this much."

"At least give me a discount. Give me one on the house and I won't charge for the beer."

I was pissed, I thought she had enjoyed the crystal cue, she said she had but needed to charge. It was the same as me drinking the bar's beer or giving coffee to whoever came in. I agreed, since I was facing a competent pro, I even paid a little extra; after all, she had missed her train and lost her fare. It's not that I'm a nice guy, I just wanted to please her. Three, four, eighty trains came by, and she let them go. When the locomotive pulled into the station, I would look at her, fearing she would leave. The whistles and bells announcing arrivals would cause me such anxiety that my skin tightened, like someone who'd had too many plastic surgeries. Heloísa helped me, and the bar was making money, packed with people, I had to reach an agreement with the railroad not to charge admission to those coming into the bar. In those days people had to pay to go onto the platform. Heloísa sang well and sometimes, between the 11:00 P.M. and the 2:00 A.M. trains, we would lock the doors and she would dance on the counter. Later I hired a second dancer, but the railroad didn't like it and I lost the concession. It was a very strict company, the railroad workers were almost slaves, they were terribly afraid, and they were all forbidden to frequent the bar—by order of one of the directors, who was also in love with Heloísa and was there night after night. A tall guy nicknamed "the Hungarian," who wore shiny boots with enormous laces, gold-frame glasses, and when Heloísa danced he would get all excited and make a funny sound with his throat, like gargling. One day the railroad company sent a notice: that's it, it can't go on anymore, the station isn't a whorehouse. It wasn't a whorehouse at all, this city has always been moralistic, uptight, a bunch of repressed hypocrites. You know of any city with more cuckolds? That was when Heloísa rented the dairy store, remodeled it, and opened the cabaret. She brought in women from everywhere. I never saw anyone with a better nose for finding whores. Here in the city she got some thirty girls, the finest, taking them from orphanages, and the nuns, crazy to get their hands on some money, provided them and promised to find more. Heloísa said the girls were going to study in good schools, and since nuns don't hang out in cabarets she was never found out. In those days you could go to a cabaret and sleep with any of the women. It's not like today, when you go to bed and catch AIDS. And it kills you! It kills you for a two-minute fuck. It's like sticking your dick in a bowl of acid, it eats you up, eats you all up, pussies and assholes have become dangerous, radioactive, tunnels of death, wolves' mouths that take you to the cemetery. No, my son, this is not a good time to live the happy life. You can't even have fun anymore, they've abolished pleasure. That's why guys get their kicks running around on motorcycles, racing cars on public streets, brawling at the stadium, killing themselves, spending all day on video games and video poker, snorting, typing at their computer keyboards. Now they have to sheathe their dicks if they don't want to die . . .

"Enough raving! I've never seen you like this. What is it? The letters? The letters, father! Who wrote them?"

"Who wrote what?"

"The letters from my mother!"

The Godfather reflected for a moment, as if he didn't know what Antenor was talking about. His vacant gaze suddenly regained a bit of expression.

"That bastard scribe at the notary's office, he was in love with her."

"Then he knew everything, about you, about me."

"He knew, but he's not doing anything with what he knows."

"Where is he?"

"He died."

"You killed him, didn't you?"

"He died of old age, he was seventy-eight when he wrote the letters. He was an educated man, the only person in Arealva who had read somebody named Camilo Castelo Branco!"

"You're not making sense, you're delirious. I know you, and half of what you're saying isn't true. The other half is a lie. My mother wasn't a whore! It can't be, because I'd have known a long time ago . . . And now this rain on top of everything!"

The lake was splashing in the storm. The Godfather and Antenor were soaked. Boats were quickly returning to shore.

"She didn't die, did she, father?"

"She's at the bottom of this lake. Drowned. The blind woman from the pink house pushed her out of a boat, the *Merci Bon Dieu*. I called her and the blind woman came up to the Snooker one day, I wanted to know about the music she played so much. She replied: only if you teach me how to play pool. I've seen a lot in life, but never a blind person shoot pool. Okay, let's try it. First she has to learn how to hold the cue. She learned, blind people learn quickly. Since they can't see, they develop other abilities. They're excellent at manufacturing brooms. The blind woman from the house was attractive, she would put on the record, she had a phonograph that replayed automatically, and I would direct her on how to grip the cue, showing her what to shoot, she would feel the ball and hit it. She seemed to see the geography of the table, where the pockets were. Of course she couldn't distinguish the color, or maybe she could, because at times she'd pick up a ball and say it's the green one, the yellow one, beats me whether she was just guessing or she could feel the texture of the ivory, but at the table she had no idea where they were located. Doesn't a gambler mark cards without anyone seeing it? That didn't matter, what was important were the cushions, the combination shots she made. She was the attraction of the house for a time. One afternoon, when she asked for the cue, I took mine out and put it in her hand. She was furious, and I tried to grab her. I was dying to screw a blind woman, with her rolling those lifeless eyes and me trying to do right by her, to light up those eyes, I was certain that a good screw would make her see again. But she went away and I lost a lot of customers because the blind woman was a sensation. I tried going downstairs and talking to her, but she refused to see me, her mother threatened to kill me. One day I found a note taped to the draft machine: Godfather, *Merci Mon Dieu*. I knew what *merci*, *bon* and *mon* meant. Me, the god of billiards."

"Sonofabitch! Have you gone crazy?"

Antenor tried to take shelter under the roof of the pier, while the Godfather went on talking, his eyes fixed on the tall waves raised by the wind. As a child, Antenor had dashed off to the Snooker to hear adventure stories about the men who had opened the railway into the backlands or about the arrival of the Hangman in the city and the hotels and boardinghouses refusing to rent a room, no family willing to house him. Everyone knew he had come to hang an innocent man who hadn't killed his children. Nevertheless, the entire city had gathered at the Largo da Boa Escrita to witness the hanging and had even applauded the Hangman's skill as a man who knew his craft. The Godfather liked to recount the battles he had won, describing each victory, each punch, each opponent's fall. You were never defeated, father? No, you can read what the papers said. I don't know how to read, read it to me. The Godfather would read frightening narrations, great encounters, blows, adversaries whipped. He remained the champion for years, no one dared face him. Antenor loved those fights, fallen giants spurting blood through the mouth. From an early age he liked seeing bleeding people, heads severed, arms wrenched off. Because of this, every time the Good-Bye Angel attacked, he would run to see the mutilated body. He bribed the police to alert him, he wanted to see *in loco* bodies still bleeding, not clean and washed cadavers. Thinking about the ones he'd seen, he again felt a shiver of pleasure. And a very great tenderness for his mother, how she must have suffered in this city, being what she was.

2

At each passing of the extremely long trains, the sweetish smell invades the area. Day and night, millions of pineapples make their way into the juice factories.

The Focal is located halfway between the truck terminal and the Industrial Village to the west of the city. The tracks were reclaimed from the spur that went from the Focal to the cotton port, sixty years earlier the busiest spot in the city, located next to the railroad station. After the fire, for fifteen years the tracks rusted under sun and rain, weeds grew between the ties, the signals rotted, spikes were stolen by Spanish junkmen, the roadbed stones were taken away to be used for construction. Only the rails were left, because they were extremely heavy, the first in Brazil to come in two-hundred-meter lengths, which was the state of the art in that period. The Focal, even without the fire, was living on borrowed time. Before the sixties, cotton had been eradicated from the region and replaced by oranges, passion fruit, sugarcane, and soy, more profitable and a guaranteed export. There was a struggle over the land, comprising several acres, which left real estate speculators dreaming and fed the fantasies of environmentalists anxious to establish a Green Reserve.

To date there were no explanations for the nonoccupation of the place by the landless and the homeless. Perhaps superstition and fear spoke louder, for no one doubted that souls in torment roamed the site, desperate, still fleeing the flames forty years later. There's not a single locomotive engineer who hasn't heard laments, cries, screams, pleas for help, moans. Others have glimpsed lights, smoke, crumbling walls. One actually saw the entire fire while his locomotive crossed the terrain, like a holographic video or an electronic spectacle at Disney World, the flames reaching the 160-foot mark on the towers that housed the barrels of oil.

On that night in 1953, the tanks burst, the incandescent oil descended like lava, transforming wooden shacks into smoking toothpicks, burning vegetation and scorching the ground, until it reached the river. The burning oil plunged into the water with a deafening sound and was repelled. A tidal bore that fed the imagination. Boiling oil and water in combat, the water rising in whistling jets of steam, illuminated by the yellowish flames. More beautiful than any fireworks display, it was said at the time. The population gathered at a convenient distance, mesmerized by the spectacle.*

Efrahim's mind was at ease. The pink package in one hand and in the other, his unfailing umbrella. He was never seen without it, it protected his exfoliated arms, a result of skin cancer. Pedro was hidden behind a bush next to a dilapidated switch box. The café owner went down a set of stairs, closed his umbrella, entered an opening to the side—the door had long since rotted, burned, or been stolen, it mattered little. Pedro ran, he mustn't lose sight of Efrahim. He crossed through the opening and found himself facing enormous solid wood frames, mixed with corroded iron, in the open air. A gigantic thing! He was amazed. Pedro was fascinated by deserted places, he frequently took the scooter and rode out of the city to ensconce himself in some plantation with a book in his hands, where he would remain for hours with a can of soda and a package of munchies. He had to explore the Focal, do a photo-essay, as soon as he got a camera.

---

* Hans of the Deluge, in his shaky Portuguese, said that only the bombing of Dresden by the English, at the end of the war, had produced similar flames. The photos of that night are in the archives of *O Expresso* and *A Lista* and can be viewed at the Lev Gadelha Museum.

Efrahim moved in the direction of the press* and disappeared. Pedro, drenched with sweat, carefully navigated the floor clotted with broken glass, rocks, wood, nails, small pieces of iron. Unbearable heat, smells of every kind, mold, dried oil, iron, urine, crap—so people did come here, despite the ghosts—rotted wood and something else, indefinable. Quimera was sensitive to smells, almost to the point of a mania. From time to time he would fight with Yvonne when he smelled a slight odor from her underarm, which would leave him in anguish and hors de combat in bed. Then he heard the snoring. Loud.

Dodging between beams and pieces of boards—they appeared new, that was odd!—Pedro arrived at a position from which he could see Efrahim standing there, staring with a clinical expression at the snoring Nighttime Shoeshine Man. A snore that had reduced the city to laughter. A lawsuit was under way in the courthouse. Neighbors of the Shoeshine Man had sued to force him to move, saying they could no longer put up with his snoring. They sent officers to the Shoeshine Man's home to measure the decibels of the snoring. It took some time, as the man lived at night, circulating about the city from bar to bar, nightclub to nightclub. He practically lived in the brothels on the outskirts, vestiges of the old bordellos that in the forties and fifties had made the city famous. Nostalgic types spoke of the Majestic and its madam, Heloísa, known as the Cleopatra of the Tietê for her habit of cutting her hair like the Cleopatra of the film.** Heloísa, owner of a business

---

* The equipment startled the city when it arrived from Alsace-Lorraine in 1937, transported by trains that took days to unload the parts. The enthralled population brought lunchboxes and spent Sunday having picnics.
** The one with Claudette Colbert, directed by Cecil B. DeMille, and not the one with Elizabeth Taylor, directed by Mankiewicz.

that had prospered following her retirement after teaching several generations. She invented the sandal that became a beach slipper, which enjoyed great popularity and was exported to Europe. A legend in the city, she lived in a penthouse, cloistered from fear of infections. Terrified of AIDS, the Ebola virus, typhus,* she never turned on TV in order not to see the war in Bosnia.

The Shoeshine Man was a messenger. He would carry notes, take information, such-and-such a nightclub is full, this or that bar is empty, there's a bunch of girls begging for it at the Top-Toque, the city's most famous spot for call girls.** A picturesque character of indefinable age. No one knew where he came from, who his parents or relatives were, or whether he'd ever been married. At least not in the city, where he had lived for the last thirty years. Efrahim shook the Shoeshine Man, who showed no sign of waking up, as loose as an empty sack.

"High! The skank!"

The café owner took his umbrella and poked the Shoeshine Man's chest.

"Wake up, Aristeu! Wake up!"

The Shoeshine Man muttered a few garbled words. New pokes, whacks. The Shoeshine Man opened his eyes, not knowing where he was. He moved his hands, trying to right himself. Efrahim warned:

"Watch it! Careful of the vomit, you pig!"

"Efrê, what's the matter, Efrê?"

"Efrê my ass. Didn't I forbid you to call me that?"

"You're hurting me, Efrê, stop it!"

---

* Typhus in 1995? With Brazil's perfect system of sanitation? Thus did the authorities distort reality.

** Their honorariums range from $500 to $1500.

"Then get up. I brought food, but you're not hungry, you need something sweet, you've got the munchies. High. If you start using what you sell, you're toast."

"It was just one hit, Efrê!"

"A hit for an elephant! I can't even see your eye! It's all cloudy. You've got to get out of town."

"They'll kill me, Efrê! They'll kill me. I won't get away this time. I shouldn't have done what I did."

"You've gotten out of lots of jams."

"They screwed me, this time they screwed me good."

"There wasn't any other way. Damned if you do, damned if you don't."

"Antenor, the Godfather, Portella, everybody's after me."

"You're worth a lot, let's negotiate that. Make some dough. Leave that part to me."

"You're gonna sell me out, Judas? You're gonna hand me over, aren't you?"

"Take it easy, you're going to make a lot of money, just keep calm, it's all one big con!"

"If you give me up, I'm giving you up too. They'll kill me."

"The Godfather, maybe. Not Antenor! He's a chickenshit."

"I know those people! Besides that, the ones who owe me money will love to see me dead."

"I can negotiate you with Portella. He won't kill you! He needs an ace up his sleeve against Antenor."

"I shouldn't have gone along with the proposition. But it's done, what can I do? And you abandoned me, you double-crossed me!"

He was muttering, frightened.

"I've got just one friend, Efrê! You!"

He tried to grab Efrahim's hand. The café owner pushed him away, and the Shoeshine Man fell limply to the floor. Pedro was surprised at Efrahim's strength.

"Don't kiss my hand, not here. I don't have anywhere to wash it. And listen to me, I need to wash it! I really need to!"

Another four or five solid whacks with the umbrella. The Shoeshine Man moaned, cowed.

Then they heard: Efrahim, Efrahim! And the café owner slipped away, skirting past a piece of equipment resembling a large armoire and disappearing from sight. After a few minutes, an argument broke out, in voices familiar to Pedro. There was no way to observe without showing himself. If he moved even a little, the Shoeshine Man would see him. The argument increased in volume, calmed down, then regained its intensity. Those voices, one belonging to a woman, the other rather hoarse. Pedro came to the conclusion that he would never be a detective, for an investigator must be able to identify people by their voice, that's what you see in books. Efrahim shouted: "They're not going to do that, they can't, it's madness. No way! Over my dead body."

He had barely spoken the phrase when the shot rang out. Pedro didn't realize it was a gunshot. He wasn't used to such things. The sound was muffled, unlike in films and on television. He saw the Shoeshine Man come to in a second and throw himself to the ground. Efrahim hid behind a pillar. The shots splintered the walls, the wood, ricocheting off the metal. Pedro Quimera was afraid, even knowing he wasn't in the line of fire and was out of sight of the shooters as well as Efrahim and the Nighttime Shoeshine

Man. Protected by the semidarkness, he squeezed his fat body into a hollow of the machinery, a small grotto of indeterminate purpose. What terrified him and made him shrink like wet cotton candy was the fear of stray bullets. Shots ricocheted in absurd directions. He had read about the actor in Rio de Janeiro killed as he lay in bed by a shot coming from the hillside shantytown. And about the woman in Campinas hit in the chest as she was bathing. The bullet was fired by a thief who was fighting in the square, fifty-plus yards below. This imponderable frightened Pedro, who preferred logic and straight paths, nonexistent in life; hence the insecurity in which he lived.

The acidic perfume of pineapples, powerful and thick, arrived before the train. Then the sound of the string of cars as they passed, their couplings clanking. After the gunshots, the silence seemed immense. Heavy drops of rain began to fall from a darkened sky. Efrahim dashed back, took shelter with the Shoeshine Man, protected by a cement mixer. They were whispering, and Pedro saw the revolver in the café owner's hand. Aristeu looked terrified. Four shots in a row. No one moved, anywhere. The shooters seemed to be testing, pausing, waiting for a response. They probed to see if the others were armed. Perhaps they were planning an attack. Very experienced types. An innocent, Pedro wondered how it was possible to have gotten himself into this. He had gone out with Yvonne on Saturday to the movies. She hated *Jurassic Park* and refused to go to a bar, claiming a migraine, she preferred going home. Pedro, suspecting their affair was over, was tense beside her. In his kitchenette he watched most of *The Ten Commandments*. That was when the message boy from the newspaper showed up and he ran to the How Come Pharmacy.

Two shots, with an interval between, brought Quimera back to the present. Slowly, thinking agreeable thoughts—the method he had discovered to flee from reality when it becomes grim or when he contemplates his own misshapen body. Luisão wouldn't believe it when he told him about the shooting. If he was lucky enough to get out alive. He was terrified. The possibility of death was no longer distant, it was on the prowl, palpably.

The last freight car went by and the smell of pineapple lingered. One of the shooters approached, stepped on something, causing a cracking sound. They must have taken advantage of the noise from the train to come closer. Efrahim fired the first shot. The Count's face could be glimpsed behind a peeling column, his white hair glowing. His expression was different from the one Pedro was accustomed to seeing in the café. His muscles rigid, standing out on his cheeks, his forehead reddened and his mouth shut.

"Come on, you bastards!"

Silence. The sound of feet dragging, cautiously. Efrahim was exposed, a silver pistol in his left hand.

"Give us Aristeu! All we want is the Shoeshine Man. You don't concern us."

"Hand him over? Aristeu isn't mine!"

A shot, the café owner didn't move. He's either brave or crazy, thought Pedro in amazement. Efrahim let out three shots.

"You're gonna run out of bullets, Count!"

A woman's voice. Efrahim, his expression unchanged, patted his pocket, checking. Another shot, the bullet ricocheting off iron, a metallic sound. Pedro looked behind him, there was a tunnel with a single track over which perhaps small wagons of cotton-seed had run in earlier times. He decided to move away, though still curious to find out who the familiar female voice belonged to. He started breathing heavily, tight places made him uneasy, he had to get out immediately, he knew that the noxious smell would overwhelm him and ooze from his pores. He saw his mother's face at the other end, with the cord from the iron, which she placed in his father's hands. When he'd see the cord detached from the wall, he'd run to the large pipe that drained into a stream, a tributary of the Tietê. He'd lie there, with the thick, dark water coursing over his body. And the nauseating smell had overwhelmed him to such an extent that it never again left his skin. All he had to do was become nervous and Pedro could feel it returning, in his perspiration. Often, when he rose from Yvonne's sweating body, he noticed that she was sniffing the air, her sharp sense of smell detecting the stench that was neither gas nor halitosis nor foot odor.

Pedro alternated between fear and curiosity. He was certain they didn't know he was there. If he left, he'd give Yvonne an open-ing. And if he left and said nothing, it would be a letdown. These things were happening on a Sunday morning and weren't a video-tape or a novel, it was incredible. And happening to him! At last, the absolute boredom that dominated him and kept him tied to the bed on Sundays had vanished. He found himself in the middle of a gunfight, scared shitless, because of a socialite who was one of the few interesting people in this monotonous city where you endlessly saw the same habits, manner of speaking, procedures, rules, norms, and fashions.

He had run into Manuela a few times. She burst into his life at a benefit party at the High School for Athletics, dancing the tango "Duelo Criollo" in a tight white dress. So tight that it clung to her body, and there was no sign of underwear. That night, she displayed the glowing face of a brunette Sharon Stone. Ever since, Pedro had gone to the newspaper's morgue and contemplated the photos of Manuela. He had ordered a copy of the famous pose with her breasts exposed. Research in the society pages for the previous year showed her name appearing 1,296 times, which means twenty-four times a week, cited six times by each of the four society columnists. The feeling was that he knew everything about Manuela. Her life was an open book. At a vernissage, Quimera had gone up to her, attracted by her Samsara perfume and her nearly transparent dress.

He was aroused; she had told a magazine that she had given up on panties, preferring men's undershorts, more comfortable and exciting. "At least my husband loves them." Which generated comments. It must not be the husband. Who could the woman's lovers be? So often mentioned, never named, never seen? Despite his bedazzlement—and why did she excite him so?—Pedro did not find Manuela as impressive as was rumored. She wasn't tall, her eyes were hidden behind dark glasses that she twice changed (Bella Golzer and Ventura, he read the next day), and her feet seemed large. He always looked at women's feet, and that was what attracted him to Yvonne. Perfect feet, toes proportional, toenails well cared for. And her masculine face. Yvonne had hard features, strong, well defined, she was authoritarian and he enjoyed obeying.

On another occasion, Manuela was leaving the How Come Pharmacy in Lee jeans torn at the thighs and a T-shirt with a name in gold. What was she doing at that cheap place, far from Hydrangea Gardens, where she lived? Unless Antenor was at the Coral Whale.

"Your last chance, Count! Hand over Shoeshine Man!"

"He can't come now. He's shining my shoes."

"Count . . . Answer me this. Suppose you had your cell phone. And it rang. And the voice of the Good-Bye Angel told you your daughter Rita would be thrown out of an airplane from thirty thousand feet over the ocean. And we know you have a daughter. One you love and sent away from the city to protect her. And the voice said: the only way to save your daughter is to blow that damned Shoeshine Man's brains out. What would you do? You'd fuck that shitass drug dealer!"

That voice! The question. It's him. What's his connection to all this? And what about the woman's voice? Everyone in the city knows that woman's voice!

REASONS ARE INVENTED WHILE
WAITING FOR THE ILLUMINATED WHALE

1

The How Come Pharmacy. For years people have called it that.
Ever since Evandro began asking uncomfortable questions. It
started as a nocturnal amusement to kill time. For years the
pharmacy had been the only one on that side of town to stay
open all night. The steel doors weren't rolled down for a de-
cade. Gears rusted shut. Times when business was good. On a
single day, Evandro wouldn't show up. Dona Idalina, known as
the needle woman because of her fondness for shots, would wait

on customers. She knew the location of every drug but refused to do injections. On Good Friday he spent the day wearing the scarlet clothing of the Brothers of the Most Holy, kneeling at the feet of the casket of the dead Lord, in the Cathedral.

The elevation of the church to the status of cathedral was recent, less than fifteen years ago. The Bishopric came about with the growth of the city, which in two decades increased sevenfold, thanks to tax exemptions for industries, free land for banks, concessions for construction of buildings of more than fifteen stories. With the growth, new businesses flocked in with blinding speed. The rich area of town became middle class and then lower-middle. The Koreans, all illegals, took over the garment industry, displacing the Jews. The Italians, struggling against the Lebanese, kept control of dining and invented all-you-can-eat pizza and food-by-weight for the masses. The Industrial Village, with the connivance of the city council, spread like a belt, flouting zoning laws, and retail business swelled haphazardly, battling the street vendors and their political protectors. The progress of the seventies became worrisome after the 1982 crisis, alarming in 1990, and catastrophic in 1995, when the liquidity of money ended.

Large American-style chain drugstores took over the pharmaceutical market, and when Evandro realized it, he was geographically disadvantaged, far away from those who mattered. Despite the futility of staying open at night, he still did. Evandro never failed to show up at night. There was always someone in need whenever the popular clubs, scattered in the vicinity, held dances. If there was no one, he stayed on, reading biographies of painters or shifting the boxes of medicine around. He would go to the rear, take a few tokes of marijuana, then quickly use sprays to get rid of the smell. If he was in a state of anguish more than on other days—he felt he should resist, suck it up, suffer the anxiety to its fullest, because that was what made the artist—he risked doing a line of blow to untie the knot that dwelled at the base of the nape of the neck, causing unbearable headaches that lasted for days. Now and again someone would ask how Manuela had escaped dying that night when she had taken amphetamines of every kind and collapsed onto the counter.

The questions game began one June night at the time of the St. Peter's Dance, an Arealva tradition. Orchestras would come from other cities, and that year Gal Costa was guest of honor because of the success of her song "Festa no Interior." The dance would begin at midnight with a fireworks display, and the city would stop for twenty-five minutes; people would wake up and go to their windows. At the end of the fireworks, an illuminated whale would appear, floating in the sky for a few seconds. The pharmacy was strategically located for watching the show, and Evandro would provide benches and chairs and hand out whiskey and chilled Pedialyte. Those who came belonged to the Gilda Parisi Chorale and as they waited would tell stories, comment on operas, and needle Evangelina, curious about what she had done in São Paulo in May 1979. It had been something really serious, a secret that she kept behind her absorbed and mischievous smile. Because she had withdrawn from the chorale's trip to Europe, sponsored by a French institute.

On the night eight years earlier, working on his fifth shot of whiskey but still sober, Evandro clapped.

"I want to see who's brave in this group!"

The people sang passages from operas, interspersed with Beatles songs (they were good and won over the youth crowd) and even ventured to interpret hits of Jim Morrison, one of Evandro's idols. He died so young and became a myth! I've missed the chance to die young, I should've committed suicide that night. That damned woman, how I hate her.

"Brave?"

"What does that mean?"

"I have to be brave to live."

"And to live in this city."

"Isn't it brave to have to put up with all of you?"

"The bravery to answer a question."

"Twenty. Thirty. Go ahead, ask. We'll answer anything. What's the prize? Anything for money!"

"All I need is honesty."

"All drunks are honest."

"Imagine your mother has been diagnosed as terminally ill. AIDS. There's no way to save her."

"That's just what I want to happen to my mother," said Evangelina.

"All right, since mother is controversial, each of you think of whomever. A person you love."

"I love myself very much," interrupted Evangelina a second time. "Nobody in the world loves me as much as I do myself, unlike you."

"Crap! This isn't a therapy session. This beloved, idolized person can be saved. By sex."

"Sex with your mother?"

"To save our mother or whoever it might be, we have to change. Heteros become homosexuals. Homos become heterosexual. It's the only chance."

"Asininity! What're you driving at?"

"The whys of life."

"That's stupid, man!"

"See? You don't even want to think about the subject."

"A really foolish subject."

"Life's a foolish subject!"

"There you are. A philosophy of foolishness!"

Silence fell. Some decided that the mother or the loved one would die, they would never change their sexual preference. The men were furious at the ridicule from the homosexuals (they had beautiful castrati voices, the only chorale in the entire state of São Paulo to have them), who kept asking for a little kiss. Once the strangeness had passed, the group decided it had found a good source of amusement, and ever since then meets on a weekly basis to formulate awkward inquiries that defy moral and religious values, raise doubts about ethics, and unmask hypocrisy. The group became audacious, to the point where many admitted they would commit crimes for almost no reason. For some time the number of people at the pharmacy grew, and the participants in the How Come game enjoyed themselves. The pastime outgrew the pharmacy, caught on at the clubs, with many at the Crystal Night inventing embarrassing questions. The *whys* ransack private life, using insinuation, rumors, gossip, cogitation, and supposition. Enmities, fights, even separations resulted. There were many who attributed the wave of anonymous letters that flooded Arealva the year before to the groups that hung out at the pharmacy on How Come nights. The letters had wreaked havoc. They included lists of who was cheating on whom. Well-known names were there, stories heard. Even a crime was revealed in the letters. Panic reigned.

Pedro frequented the pharmacy, even though Yvonne, suspicious, refused to go. The difference is that Pedro would take a recorder and had dozens of tapes with hundreds of questions that he typed up and selected, classified by topic. He even suggested to Evandro a section in *O Expresso* with a question each day. Or perhaps a paperback book with the 666 most provocative questions. Pedro shared the pharmacist's hope to publish *The Book of How Come*. He smelled a success, a guaranteed best seller. Hadn't that young writer, hailed as the new Françoise Sagan and the most successful on the list with her short novel, startling for someone only seventeen, come from Arealva? The book that talked about the sex life of day laborers who worked harvesting pineapples, passion fruit, apples, and oranges? Compared by critics at the time to Steinbeck's *Grapes of Wrath*. Seen as the best nonfiction novel of the year, whatever that meant. Critics hailed it as the greatest work of its kind, second only to Truman Capote's *In Cold Blood*.

Evandro had become an expert on questions and ended up turning unpleasant. He attacked incessantly, displaying his bitterness, dripping with anguish that disturbed others to the point that people began to avoid him. Now, the pharmacist and Evangelina were there, shooting at the Nighttime Shoeshine Man and Efrahim. The voice was Evangelina's, and so was the way of asking a question. Why was she trying to kill Shoeshine Man, if he was nothing more than a witness who wasn't sure what he had seen in the rain? Considering who Shoeshine Man was, would he be believed? It was weird to picture Evangelina holding a revolver. Was she there in support of Evandro? The four traded shots, without stopping, the bullets whizzing past. Pedro Quimera wet his pants out of fear.

Evandro shooting didn't jibe with his quiet, passive image of a person with introspective, dreamy style. An introverted guy who longed for glory that would come from somewhere he didn't know; he had no aptitude for anything that could make a man stand out. At most, he would get a certificate and medal from the Chamber of Commerce for being the indefatigable worker who kept the doors open for ten years. But who would be moved by that or even care about it? Certificates just gather dust, medals tarnish.

Evandro wanted something that was impossible. He wanted to be famous—anonymously. That was the great move, the innovation, the insoluble paradox. All creative people are labeled utopian, he would shout, seeking impractical things and ending up proving they were right. The ideas of geniuses were branded as ridiculous. If they were, we wouldn't have lightbulbs, the movies, the wristwatch, or television. He would proceed to enumerate a long list. Merely to show how much he knew. He knew who invented what, and enjoyed telling stories that were part of useless culture, good for cocktail party conversation. Evandro had read the *Dictionary of Inventors*, the *Guinness Book of World Records*, almanacs, fascicles like *Discover*, publications like *Superinteresting* or *Popular*

Mechanics. Sometimes it was boring to hear about the invention of the Band-Aid, the condom, the rubber tire, the tampon, credit cards. There was a time, in late adolescence, when he would sweep up all the prizes—records and magazines, stockings and bedsheets—offered by radio programs that quizzed their listeners.

For the last two years, an obsession had dominated him: to cast off his anonymity. For him, going through life incognito was profoundly painful. Not being known, destined to die behind the counter—the thought endlessly anguished him. To the point that he couldn't breathe when he fixated on the subject, which tortured Evangelina. Evandro's goal was to be one of those people who act behind the scenes in history and exert influence, for whatever reason, by means of a very gentle, subtle, unconscious movement. People who determine changes in the life of others but remain anonymous.

Ruy Banguela took a photo one night of the group gathered at the pharmacy to play the How Come game. The photo was published in the biweekly magazine of the Regattas and Navigators, without Evandro's name. He reflected that when he was dead and no one remembered him, someone would pick up the photo and classify it, putting the caption *unknown* beneath his face. There was also the hypothesis of the photo becoming part of the archives of the Museum of Image and Sound. It would be published in albums dedicated to Decades of Arealva's History. For years, Evandro had been working on a book about the pain of the anonymous, based on photographs in newspapers, magazines, biographies, and albums. He rummaged through everything, looking for characters who weren't even secondary, nothing more than small, ephemeral comets, nameless. That changed or could have changed their routes. Like the young eighteen-year-old Swiss woman who had an affair with Kafka in Riva, near Genoa, in 1913. The affair was brief, lasting ten days, and the girl demanded absolute discretion. She asked that there be no future contact, no letters, and that not even her name be cited. In other words, she came on the scene and departed, when she could have left a footprint in history just like Felice or others loved by Kafka.

Evandro saw himself as the anonymous one of Arealva. An unidentified face, gloriously seen and reseen by generations who would ask, intrigued, What about this one? Who is he? What did he do? What was he thinking when they took the photo? And what if some curious type undertook to research his life? That's why he had organized a portfolio, with texts, thoughts, general ideas, readings, photographs, recordings of conversations, questions from the How Come game, newspaper clippings, letters, and a diary. All that was missing was some grand gesture. He needed to come up with a climax that would move people and justify that unlikely future biography. I'm dreaming, as usual when I think about this stuff, thought Pedro Quimera, seeing it all as a way of warding off fear.

A pause in the shooting. Pedro knows it's the pharmacist. And the woman can only be Evangelina. They're never apart. Chair and cushion. Intestine and crap, in the words of those who didn't like the gossipy couple. Every time he went to the pharmacy the reporter would observe the two, curious about the relationship. He never learned—he investigated—of any women in Evandro's life. Or men in Evangelina's. There are guys crazy about her because of her *Playboy* breasts. When the chorale puts on an exhibition, she wears very low-cut necklines and removes her glasses. Near-sighted, she memorizes the scores. The Gilda Parisi Chorale was the first story that Pedro wrote when he arrived in Arealva five years before, drawn to the New Methodist University, the only one with a decent communications major. He left Corumbataí thinking about Rio Claro, cities still in their early stages, which made him dizzy. Besides that, the streets and avenues didn't have names—they were all 1, 2, 3, 34, 56. All that was merely an excuse; he had gone after Yvonne, but she, as soon as she saw him in the city, moved to Arealva without leaving a trail. It took six months for Pedro to locate her, through a spot on the seven o'clock Regional Newscast, where she appeared at a rally on the Methodist campus protesting poor teaching.

When he arrived in Arealva, he discovered she had been expelled from the university and was surviving as a contact person for the embroidery stores, the major craft in the region. She seemed meek, disappointed, because no other college had accepted her—the information was spread through the Internet. Thus her bitterness and aggressiveness, which Pedro understood but which was starting to become unbearable. She demanded of him what she herself had failed to achieve: to reform society. And he wasn't thinking about any such thing. He was waiting for the great stroke of luck, the twist of fate that defined the moment that changes people's lives and propels them to glory. He played the lottery, obsessively, we have to pursue wealth. He would cite clichés, like the apple falling on Newton's head or Alexander Fleming discovering penicillin when he forgot the cultures in his petri dishes and found them full of mold. Readings from almanacs, Sunday supplements, knowledge from television programs. He believed in twists of fate and allowed the boat to follow its course, certain that it wouldn't crash into the rocks. He was interested only in the decisive moment. At the paper he was known for being lazy, to which he would reply that he wasn't, he was merely saving his energy to use when he entered the home stretch and saw the winner's flag.

From time to time he would catch a small stroke of luck, and a terrifying gunfight could signal the entrance into another dimension. While the pharmacist shot at Efrahim and the Shoeshine Man, he pictured himself on television with the solution to the crime. If he solved everything within twenty-four hours, if he managed to connect all the dots, he would be on national TV. No! First he had to make the story into a case that would rock the country. Pedro's head was swimming as he searched for the hook that would let him expand beyond the limits of Arealva. Some time ago a national magazine had done an article on the city, its wealth, the GDP, the First World leisure activities, a combination of Texas and Florida. Antenor is rich but he's merely a local millionaire. He wants to be governor. For now, he's nothing. Still, his role model is the politician from Alagoas who went from unknown mayor to president, did what he did, and ended up impeached. Millionaire Kills Beautiful Wife.[*] The drugs added spice, but they're old news. Sex, drugs, power, politics. Clichés, repetition.

---

[*] Fat Cat Kills Social Butterfly. They Wrung Her Neck and It Wasn't Even Christmas. Pedro Quimera thinks of all the headlines. He even imagines: Reporter Unmasks Mystery. He starts elaborating what he'll say on the *Fantástico* show.

Isn't that what the public loves? Seeing celebrities brought down, as Iramar Alcifes screeches.

There were several problems ahead. Proving that Antenor was the killer. Discovering who was Mariúsa, the name the Godfather had mentioned. Could that name have been in Maciel's pocket? What was Maciel's connection to the Nighttime Shoeshine Man, the Godfather, and Antenor? Why does Evandro want to kill Shoeshine Man? Who killed Maciel? Where did Antenor go when he left the orgy at the Nove de Julho? Why did Evandro faint when he recognized Manuela?

2

What if he went to Portella? What kind of help could he get? Would he unearth hidden questions? No, he couldn't, he had done a series of stories about accidents involving illegal buses circulating around the outskirts. A monopoly run by Adriano, who would buy up ramshackle auto bodies, easily licensed. He dominated the transport of the dayworkers who picked fruit and was now penetrating the area of telephones. In traffic, he would display a golden cell phone, protected by the bulletproof windows of his armored Mercedes.

If Pedro went to Portella and told him about this senseless gun battle—at least senseless to him—what kind of deal could be reached? Some lead, some clarification, a clue? Feverishly, he jotted down on his notepad whatever came into his head. The modern reporter can't be without instruments compatible with the new century. Still, what good is technology if people lie and everything we see is continuous staging, a set of fun-house mirrors? Words heard, scenes witnessed, when filtered through the newspaper or the small screen lose their original meaning. Spoken words are different from the ones we think, there's no such thing as original thoughts. Pedro felt hunger, fear, panic, sweating behind the ears. The gunshots had stopped and he realized Efrahim was alone. The shed was pelted with rain and another pineapple train rumbled by, leaving behind its sweetish smell. Shit, who's going to drink so much pineapple juice? Isn't there some other fruit? Pedro's stomach contracted. Evangelina approached and pointed the revolver at the café owner's head.

"The Shoeshine Man, where's Shoeshine Man?"

"He's out shining shoes; he had an appointment."

"That's enough, asshole! Hand over the man!"

The Count rubbed his hands together, his habitual gesture, and smiled. Evangelina was panting, her enormous breasts like cowcatchers.

"Get out of the way. Out of the way, damn it!"

Evandro had approached, a steel-blue pistol in his left hand, the same hand with which he smoothly applied injections with a skill that no other pharmacist in Arealva possessed.

"Where's Shoeshine Man?"

"Shoeshine men are like rats. They know the holes. Aristeu knows every hole in town. Didn't he go into yours, Evangelina? So, Maria Callas decided to make an appearance. You want Aristeu? Everybody wants Aristeu! Some people change opinions really fast!"

Evangelina fired two shots. One in the shoulder, one in the knee of Efrahim, who stared at her in disbelief.

"You through, wop?"

"A wop like his father," added Evandro.

The pain hadn't yet reached his sensitive nerves. The café owner displayed surprise at the unexpectedness, like someone finding his mother in the centerfold of a pornographic magazine.

"His father hated it when I called him a wop. Same with this lowlife. A wop like his father! What about it, wop? You've got one minute to hand over Shoeshine Man."

With a finger, Efrahim pointed behind him toward the darkness. Then he fell. Evandro leaped upon the body, shouting.

"Why'd he have to show up here? He stinks like shit! Like rotten meat."

Evangelina followed him, their footsteps fading in the distance, plop, plop, plop, feet in water. Curses. Pedro waited a bit and went up to Efrahim. Blood was coming out of the wound in his shoulder. The bullet in the knee must have hit bone and cartilage, everything was shattered. Pedro vomited. How could he get the man out of there? The Count was heavy and moaned when he was pulled. He opened his eyes.

"What're you doing here?"

"I followed you."

"What is it you want? To get killed?"

"I smell a story."

"You're going to die!"

"Why does the pharmacist want to kill you?"

"He's crazy, he's a junkie, an alcoholic, he takes it in the ass from that dyke."

"You haven't answered the question . . ."

"They want the Shoeshine Man."

"What the fuck for?"

"Are you nervous? I'm the one who's shot and you're nervous? Fat people are usually calm."

"What's the story?"

"I was defending the Shoeshine Man."

"So?"

"Shoeshine Man saw the pharmacist with Manuela before it rained. And he saw the guy who took Manuela out of the trunk of the car and threw her under the Whale Ship."

"Manuela used to hang out at the pharmacy, that I know."

"She would stock up on pills, all types. She used to practically live at his house, the three of them would get together every night. Evangelina was in love with her."

"In love?"

"Passionately. It began in my café, in the back room, at the party where Iramar Alcifes handed out prizes to the people most cited in columns during the year. A sham, because everyone pays to be mentioned. Manuela was wearing a strange dress that went over big. It was made up entirely of credit cards held together by gold rings. She was almost naked, and looking hot. Another ploy, she would get cash from the card companies. Evangelina was the chosen one because she had sung the best operatic arias. Her and Manuela . . . side by side. Everybody laughed, beauty and the beast! Others said: powder and dust. They might have meant gold dust, but it was cocaine, and the dust actually was dust. Evangelina stole one of the cards from Manuela's dress, a fetish, and that's when Antenor's wife found out about the other woman's love. Never requited. The good thing is that Evangelina is shy, not pushy, but she had an accomplice in the pharmacist, and he tried to intercede for her."

"Did they have an affair?"

"I think so. That business of going to his house every night, that gas station, was strange. Something must've been going on!"

"Where are the two of them?"

"They barged into this hole like maniacs! Take my cellular and call Cassio, my manager."

Efrahim gave him the number. Pedro didn't know how to use the cell phone. The Count laughed, a laugh that provoked pain. No one answered.

"You're not scum, young man! Don't get involved! Stay away from Antenor, the Godfather, and the Shoeshine Man."

He stopped talking, his breathing labored. Pedro wanted to know more. They were stories that would never see print, but he was driven by curiosity. He was enjoying himself; it would be good if somebody died every week, so he could investigate.

"Do you know who Mariúsa is?"

"Mariúsa? Where'd you hear that name?"

"It was on a piece of paper that the Godfather took out of Maciel's pocket."

"Maciel's pocket? You saw it in the Godfather's hands?"

"Yes."

"Did you see him take it out of Maciel's pocket?"

"No."

"What a sonofabitch that old man is! He wants to scam his own son. Listen to me! There's not an act in this world that doesn't have a hidden agenda!"

"Hold on . . . Hold on . . . Son? What son?"

"Antenor."

"Antenor is the Godfather's son?"

" . . . "

"It's unbelievable!"

"It's Arealva's great secret!"

Antenor and the Godfather, father and son.* No one knew it, or the few who did kept quiet. And there must be a powerful reason for them to keep quiet. Those reasons excited Pedro. It means that for years a game was being played in which the entire city was deceived. Amazing. He had to tip his hat to both of them. Moving. But he didn't understand the Godfather's insinuations implicating Antenor.

"How did they manage to keep it a secret? Everybody here knows about everyone else."

"One way or another. There's fear!"

"And how is it that you know?"

"My father and the Godfather were after the same woman. Heloísa, Antenor's mother."

"Isn't Heloísa the rich woman who invented those sandals? The one nobody sees and who runs everything in the house behind closed blinds? They say she's crazy and that a lawyer administers the business . . ."

"What a house! She lives in a sterilized penthouse. She's very clever and shrewd! She learned how to run things when she owned

---

* Anyone who thinks Pedro wasn't surprised is mistaken. He found it, at the time, a complete mindfuck. An expression, by the way, that Yvonne hated, deeming it very chauvinistic.

the largest bordello. She invested the money that people paid for pussy!"

Pedro smiled. Efrahim was from the days of bordellos, red-light districts, whorehouses, and waterfront brothels. A lot of money had come to Arealva by way of whores' thighs and breasts, in a remote time that the city was trying to forget, to expunge. An era of adventurers, coffee barons, rich "colonels" in politics, an Arealva that no longer exists. Today it's juice magnates, speculators in the financial market, investors, owners of the garment industry, people with houses in Miami, Learjets, polo fields. Who do they screw and where do they do their screwing?

"Heloísa grew up among whores, pimps, lowlifes. She became a hooker among the smugglers at the port. The greatest mentor of whores ever! Ah, my boy, what times! What times! These days everything's second-rate, decadent, nothing but politics and money. Those people make shitloads of money."

Every old whore-hopper turns nostalgic, mused Pedro, thinking about those characters from a romantic Arealva.

"Mariúsa! I need to find out about her."

"Ask her sister."

"What goddamn sister, if I don't have any idea who she is?"

"That cripple from the Snooker. Lindorley! Another lowlife."

"Lindorley?"

"Mariúsa was the head nurse at Maciel's clinic."

"That was a long time ago."

"At your age. Ten years is a third of your life. At my age, it's nothing. It happened yesterday."

"And what was it that happened?"

196

"She was committed to the Floral Mansion. It was all arranged by Antenor and the Godfather."

"The Floral Mansion. Was that what Lindorley was talking about when the Godfather threatened her? What kind of place is it?"

"The most expensive hell in existence. Anybody who wants to get rid of a relative, an elderly father or aunt, sends them there. Political enemies too . . . It was used years ago for important prisoners . . . In those turbulent days nobody had a peaceful life, what with people throwing bombs and robbing banks . . . Antenor, the Godfather, and some filthy rich guys from Brasilia said they were from the Ministry of Health and put together the scheme . . . The scheme was going to be national, convalescent spas. Maciel signed the reports."

"Maciel could've told a lot of things."

"That's right! Find out why he was killed!"

Efrahim grimaced and folded over.

"That busty bitch knows how to shoot. She got me good, but her time'll come."

"Wouldn't it be better to call the police?"

"Don't get the police involved in this. I can fight my own battles."

The old man is going to die. Blood oozing slowly, it must be a hemorrhage. I'm going to have a dead man on my hands. I ought to get out of here. What's all this got to do with me? I'm not going to find out a damned thing, I want to leave the newspaper, the city, go to Rio de Janeiro and lie on the beach. My stomach's turning at the smell of this hole, this fruit, it's last year's fruit, the city reeks of fruit, I'm hungry, I don't know what's going on out there, maybe they already caught the criminal. But what if the killer has nothing to do with the Godfather, Antenor, the Shoeshine Man, the pharmacist? I've never seen a man die and the first one who falls into my hands is bleeding. I'm curious, the blood flows and each drop means a fraction of time less of Efrahim's life. Only I would think about fractions of time at a moment like this. I'm curious about banal details. Yvonne accuses me of getting lost in minutiae, neglecting the essential, not seeing the significant and the revealing. What can I do? That's what I like, the details that nobody notices. I could be a cop, I don't get all emotional seeing this man dying, he can die as many times as he likes. Yvonne can die. Let them all die, Luisão, all that bunch of sly, skinny reporters. It's pleasant to think about the death of people close to you. Who has never wanted to kill their father, mother, family, teacher, boss, the guy who steps on your toe, the lottery winner, the guy who screws a great-looking woman? What fascinates me is that I deal with things that seem simple but are unknown. There are forces I don't perceive behind all this, they're unfamiliar to me, I don't know how they move, I just imagine they're not on the same wavelength as the majority. That's where this wish to know, a desire that attracts and repels, scares me. I want to go away and eat roast pork with mustard sauce, there's a real good one beside Edwiges's pinball arcade.

Pedro felt empty. Yvonne was right, he didn't care about the course of events. He dreamed about his great moment, waited, the years went by. He needed to find a fun girlfriend, someone who wouldn't pressure him to keep his feet on the ground. Efrahim groaned, his wound must hurt for real. Another train went by the detour, in the far distance.

"What do you know about the Floral Mansion?"

"Near Avaré there's a hospital. It may be in Ouro Branco, in Arandu or Macedônia. When we'd go there it was always at night, and I would be in the rear of the ambulance. It's a huge building, used to be a casino, a hotel, a hospital, then it was abandoned, later transformed into a spa. Everybody in the region knows of it. Go look for it."

"And how do I get in?"

"There's no way . . . Or rather, there is . . . But you're going to have to do me a favor. Close that door over there. That one. Close off the tunnel."

"Is there a way out?"

"There was, but it caved in. It was the tunnel that led to the river barges, a helluva long time ago. My father used to extract cotton-seed oil around here, the most modern system there was, a real feat of engineering . . ."

"Your father? What's your father got to do with it?"

"He owned the Focal. The factory was a dream, and the Godfather put an end to it all. He burned it down and ruined my father."

"The Godfather?"

"He doesn't admit it, he says I'm crazy, says he doesn't kill people—because that night in '53 a lot of people died in this place. The Godfather swears he had other ways of collecting gambling debts . . ."

"No one did anything?"

"No one knows. *I* know. It was for another reason, more impor-tant than gambling debts. It was because of jealousy. The Godfa-ther has a fatal jealousy about everything. It's a cancer eating away at his stomach, his ribs, his heart. He was obsessively jealous of Heloísa. He received an anonymous letter when she got pregnant. He was in love with her and she was in love with both of them."

"Both of them?"

"Him and my father."

As he closed the door, Quimera noticed it was new and strong.

"What about the letter?"

"It said that Heloísa's child was my father's."

"Antenor has a brother? Antenor's your brother?"

"I don't know, a whore is a whore, she puts out to so many people! Even today the Godfather has that doubt. From time to time he gets anonymous letters. Where do the damned things come from? That's what makes him hate me."

"How do I get into the Floral Mansion?"

"There's a key at the café. Ask the boy at the register. It's No. 6. That's the code . . . The key opens a door at the rear of the spa. Anyone with the key can come and go as he pleases . . . It's warm, I'm sweating, I'm thirsty, very thirsty, very—"

"Someone who's bad off doesn't talk so much."

"It's fear. Fear is what keeps me alive. Get me out of here."

That was when the idea came into Pedro Quimera's head. It arrived smoothly and settled in comfortably. To turn his life inside out, free himself of this torpor in which he lived. To penetrate the unknown world, *le monde à rebours*. Something that he alone would know, no one else. It would make the difference between him and the rest. No longer a common man.

"I'm not going to do that."

"Whose side are you on?"

Pedro remembered the Godfather and laughed.

"What if I were the Good-Bye Angel?"

"You? Show me the picture of the guardian angel. And the knife to carve up the bodies. Show me! You fool, if you only knew who the Angel is!"

Pedro Quimera took Efrahim's pistol, placed the barrel against the center of the café owner's forehead, and fired. The Count's head exploded.

A TRIP BY BOAT WITH TORMENTED SOULS

Zoraide was a fragile boat, tossed by the wind, lashed by the waves on the lake. One of the enigmas of Arealva was the strength of the waves during storms. Disproportionate to the size of the lake, they seemed as if created by an angry ocean. Researchers had come from the University of São Paulo without discovering their origin. Many attributed them to the hydroelectric dams that harnessed the Tietê, while others offered simplistic explanations, for Arealva is ruled by superstition: it was the refuge of the souls of the unjustly hanged woman, the lynched men, the victims of the Good-Bye Angel, and the dead from the Focal fire. One of the problems in installing the Regattas and Navigators was to decide the shoreline reserved for the souls in torment. Even today no one takes their boats to the eastern side, despite the artificial beach of alabaster sand. Sand that not even contractors dare exploit because there's a clause in their contracts when they erect buildings in the city. The sand cannot come from that shore.* On All Souls' Day, the beach is filled with candles, vases of flowers, offerings, and the people spend the night in vigil. Security men from the club gave up trying to block access, because in 1987 there were clashes, resulting in a large number of injuries. The next day they have to drag the lake to pick up the rubbish, a day when no one goes waterskiing.

"This piece of shit isn't going to hold up. We can't go back or ahead. We're going to sink right here."

The Godfather was calm, but Antenor was frantic. Fear and rage. Did everything have to happen in a single day? The papers will go wild: WOMAN MURDERED AND HUSBAND DROWNS. A juicy morsel for the city. The Godfather took from his pocket a small waterlogged cigar. He bit off its tip and chewed it like the old codgers in westerns who spit into saloon cuspidors.

Despite everything, despite its apparent fragility, *Zoraide* resisted. It let itself be carried, instinctively fleeing from the waves, escaping. They were still in the middle of the lake when the wind diminished, the rain slackened, and the heavy cloud passed.

---

* It does, of course. At night, trucks haul away as much sand as possible. They're known as sand bats.

"The souls kept us safe, we owe them for that!"

"You believe in that, Godfather?"

"They look out for good people."

"And you're good people?"

"I am, I'm damned good! Know what we are? In this middle of this lake? Jesus and his favorite disciple, Peter."

"Jesus! You're crazy! Jesus. And you killed my mother."

"You're back to that?"

"You killed her. You're jealous! There was another man in my mother's life . . ."

"I couldn't kill your mother. She was the one who threw me out, she knew everything, knew everybody, she had people in the palm of her hand. The life of the city was played out in that cabaret, where the Crystal Night is now. Except it was bigger, the lot took up the entire block. Today it's full of offices, assholes who go to work in a coat and tie and punch a time clock."

"Threw you out of what?"

Antenor suspected that the Godfather had finally, through age and the life he led, plunged into senility. He'd never seen the old man like this, talking without realizing what he was saying, as if in a state of shock. Nothing made much sense. In senility people return to certain moments in the past and cling to them. Something must have happened tonight, because between yesterday and today the Godfather had come apart. He had gone from taciturn and introspective, guarded with others, to nonstop talking. Could it be because of Manuela's death?

"The sonofabitch shattered my life with that pool cue."

"What sonofabitch?"

"I was going to win the Scottish championship. The ticket is still in my drawer. Arealva-São Paulo-Rio de Janeiro-Dakar-Paris-London-Inverness. But that con man had to come into the Snooker and challenge me, trying to show off, except that he was the kind who ripped the felt with a stroke of the cue. He was high, full of Dexamyl, that little blue heart-shaped pill. The piece of crap was no match for me, and I had a winning streak of 316 games. I could've ended the match* in ten minutes. I started slowly so as to show what a paladin was. But he started getting pissed off, he noticed the blind woman's stare . . ."

"The blind woman's stare? The one who played music? What the hell? The blind woman again? Get serious!"

"She was a famous blow-job artist. People would show up to play, take a break, go to the pink-colored room upstairs, get a blow job, and come back. They loved seeing the blind woman rolling her dead eyes . . ."

"Sonofabitch! The damnedest things!"

"I didn't succeed in winning the 317th match. I think it was because of the dog. The grifter had a dog that followed him around the table. A ferocious mongrel he called Madá that growled, barked, and snorted. It distracted me, and I told him to get the mutt out of there. He laughed, just imagine, a dog upsetting Mr. 316. Because of pride, I let him stay. My dream of making it to 508 came to an end. I was shook. And on top of that, the bastard grabbed my cue and broke it in half. That hurt. I moved toward him, he pulled a gun and pointed it at me. Heloísa shot him in the head. Self-defense, and I had forty-seven

---

* The 317th. It was always written on the blackboard, in yellow chalk.

witnesses. They were all phonies, of course, Heloísa knew how to fix things, prosecutors, judges, lawyers, police chiefs, all of them customers of the cabaret, and—"

"You're not making sense!"

"I had style. People came to watch me. The Snooker was always full. It only emptied out in the afternoon, when Manuela came to play and I would close the windows. She loved that dim light. The place was hers!"

"When I got there, she stopped playing; if I came in, she would leave."

"She was deceptive! She fell in love with you. So many people in this city and the woman had to fall in love with my son! Curse the day you came back!"

The sentence was spoken with his mouth almost closed, and Antenor was frightened. The Godfather's eyes were dry, full of condemnation, and he was afraid. He was fearful of what that impromptu, incidental revelation could mean. The Godfather also saw this, and the repulsion disappeared in a second, as if he were able to delete the feeling with the touch of a button.

The boat reached the dock, security guards relaxed as they realized it was Antenor, though surprised to see the Godfather.

"Good thing you're here. Everybody in the entire city is looking for you. The body of Dona Manuela is arriving and we didn't know what to do. The house is full of people, and the press wants to come inside."

"What about Bradío?"

"He's on his way with the body."

"They took a long time!"

"Traffic is jammed."

"Didn't a helicopter land here?"

"Nothing to do with us. A medical thing, kids ran their car into some cows on the highway, they're pretty fucked up. In Barra Bonita. There's two detectives who've been waiting for an hour."

"Detectives? Now? Even if they're Portella's men, they could've shown some consideration. Serve them some whiskey. The cheap stuff. Cops love to drink whiskey in the homes of rich people. I'm going to take a shower."

He would have to face them. He didn't want to look at Manuela again, by now she must be sewn up. Had that son of a bitch Japanese coroner talked about the needle marks? Lately her ass looked like a sieve. He discovered the truth about Manuela and it's going to get expensive, very expensive. He knows how much it's worth. The three maids, dark circles under their eyes, cried when they saw him. He took a long shower, then got dressed. He snorted a line and was beginning to crash. He took the detectives to the library with its mahogany shelves and thousands of bound books.* The second time in his life that he'd been in the library, it was useful to impress the detectives. Who seemed not to notice the existence of books; they looked at the walls, as it was rumored that the photo of Manuela at the Scala dance was in the library, larger than life-size. Except for mirrors in gilded frames, which the policemen considered tacky, the walls were bare.**

"Excuse us, sir, but we need to ask one question. We didn't even want to come, but Mr. De Castro made us."

---

* Fake books. The titles of classics and great works on their spines. Inside, blank pages or other books from secondhand bookstores. A movie library set.

** Mirrors in a library? Some decorators will do anything to earn a commission.

De Castro, Adriano's right-hand man, ran communications for the police, controlled the private security businesses, his men were in key positions close to important people and large firms in Arealva. What could he offer to get De Castro to come over to his side?

"If I can, I'll answer."

"You were at the dinner at the Nove de Julho."

"Yes, I was. Everyone knows that."

"But you left."

"I did? Not for a minute! Who says?"

"This photo taken by Ruy Banguela. You're leaving through the rear entrance to the hotel."

"He took that a month earlier, I remember it well . . ."

"So, you're in the habit of leaving through the rear entrance? Always?"

"No, just that day."

"Tonight you left again. The photo was taken this evening. Take a look! It's got the hour and date. Those Japanese cameras do that. They're real pissers!"

"Coincidence."

"Coincidence how?"

"That day, Ruy must have set the date for today by mistake."

"Mistake? A month ago, and he set the date and time precisely for the day your wife was killed?"

"Bradío. Do I have to answer? Do we need to talk about this now? My wife's body is arriving. Give me some time, tomorrow I'm going to the police station, and the two of you show up here. Act like human beings."

"Actually, it's better—better for both of you—if you do just that," injected Bradío.

But the detectives, who must be well protected, didn't blink.

"Is that by any chance a threat?"

"What do you mean, *threat*? How about some whiskey or a gin and tonic? Or imported beer? It's so *hot*."

"I just had lunch. If you had some guava or jackfruit candy, I'd take a bite."

Murmurs arose from the crowd gathered outside, turning into shouts. The clamor increased, seemingly a large tumult. Muffled, barely audible sounds, car horns, then an explosion or what appeared to be an explosion. One of the maids entered, upset.

"Dona Manuela's body arrived."

"Did they have to bring it here? Why didn't they take it to the city wake facility?"

"That place is tawdry, Antenor. Manuela deserves a grand farewell and it's going to be here in the garden. It's the home she adored," Bradío answered.

"She hated it, she hated it! She wouldn't set foot in here. You don't know how things were. This house was hell ever since the boy died. That greenhouse over the pool, it's a tomb, Bradío, didn't you know? A chapel, a monument. Doesn't it look like a mausoleum in the cemetery? She became unbalanced following that afternoon. She would spend hours on end getting drunk, shooting up, reading books the pharmacist gave her, her and that hag with the big breasts. The two of them fucked Manuela up, really fucked her up, but I'll close down the pharmacy and throw the woman with the big tits in jail where the prisoners can all take turns sodomizing her. That boy! Our son! Manuela was so happy."

Bradío looked at Antenor, surprised, as if not understanding. What was he saying? His memory had deserted him. Could it be from so much coke?

"Oh, how I adored Manuela, adored her! She was in a state of shock for years. Then she entered a different phase and went down the drain. I tried everything."*

"They never got anything out of Maciel? It was strange. Both of them were there when the little boy crawled to the swimming pool. He saw it and didn't stop it, that's what I said at the hearing. What you told me."

"That's enough, Bradío, enough. Not now, not today!"

"It's now or never. Your brain is open, spewing out things. You're going to dig up everything, free yourself of it."

"No! There's nothing that will free me from my via dolorosa."**

Except getting elected governor, he thought.

"You know it was Maciel," said Bradío. "He threw the boy into the pool and Manuela covered for him. You killed him. You took me up on what I said, for Chrissake! At the hotel I was talking just to talk. I was smashed, dying to screw that mulatto woman . . ."

"I didn't kill anybody! If there's anything I've never done, it's kill somebody!"

"You've known it your whole life. He killed your son! To punish you. He wanted to destroy you by hurting you badly. He told

---

* He didn't try anything; he let her sink. I have statements from all the servants in the house.

** What a term! Antenor must have learned it from the Godfather. It smacks of something biblical. Lindorley said that the Godfather read the Testaments every afternoon, while Manuela played by herself.

Efrahim one night. He accused you of the death of his daughter. In the parking lot. He never recovered."

"*He* killed his daughter! It wasn't me. The cuckold, that cuckold. Everybody was screwing his wife. And when he saw that his daughter was turning out the same way, was going to put out for the entire city, he killed her, right at the time she was with me. That was it . . . Enough, enough, enough! Let's get on with our lives, find Ruy Banguela. You're going to locate the son of a bitch, now, now, now . . . Where's the Godfather?"

"Is he here? Doing what? Don't let anyone know, or see. There'll be talk . . ."

"He came with me in the boat. Everything's been happening today. Something for everybody. What's next? Listen, I'm gonna win the election! A guy who goes through all this wins elections, the rabble like dirty tricks, underhandedness, they admire underhandedness. I'm a hero, a cheat who plays clean, and if they know you're an honest cheat who plays clean they admire you, envy you, I'm a role model. Bradío, look at me. Aren't you proud to be working with me?"

He's going to explode, thought Bradío. The tension's been too much, he's going to blow up. Antenor didn't even notice when the dwarf lawyer left, taking refuge in the old changing room by the pool, where he turned on his cell phone. He made twenty calls, spoke, then made another call, feeling satisfied.

"Two things," he told Antenor, "one bad the other good. Like in the joke, first the good news. I just spoke with Portella."

"What about?"

"He was sorry about Manuela's death. It was a violent thing, he understands how you feel, and it's terrible."

"The cynical son of a bitch."

"He's ready to reach an agreement."

"So?"

"He'll call off De Castro. To loosen the knot and let you breathe. You're in the clear on this, he doesn't believe you killed your wife. He said it's time for a pact. I agreed."

"Agreed? For how much? A pact with that son of a bitch? The guy can't be trusted."

"Neither can we! Why worry? We're all dishonest cheats playing dirty."

"What about the other one, that nasty bitch?"

"I spoke to Ruy Banguela!"

"That son of a bitch set me up, we'll see to it he gets his."

"He got hold of the photo and sold it to the Godfather."

"He didn't find it, he went to Portella."

"He did find it . . . He found it . . ."

"Did they agree on a price?"

"Yes. The Godfather paid plenty."

"Then Ruy is an even bigger son of a bitch. That one's a dishonest cheat."

"No, he played clean. The Godfather paid him to show the photo to the police. To hand it over to Portella."

1

Pedro Quimera looked at Efrahim's body and experienced a new sensation. Invigorating, different, discomfiting. He felt pleasure because he was disturbed and agitated. He was no longer a thunderstruck fat man, as the diaphanous Angelica called him, or the slug who never moved unless it was absolutely necessary. At that moment he was rewriting a chapter in the city's history. The pleasure came from the chance to cause confusion. There was no earthly reason to tie him to the café owner's death; he was an alien accessory, silverware that didn't belong to the set. Killing Efrahim was executing a wrong move on the chessboard.

He heard knocking at the door to the tunnel and waited to give the impression that no one was there. The knocking became nervous, Evandro and Evangelina were shouting. Pedro let them knock, thinking: I try to find a meaning for my life. It started raining again, the wind whistled through the decaying machinery. When he saw that the couple in the tunnel were losing heart, he opened the door. They came out, irritated.

"Those rotting remains! I puked my guts out!"

They saw Quimera and had a question to ask, but before they could ask, Pedro ventured: "And that's why you killed the man!"

"Killed?"

"You blew his head off."

The two of them exchanged glances as if they had discovered the whale bones, but their expression remained unaltered. Evangelina took her hands from the multicolored jacket she always wore and which made her look like a hippie. She pointed the revolver at Pedro.

"Who are you? What're you doing here?"

"I saw Efrahim coming in with his umbrella and a package. I thought it odd."

"You came after an umbrella?"

"Never, in all the time I've lived here, have I ever seen the Count outside the café. He's famous for shutting himself in the Venetian blind room. Suddenly, as pale as a zombie, there he is in the street, in this pestilent hole, on a stuffy day."

"And you followed him."

"I was at the Shoeshine Man's backyard, where Maciel was killed."

"So, they killed Maciel!"

They showed no surprise, merely glancing at each other.

"Early this morning they killed the doctor. Efrahim was among the onlookers in the street and left quickly with his package. I followed him, saw him meet with the Nighttime Shoeshine Man, and became suspicious. I was at the pharmacy after they found Manuela. The Shoeshine Man left, agitated, after seeing some thing. Dona Idalina told me. The Shoeshine Man talked with you, Evandro. You and he shut yourselves up in the injection cubicle. Afterward, he disappeared."

"You don't even seem like the same clueless reporter. Or were you just pretending?"

Pedro Quimera let that pass. He was accustomed to being put down and had a thick skin. It had attached itself to his skin and immobilized him, becoming part of his personality. Now it was just a matter of awaiting the day of revelation, when he would no longer be obliged to listen to such things. The moment it was found out he had killed Efrahim, his liberation would come. Holding the gun, Evangelina had a determined look on her face.

"I was trying to find out what Efrahim and the Shoeshine Man were saying when you two showed up shooting. Shit! This is a Sunday full of surprises, like some TV show. You killed the Count and tried to escape through that tunnel, thinking it led to the river."

"We didn't kill anybody. We shot into the air. And we went into the tunnel looking for Shoeshine Man. Efrahim said he'd gone that way."

"You blew his head off. What did he know that he couldn't be allowed to tell?"

"If you were here, you saw that we didn't kill anybody."

"I stayed hidden. Afraid of stray bullets. When I decided to take a look, the man was dead. I was terrified, I walked around, to catch my breath, I felt dizzy. I don't like firearms, gunshots, violence. I came back because I'm curious, then you banged on the door. Who told you Shoeshine Man was here?"

"Efrahim phoned . . ."

"Why should he phone?"

"Shoeshine Man went to the Crystal Night and Efrahim brought him here. Then he went to the pharmacy. He knew Shoeshine Man had seen something, standing in my doorway! When I told him who, he was both frightened and happy. He never was brave, it's amazing he did what he did. He always relived the trauma of the Focal fire. He saw the man who set the fire. Efrahim was getting it on with a packer and would go to the factory every night. There weren't any motels and he couldn't take the girl to a regular hotel, they wouldn't let them in. His father was against it, a social-class thing. When immigrants get rich they become prejudiced . . . The Focal belonged to Ulisses Capuano, his father, an enemy of the Godfather. There was a quarrel between the two, something mysterious. Capuano lost everything at the gambling tables bankrolled by the Godfather. That night in 1953, when Efrahim showed up to fuck his girlfriend, the fire had already started and a tall, thin guy ran toward the tracks. The Focal ended up like it is today, a lot of people died, even the Count's daughter, who was sixteen. Efrahim knew the man and why he had done what he did, and he spent his life planning to take the guy by surprise. Except he was afraid, the guy's extremely dangerous. He didn't want to kill him, just cripple him, hurt him, take away something the guy needed and loved a lot. That is, if the man actually loved anything at all besides money and being a bastard."

"Who is he?"

"It's better you don't know!"

"You can tell me, Evandro! The fat man wants in on the deal. The big deal. Sunday slaughter in Arealva. We're going to run a lot of pages today."

"Not today. I don't have the strength."

"We're going to do it! There's time before nightfall, I just need an idea for the dough boy."

Evangelina was having trouble breathing, as if she had asthma.

"Who was in the car?"

"The Godfather."

"The Godfather? No way! Why would he kill Manuela?"

"And what if he didn't kill her? And he's covering for his son? He was the one who hid Manuela in the bushes in the square."

"I'll be damned!"

"He saw Shoeshine Man at the door to the pharmacy, drove up to him, opened the car window, and made a gesture, bang-bang, with his fingers. Then he brought his hand to his mouth, meaning silence. Shoeshine Man shit in his pants and went to the cubicle to clean up with cotton and gauze. Idalina, the needle woman, was in the bathroom. She takes a piss before her evening injection—she's a sicko, she does it with the door open so we can hear her pissing. It turns her on . . ."

"But why'd he kill Manuela? His son's wife?"

"Who's the son of who?"

"Antenor is the Godfather's son."

"Fatso's gone over the edge, it's the heat, the smell of rotting carcasses in the tunnel."

Quimera realized he was holding a trump card, something they didn't know about. He recalled a book on Richard Sorge, the Russian spy who had set up a network in Tokyo during World War II. Sorge had originated one of the principles of the profession: the successful agent is the one who himself is the source of information. If Evangelina was as cold and obsessed as she seemed, he was in danger. She wouldn't want to expose herself. Efrahim's pistol was in his pocket; he just hoped it still had ammunition. What if he killed both of them and hid them in the tunnel? The thought surprised and excited him. What was going on inside him?

"Why did you kill Efrahim?"

"We killed him about as much as you did."

"Then who was it?"

"Maybe there was a third man . . ."*

"A third man . . . I saw Evangelina shoot him in the knee, then in the shoulder, and finally in the head."

"I shot him in the knee, the knee . . . The knee is here, you lard bucket . . . I shot him in the knee, not the head! But I can shoot *you* in the head."

Pedro sensed something was coming unraveled. The couple hadn't insisted on knowing whether Antenor was really the Godfather's son. They let it go. Unless they already knew.

---

* *The Third Man* (1949) by Carol Reed, with Orson Welles (Harry Lime), Joseph Cotten (Holly Martins), and Alida Valli (Anna Schmidt), based on a Graham Greene novel. Whenever he can, Evandro cites films.

"You knew they killed Maciel," he said. "When I told you, you weren't surprised."

"It was . . . was . . . it was on television . . . On the *Morning News Show*. The city's one big rumor mill. Antenor's disappeared, he's on his way to Uruguay."

Evangelina was impatient, angry.

"Let's get out of here, we've got a lot to do."

"I'm not going anywhere, Evangelina, I'm not going, I'm tired. I don't have the strength. Manuela's death destroyed me."

"Manuela's death is your glory. Tomorrow we're going to take your masterpiece to television, you'll even be on *Fantástico*. Your time has come, Evandro. From Arealva you'll go to Paris, live like a bohemian in Montparnasse the way you always wanted. You can hang around looking for Anaïs Nin."

"And you with me."

"No, I'm not going! I've had it with weak, indecisive people. There's nothing but rabble here, everything's fifth-rate, I'm the only one who injects a bit of adrenaline into the people, nobody else does. I'm going to stay, carry on. Somebody needs to persevere. Keep the city under tension, make it afraid. They're afraid, Evandro. We filled this city with fear. We're more powerful than the Godfather, Antenor, Portella, the ministers of God, the people in Hydrangea Gardens. Remember how they got when we sent the letters? Everybody was in a frenzy. They almost caught the Shoeshine Man sliding them under the doors and sticking them in mailboxes. Maciel could've helped me, because he harbored the same rage. That was what united us. The hatred of Arealva, which took everything from us, everything."

Which united us? What was she talking about? What Evangelina is this? Pedro Quimera wavered and was beginning to feel afraid.[*]

They left, crossing the tracks under a closed, threatening sky. Evandro's car was a Corsa, the first one out of the showroom in Arealva, because of Manuela's influence. Quimera sat in the rear.

"We're pretty calm for someone involved in a murder."

"We didn't murder anybody, you fucking fat blob."

"But why did you want to kill Efrahim and catch Shoeshine Man?"

"We want his notebook, our names are in it. If anyone gets their hands on it first, there's going to be a messy blackmail. He works on two fronts, with the Godfather, who distributes crack, and with Efrahim, who handles rich people's drugs—cocaine, heroin, stuff like that. He uses the pharmacy as a site; customers stop by, pick it up, and leave."

"Why're you telling me all this? I might write it."

"You're not going to write anything, fat ass. We need to find out what you know and why you killed Efrahim. Then you'll join him."

If I believe it, I'll panic. The two of them don't look like people who go around killing. Maybe the shot in Efrahim's knee was an accident. Wait a minute, wait a minute. Today's Sunday, there's no *Morning News Show* on television.

"We heard the shot, and you were the only one there. Now we're nervous that maybe you're not the melted lard we thought you were. We need to find out who you work for."

"Find out who I work for? *O Expresso.*"

---

[*]   Pedro Quimera is totally unstable, so he becomes difficult.

"We've suspected you since you showed up at the pharmacy, interested in all the how's. Too much interest in nonsense. Writing a book, a best seller with all those questions. Stupidity, we kept our eye on you to discover what you were up to. You're no dummy."

It was a crazy conversation, Yvonne should hear it, Pedro thought, finding it all quite amusing. He should call Luisão right away, call Alderabã, call diaphanous Angelica and tell them all to stick it, to shove the newspaper up their ass. Evangelina had her weapon pointed at Quimera's head. Why? He was getting into a situation of unknown dimensions. He couldn't figure things out. Nevertheless, he was excited. The buxom woman wasn't the same fragile, shy person who on stage wrung her hands nervously. Her breasts peeked out of her neckline, and Pedro felt like taking them in his hands and seeing what the nipples were like, he liked big nipples, a woman with big nipples is hot, nervous, and screams when she screws. She began to hum "Non sapete quale affetto" from *La Traviata*. Pedro Quimera knew nothing about opera, but he was enraptured. Evangelina was a marvel, why hadn't she become a professional, why hadn't they given her an opportunity in São Paulo, on that famous trip in 1979?

"Get out, you sweaty pig. You smell like crap."

The smell of childhood coming back? He had been afraid of his father, just as he was afraid of Evangelina. Not of Evandro. They had arrived at home. Finally, the chance to see the gas station from the inside. The small garden was balanced, highly colorful, its flower beds forming abstract, slightly Zen designs.

"I design each bed, pick out the flowers, change the colors. Do you like it?"

It was cool inside. An air conditioner purred softly. They went into the living room, a mixture of parlor and studio where Evandro's canvases (so he actually painted?) were piled onto easels against the walls. They turned on lights; the closed curtains prevented the entrance of outside illumination. Pedro Quimera was astonished. The paintings showed fragments of headless bodies. Massacred legs, exposed bones, eyes out of their sockets, necks with large gashes, fingers being spit from mouths sticky with red, bellies displaying entrails, hearts cut in half, open toothless mouths, bleeding gums.

"Our series! The blood of the city. To honor the city of blood," added Evangelina. "Woe to thee, bloody city. Do you remember Father Gaetano's prophecy?"

Evandro painted well, hyperrealism, conveying a three-dimensional feeling.

"Too bad the rain washed away the blood of that guy who killed himself in the square. I saw it all, a thing of beauty. I'm going to paint it from memory, using my imagination. My first canvas from imagination, I can donate it to the Lev Gadelha Museum. They won't accept it. They've never accepted any of my paintings, the curators are conservatives: 'We do not allow anything that may sully the image of the city.' So I'm preparing the *Blood of the City* exhibition. I'll exhibit it in the streets. The world's first exhibition in the streets, with the works hanging from lampposts and trees. This damned Arealva is going to see itself again and again."

Quimera realized that some of the faces were vaguely similar to those that had been published in newspapers.

"You don't paint anything from imagination?"

Evandro saw what Pedro was getting at.

"No, I look for models."

"Are these the victims of the Good-Bye Angel?"

"Some of them. Others are people I'd like to see dead. I kill them in my paintings."

"Are you the Angel?"

"Not me! Maybe Evangelina. She's violent."

"Maybe me? Violent? I'm sweet and gentle . . . Evandro, show him your masterpiece. The last thing he's ever going to see. The city's passion, the bitch that took Maciel away from me."

"Stop it, Evangelina! Stop with this torture! No one took away anyone, you're just obsessed. Manuela never cared for sex, she didn't give it any importance. She wasn't like everyone else. She was very special, too special!"

Pedro was led to a small house in back. He found himself looking at a painting that occupied an entire wall. Manuela, her arms open on a cross, her face covered in blood that flowed from a crown of nails, her breast pierced by scalpels that hung from her flesh, her knees spread, her feet torn off. Her vivid, shining eyes were the only intact element in the painting—for the first time, Pedro saw her eyes without glasses, painted so that they followed the observer from side to side.

"Those breasts are from the photo of the Scala dance."

"No! She posed for me. She loved to pose. It's unfinished. I'm not going to have any way of completing it. For years we've been working on this painting. Manuela would come, lie down on that lounge chair while I worked. She would offer hints, suggestions. She wanted to see what she would look like quartered. I don't know how it's going to be from now on. I just don't know."

"Show him *The Good-Bye Angel* series."

"Why?"

"Now he's going to be part of it."

Evangelina was enjoying herself, a torturer who shows his instruments to the victim.

"Not today, Evangelina, not today."

"Today, goddamn it. Today's the apocalypse of the city."

They went into a hallway that smelled of mothballs. A new room, full of canvases. How long had Evandro been painting secretly?

"Here's Manuela."

Each painting was a different body part. The severed head, nerves, muscles, veins dripping blood. Arms, hands, fingers, fragments of belly, the pussy, all the details of a totally dismembered body. Deposited on silver serving trays brought to the banquet table.

"It took me two years to complete this series. Manuela planned to show it at the Coral Whale. First she would kill Antenor."

"Were you in love with her?"

"Him? About as likely as a black communist being president of the United States."

Evangelina laughed sarcastically.

"Him and Manuela. That's the funniest thing I've ever heard. Evandro doesn't like women, or men either. He's scared to death of AIDS. He hasn't screwed in twenty years. He loves hand jobs. What do you think Idalina does for him when she gets her shots? What about you, Tiny? You screw anybody? How can you do it with that belly? Can that stinking bitch of a teacher stand you?"

Quimera was bothered by Evangelina's incessant aggressiveness. A rage began growing in him that, if it exploded, he knew would be beyond control. It was the change in her expression.

The transparent hatred brought life to her skin, made her teeth glow. She had excellent teeth, but who was brave enough to kiss that mouth?

"I'm no limpdick, you bitch. Never have been. I'm a saint guarding the Holy of Holies! That man of yours, okay, his didn't work."

"It did work! And how. I'm the only one who knows how it worked."

"Drunk, drugged, neurotic."

Evangelina sobbed, Quimera couldn't tell whether from anger or tenderness. Even when she cried, it was impossible to feel sorry for her, a disjointed puppet with leaping breasts.

"Maciel loved me. For three months I was the woman he wanted most in the world. There was no one else. Not even Manuela, who the whole city wanted to bang."

2

From the age of fifteen Evangelina had been in love with Dr. Maciel. She did everything possible to get her mother to take her to the famous, sought-after gynecologist. At sixteen she swore she was pregnant by the owner of the Cine Esmeralda—no other excuse occurred to her at the time, and only later did she realize how absurd this was, but she was always running into that nobody, Evandro's father, at the pharmacy. Her mother, who knew the city and its characters well, was dubious: "That old geezer hasn't been able to get it up for a long time, he drools, he's useless. And he wouldn't want a troublemaker like you anyway." The girl who was coming out of adolescence seeing her friends pull away in cars, through canebrakes and orange groves, was dying to sit down in front of Maciel and open her legs. She wanted to feel the touch of his hands, delight in the doctor's peering deep inside her. She would stand outside his office at the end of the day, waiting for him to come out, follow him to the Nove de Julho hotel garage where he kept his car. Every evening she dreamed of being with Maciel, redolent of cologne, wearing a gold watch, voluptuous in his white suit, impeccably creased linen pants, the expensive rayon shirts still unavailable in the stores of Arealva but brought from Rio de Janeiro by a lover. She imagined herself at the hotel known to the entire city as high society's trysting spot, although no woman had ever been seen entering with anyone. *Tryst*, an anachronistic word uttered cautiously, replete with lasciviousness, aroused in Evangelina indocile instincts; it wasn't something a young lady said, involving pleasures not in keeping with decency. There was a secret entrance in the rear, through a lush orchard, but however much it was watched, and everything there was watched, no one had ever caught adulterers surreptitiously coming or going.

I've always wanted to be a whore, Evandro, she confessed excitedly. To put out for everybody and get paid. I'd run things well. You'd be my pimp, spiffy in white suits and two-tone shoes. Except no one wants to screw me. No one! I've tried everything, but the bastards shy away from me in disgust. You don't know what rejection is like. Someone looking at you like you were a slug. That's what that guy with the freckles said to me. And what happened, happened. Sitting in the garden and crossing my legs. Showing everything and no curious kid would stop to sit on the opposite bench to look and run off to the bathroom. Not a single one! Not even you, who're my friend, help me, that's what friends are for, and getting it on with friends is wonderful, there's a lot of affection and no obligation. I forgive you, I know what you're like, what holds you back, but would it be too much to get naked with me here in bed?

In high school days, Evangelina would leave in the middle of class and go down to the boys' bathroom, eager to discover her name behind the door. All she saw was *Marinhalva shaves her pubes, Vanda takes it in the thighs, Veronica has a loose ass.* Then she would write *Evangelina does it all, Evangelina gives good head, Evangelina likes it hard.* She hoped that at least some curious guys would approach. She didn't know that bathroom graffiti are like anonymous phone calls, satisfying the one who calls or writes, the shy, the incompetent, the joker. One rainy afternoon, she was leaving the bathroom when a blond boy, freckled and pimply, caught her with the ballpoint in her hand.

"What're you doing in the boys' room?"

"I made a mistake."

"Dyke! Just like people say."

"I'm not a dyke. I made a mistake!"

"The girls' bathroom's on the other side of the courtyard! What about that red pen? Aha, red ink! So that's what it is? You're the one who's been writing that *Evangelina likes it hard*?"

"I didn't write anything, I just came to copy it to show my girlfriends."

"No way! Everybody wants to know who's the pervert writing about the girl with glasses and big tits. Of course—there's no pervert. There can't be. Who'd be able to stomach you? You're the pervert."

He was in control of the situation, Evangelina was cornered. What she didn't know was that the freckled boy also crouched down to write things. He was a large, timid kid, a pissant who would masturbate in the balcony of the Cine Esmeralda and watch the come drip onto the heads of the audience below.

"It'd take a monster or a raper to screw a pig like you."

"It's rapist, you dummy."

"Piss off, you hunchbacked, ostrich-bellied midget. The school's going to love knowing it's you. Nobody'll want to miss out on this. This is funnier than Valquíria, who lost her panties at the debutantes' ball. Remember, her panties fell off and she tripped right in the middle of the dance floor?"

"You wouldn't dare."

"It's gonna be the best thing this year!"

"Don't open your mouth! You blond weakling, you faggot. Yes, you! Who'd want you with that pimply skin of yours? You look like a leper!"

"Faggot?"

"Everybody knows about it, you like a fat dick. You take it in the ass at the Esmeralda balcony."

Evangelina, frightened, said the first thing that came into her head. If the boy blabbed, if the story got around, she would be cursed. A scandal. She foresaw ridicule, humiliation. Valquíria had had to leave Arealva, the city was merciless. Her pain increased when she thought of Maciel mocking her in his office, a hotbed of gossip, the patients beautiful and naked, the doctor examining them, putting his fingers inside them. She bent over, clutching her chest as if suffering a heart attack, a piercing twinge in the neck. It always struck her when she became nervous and was about to go on stage. Her bladder released, she felt warm urine trickle down her legs. It was no good to deny it, to say no, the word would travel with unparalleled swiftness; the speed of light was a turtle's pace compared to rumors. Her shoes were soaked; if the freckled kid looked down she was lost, her via sacra completed. What would they say when they found out Evangelina wrote dirty words in the bathroom and pissed on herself?

Sweating, waiting for the recess bell to ring, looking at the deserted courtyard, she made a decision under intense pressure. Later, she told Evandro, I felt like my heart was in a vise and was squeezing out all the blood, like that duck in the restaurant in Paris where you want to go. It was an internal hemorrhage, my belly was swelling, it was going to explode and flood the bathroom with blood, I began to see a red haze before my eyes, like a curtain, and the freckled boy's teeth were chewing at the curtain. I saw I wasn't going to survive.

"Want to see what I just wrote?" she asked the boy.

"Huh? What was it, what was it? I want to, show me!"

"You'll see. A fucking dirty trick."

"A dirty trick? A bad one? Do you like dirty tricks? Ever think about sucking earwax or licking greasy hair?"

The freckled kid's eyes shone. They went to a toilet stall.

"Go on in. It's behind the door! I'll stay out here, there's not room enough for both of us."

With his back to her, Evangelina removed her high-heel shoe: latest fashion, with a thick sole, a mixture of Carmen Miranda and Marilyn Monroe, a futile effort to make herself attractive. The girls in normal school were exempt from wearing uniforms. She took a deep breath. God's will be done. She mustered every ounce of strength, linking hatred to fear. She brought the heel down on the back of the boy's neck, exactly as she'd seen done by Cleo Moore in Hugo Haas's classic black-and-white B film. Praying it worked, O my guardian angel. The boy fell forward, the door opened, he hit his head on the toilet, blood spurted. Evangelina moved in calmly, pushed his head inside the toilet, forced him down with her foot, and flushed. The boy seemed to come to, struggled lightly, breathed and resisted, but she kept her hands taut, grasping his head, for a long time, until he was no longer moving. Good-bye, my angel. She left. From the auditorium came the sounds of choral rehearsal singing of the gabby peasant, *Oh oh oh, the gabbiest peasant we know . . .* She went to the side wall facing the church property where festivals were held, leaped over, slipped in a crouching stance between the booths. Except for her wet feet, she felt fine. Relieved. There was no more humiliation, no laughing at her. Who needed some freckled kid anyway? There are unnecessary people in the world, and it's not hard to get rid of them. She was floating. I'm an angel. She could see the city below her. Angel. Good-bye, my little boy, you're never gonna bother anybody again. A good-bye angel, maybe that's my mission, besides singing di-vine-ly the way I do.

It was never discovered who killed the boy, the grandson of Lithuanian immigrants who had fled from communism during the Cold War. No one had seen anything that afternoon, the classes had tests, the monitors were assigned to oversee them to prevent cheating. Evangelina arrived home with a fever and was put to bed; they called the doctor, who diagnosed a virus. The death in the stall was the topic for months, and in that period she decided she should take a break, putting her studies on hold, and go to São Paulo. It was 1979 and she was almost eighteen years old.

The city had a penetrating, metallic smell. She took lodging at a hotel on Rua Guaianases, downtown, and for the first few days barely left her room. On Saturdays she would go down to the street, jammed with urchins playing soccer. The aged buildings exhibited clothes drying in their windows like colorful banners. Shoe stores, locksmiths, launderettes, brokers, clerks, tailors, greengrocers, automotive electronics, copy stalls, bars—all that small business carried out by the poor, Northeasterners, Koreans, blacks, people from Minas Gerais. Women would shout from one window to the next, call out to their children in the street below. Later, at the end of the afternoon, she would wander about the street, bumping into men in drag or hurried, heavily perfumed women. She followed two of them and saw them enter the Cine Áurea, which showed porn films. In the intermission, live stripteases. From that time on, she would spend hours in the theater watching films that didn't excite her unless the actors vaguely reminded her of Maciel. When the film ended and the lights came on, the men would make a dash for the front-row seats in order to see the puffy strippers with their big asses. Evangelina discovered that the women worked in three, four places at the same time. They would leave the Santana Theater and go to the Áurea, and from there rush off to the Los Angeles, then to dives along Avenida Rio Branco. In the early morning hours they would be having steak with garlic and oil or feijoada. What if she herself did a striptease? She had such a desire to expose herself, it was like sitting with crossed legs in the garden. She didn't have the courage to try.

One May morning, descending Avenida São João toward Vale do Anhangabaú, she looked into a shop window and felt herself slipping on the ice. A pleasurable, agreeable sensation. In the window of the Ao Gaúcho shop she saw the small, shiny revolver. She went in and bought it, along with boxes of ammunition, received the caution she needed to carry a weapon, filled out a form, and left with the gun in her purse. Evangelina was getting along well in São Paulo, lost in the midst of the crowd, where no one looked at anyone. A beautiful city in which to kill people, the world is too crowded, it suffocates me. But what I really want is to return to Arealva, I want to terrify the world, I want them to live in anguish. The thought made her float like an angel.

THE EXHIBITION OF WILTED HEARTS

Evandro, the pharmacist, had put on a Plácido Domingo CD, *Mi Alma Latina*.

"I can't believe it! You, Evangelina, are the Good-Bye Angel? No, it doesn't make sense. It's your imagination, delirium!" said Pedro Quimera.

"Everything that doesn't make sense has a meaning," said Evandro, who was given to epigrams.

"You're intelligent, Evangelina. You can't go around killing because men find you unattractive. If it were like that, there'd be few people left in the world; humanity is a horror."

"Take a look at yourself."

"Know what I think? What consoles me? There has to exist in this flaccid body of mine something, a pore, a hair that one day will soften a woman's heart . . ."

"Ha!"

"The city admires you, Evangelina, you're loved, people go to the theater to hear you sing."

"I don't kill because they look at me strangely. That's silly! Don't play the analyst, it's nothing like that. I kill because I feel like it. For the game, for pleasure, that's something you're never going to feel. The seduction of seeing a person terrified. You can see he's aware that he's come to the end, his life is over. The surprise of discovering that some face it with joy, they want to die and don't have the courage."

I'm not going to say that I know this feeling and that it makes us equal, thought Pedro Quimera. We belong to a special circle, even if I'm just a beginner who's barely passed his weapons test. Maybe it's destiny. Our function in the world, a responsibility. Maybe it's even an excuse.

"And all these years you've gone on killing?"

"Not all the dead were ours. Someone, before, killed, mutilated. One day we found a quartered body and Evandro had the idea of placing the religious image he was carrying in his pocket, with the picture of the guardian angel. He'd received it at church, from a senile priest. It was ironic. The Good-Bye Angel was born. Evandro had a stroke of genius when he thought of the religious image; he reads a lot, sees films, and felt it was a cinematic touch, a feature if someday they made a movie of our lives. Or a television special.

Because we're the new Bonnie and Clyde, Lampião and Maria Bonita, incognitos, except we don't rob. We're kindred souls, brother and sister. We were united before birth, in other lives. He was a Roman legionnaire, I was a servant of Messalina, very beautiful, I had my phase of sensuality, but I'm not complaining, I live with myself. I would go out after dark through alleyways to brothels, spending the night with troops who reeked of blood. The pleasure was greatest when they would arrive fresh from war still bearing the bitter smell of battles, after having put thousands of prisoners to the sword. It was the legionnaire Evandro who had the idea of slicing up the dead. Of course I considered it a cliché, we're not common murderers, we're not murderers at all, we're executioners. The Good-Bye Angels, we dispatch people who need it."

"How do you know who needs it?"

Surprised, Quimera discovered a different being in himself. He was taking part in the conversation naturally, and Evangelina had become transfigured into a lovely woman as she passionately narrated, her face illuminated, in ecstasy. He was certain she floated after killing, truly becoming an angel watching over Arealva.

"Intuition, scent, gaze. Those nearing death exude a light perspiration, delicately floral. Only people like us can perceive it. It's fear emanating from them, the dread of the unknown, the attraction. Death is seductive. Candidates for death come to us, demand, beg, and we can only accept the mission."

"It's the bloodiness that bothers me. If I killed, everything would be clean."

"The blood provides the proof. Faced with it, we must be strong. It smears, sticks, sickens, disgusts, especially the smell. What did the Jews do in the Temple? Sacrifices purified by blood. It's my mortification, the means of showing myself worthy, of purifying me. I have to bear it. I come away wet from head to foot, especially when we cut arteries, the blood gushes, the body has a powerful little pump. When the blood is exhausted, the heart wilts. That's what Evandro and I call those dead people. Wilted hearts. We have to do everything slowly, because that one there"—pointing to Evandro—"stays at a distance, drawing the sketches so he can get home and paint. He spends days and days painting furiously. That's why he returns from São Paulo with piles of drawing pads and canvases. Every night at eight o'clock we go upstairs, that's the time when we have the most energy, and work. In that tunnel at Focal there are hundreds of canvases picturing dead people. Efrahim showed us the tunnel, we added the door, the only place where no one ever goes because of fear of ghosts and miracle workers. No one knows that Evandro paints; it'd be a real surprise for Arealva. The great exhibition of wilted hearts, to be opened as soon as his mother dies, but the old bag doesn't die. I've felt like killing her without Evandro knowing. I didn't have the courage, it would mean hurting my brother, insulting the legionnaire. After the exhibition, they'll find us in the square, hanged. Every day we want more and more to put an end to all this."

"But what about Paris, the dream?"

"Fuck Paris! Paris is through, nobody goes there to paint anymore. Evandro found that out years ago, and it was a huge shock. To have to live in this city. Forever! A man of forty doesn't abandon his roots, doesn't leave the place. We're prisoners, stuck here, bronze statues, bushes in the square . . ."

"Mosquito droppings on the yellow ceiling," Evandro said.

"This city that condemned us needs to pay for having sacrificed us."

"So you two killed Manuela? It doesn't fit."

"It wasn't us."

"You say that, but you killed Efrahim."

"Efrahim was you. We heard the shot. The only reason we didn't kill you was because we thought you were also a good-bye angel come to join us."

Of course not, thought Pedro Quimera. If someday I do it, I'll act alone. Everything a man does alone he does better. There are no trustworthy partners.

"Why Manuela?"

"It was Efrahim."

"Efrahim???"

"Efrahim is unbalanced. Was. Kind of a laughingstock, he pretended for many years to be on the Godfather's side. It was convenient for someone who needed drugs to distribute. That café of his always lost money, he was a rotten administrator, didn't inherit his father's competence. Ulisses Capuano was a pioneer. But he gambled. Being a businessman is a gamble, you have to be bold, unscrupulous, know how to bluff, to cheat, know when to bet and when to fold. But Ulisses challenged fate. He wanted total power. Everyone said yes to him, except the cards. And that exasperated him, challenged him, he wanted to dominate cards too, to exercise power over the deck. And so he went further and further, getting in deeper and deeper. The cards resisted, told him no, they're the ones who subjugate, which drove Ulisses insane. He lost everything at the hands of the Godfather. Of course we knew that Antenor was the Godfather's son, but the secret was valuable. Even if we didn't know how to bargain with it. Manuela, when she found out, was unsettled because there was something between her and the Godfather. We don't know what. But there was, because the Godfather was obsessed, in love with her, jealous, violent, corrosive. Unable to get closer, he came to hate Antenor after he married Manuela. It wasn't hard for him, hate was in his blood, it's natural, what he lives for, what keeps him going at his age. And it was said she married him to stay close to the old man. The Godfather has a great deal of affection for his son, his only son, even though Efrahim thought he was also his son. It was Babylon, because Antenor's mother, the madam, had an affair with Capuano. The Godfather set fire to the factory out of jealousy. It wasn't because of gambling debts, the miser. He never needed money."

"Efrahim killed Manuela! Unbelievable! But they saw the Godfather placing the body behind the Whale Ship."

"No one saw it."

"The Shoeshine Man did."

"Efrahim put the body there. Then he came to the pharmacy. Shoeshine Man was here. He owes Efrahim a fortune, because he's a dealer but also a user. So we set it up for Shoeshine Man to spread the word that the Godfather put the body there. You know? A rumor spreads, it can't be disproved, especially in this city with people like Iramar Alcifes. Shoeshine Man agreed, then he got scared of Efrahim, he was certain he'd be killed to keep the truth from coming out. He had no choice. Efrahim hid Shoeshine Man and informed us, he wanted us to do the job. It would be the first contract work, a new milestone in the Good-Bye Angel's career. I once told Evandro I wanted to be a whore, get paid for giving myself. At that moment, when we accepted Efrahim's offer, we felt like whores, we were doing it for money. We hadn't perceived any death wish in the Shoeshine Man, just the opposite. It was a new experience, unexpected, that made us ponder all night. We finally decided it was our duty. The Shoeshine Man was an unnecessary person, a throwaway in the world. There are millions like that."*

"Too bad we've got neither time nor ammunition to eliminate all the superfluous people in the world," said Evandro, excited again.

"We went to Focal, but we didn't know that Efrahim was still there. Or you. He ordered Shoeshine Man inside the tunnel as we had agreed, and we went in after him, except I couldn't resist and put a bullet in the Count's knee, and that's when he knew he was about to die and tried to keep us there till he could work things out. Everything was mixed up, out of control. Manuela's death left us all confused. The only person in the world that turned on Evandro. When he went into the tunnel, Shoeshine Man arranged his own execution, he was going to discover the paintings, find out the truth, he'd hold a trump card against us. We decided to kill Efrahim too; the blame would fall on Antenor, or so we thought. We took pity. For the first time, we felt mercy, a horrible sensation that means the end of a career. Good-bye angels have no feelings. He was someone we knew, because all the others were nobody to us. And I felt bad, I was weak, I vomited a lot after I finished off Maciel. Killing—"

---

* Placido was singing "Moliendo Café" at this point.

"Wait a second, stop right there . . . Maciel? We were talking about Efrahim. Where does Maciel come in?"

"I killed him."

"That asshole doctor? What did he ever do to you?"

"Killing someone you love is to attain the supreme, break with everything, cut yourself into pieces, then resuscitate. He was the Good-Bye Angel of my emotions.* When we come out of it, we're a new person, we have a new identity, we need a new ID card. Even my face was transformed."

"You mean Shoeshine Man is dead?"

"In this heat, he'll smell before nightfall."

Evandro realized, by his perplexed expression and his silence, that Pedro had been affected. And he took charge of the rest.

"This is painful for her, she's not going to be able to tell the story. It came out, it must have been very strong. I'll tell you the rest."

---

* Evangelina may kill well, but she's a pitiful phrasemaker.

THE SET TABLE PROTECTS THE GOOD-BYE ANGEL

1

When Manuela left the café, Efrahim followed her. The bouncer, who was hanging a car key on a board and had his back to the door, didn't see him. Upon leaving the café, where she drank Bloody Marys loaded with vodka, she headed for the How Come Pharmacy. She isolated herself in the antibiotics storeroom, where she sipped whiskey with Pedialyte. And she talked and talked, as if the storage area were a confessional or a therapist's couch. Every day she conversed more with the yellowed tiles. It seems the tiles were magic, because away from there Manuela was close lipped. Several times, Evangelina offered her a line and she refused; it had been years since she had taken pills of any kind. I have to fully bear this pain, she would say.

Yesterday she was more agitated than usual. Perhaps because she had made a decision. Without her being aware of it, I left the recorder running, as always. I have all the tapes, you can listen to them, I've separated the interesting parts. Just FYI, the condemned man has the right to a last request, so let's pretend this is yours, even though many things must remain hidden. (Pedro Quimera wasn't impressed. He knew exactly how he would get away.) Here's what she said:

There is none righteous, no, not one.[*]

The boy's death. I have to bear this pain, I don't want to arrive owing for an innocent life . . .

It was between three in the afternoon and sunset and now I know I must make the sacrifice for purification through blood.

He was there, beside me, I went upstairs for a moment, to get tweezers to pluck a hair growing near my nose, very unsightly.

If I had even imagined that when I came back I'd find what I found, I'd have let my face sprout a beard, like the woman in the circus. But I went upstairs, calmly. Evandro was with the boy . . .

I took a bit of time. I had to change my tampon and couldn't find the box. The servants mess with everything, and when I went back down I couldn't find the child . . .

Evandro was snoring, his eyes covered with a towel, and Maciel was staring at the pool . . .

---

[*]   Paul, Epistle to the Romans.

I went up to him and he pointed to the pool . . .

I didn't see anything, I refused to see . . .

The boy was floating face down . . .

I refused to look, I didn't have a voice to scream . . .

Maciel threw me into the pool: save your son, Evandro killed the poor child.

The poison of asps is under their lips, whose mouth is full of cursing and bitterness . . .*

And when I reached the body, he was already dead, I asked Maciel to help me . . .

He turned his back, I screamed, screamed . . .

Evandro was stoned and didn't wake up. Maciel gestured goodbye with both hands and disappeared . . .

I stayed in the water for hours, holding my son . . .

That's how they found me, I almost drowned too, and the only reason I don't kill myself is because I promised . . .

Sacrifice through purification. Maciel was the lamb of God . . .

But I wanted to get Heloísa's letters back, they'd been with him for years . . .

They had been my insurance policy, I would use them, if I felt threatened, because the Godfather was becoming more and more restless, watching me, watching, never forgetting the morning that I arrived at the Snooker . . .

That cursed Saturday morning before Easter Sunday. I could feel in his eyes, the instant he saw me, that I was doomed . . .

Their feet are swift to shed blood. Destruction and misery are in their ways . . .**

---

* Paul, Epistle to the Romans.
** Paul, Epistle to the Romans.

It was passion, but his eyes were those of hate. I beat him at the pool tables, he, the invincible, never won once. And he loved me and hated me, and let me win, and he was torn up inside when he lost, lost over love . . .

He signed everything over to me. Everything in my name. Houses, land, agencies, stocks, the hidden world that he controls. Everything that Antenor wants to take away from me, challenge in court . . .

Why did I wait so long? I think it was just an excuse, getting those letters back was foolish . . .

We found them the afternoon we locked ourselves in the boat-house. Maciel was still charming, with the traits of a man all the women were in love with . . .

It was the first time. I wanted to experiment, to find out what the most desired man in Arealva was like. He would be the first. He had to be, I would offer myself, I had thought about it a lot . . . desired. At H-hour he proved as rushed as a teenager. He ejaculated prematurely, then kept excusing himself, saying it was because he was so turned on. He asked me to be patient and understanding . . .

Which I wasn't inclined to be, he left me hanging, it was a real dirty trick, women have to stop being understanding, nice. He promised and didn't deliver, too bad . . .

He begged me not to tell anyone, and he seemed vulnerable I let him put his head on my lap, sobbing . . .

I got bored and looked around at the boathouse, it needed painting, there were spiderwebs, broken glass in the windows. I sang an Isaura Garcia song, *They've forbidden me to love you, forbidden me to see you, forbidden me to ask about you.* I saw a metal box, disguised, it was new and I became curious. I love seeing what's inside suitcases . . .

When my father would arrive home from his trips, there were so many, we would gather round the table to see him take out the stuff he brought from the cities, bras, panties, nylon stockings, lipstick, rouge, cologne, rose water, talcum, face powder, cucumber water, bracelets, necklaces, earrings, anklets. I've had an anklet since I was twelve, the other girls envied me, boys would flock around me, it was wonderful, the thing I liked best was the boys touching my ankle, pretending they were admiring the little gold chain . . .

I removed Maciel's face from my lap, he had gotten my thighs wet with his tears. How ridiculous for a man to cry because of a limp dick . . .

Why did I adore that man? . . . Why was I willing do anything for him? So suffering, so vile . . .

And I tried to open the box, but it had a strong padlock. I looked for a hacksaw among the tools and found one, rusted, so it took me a long time to saw through the metal. I found a thick pack of waxed paper, sealed with a crepe ribbon . . . The most curious part was that it was something recent. Maciel sat down beside me on the floor and we broke the seal. We found twenty-two packages, carefully done, wrapped in plastic. Each pack contained fifty letters, with the exception of one with only thirty. Each envelope was numbered by hand. Addressed to Antenor, in Rio de Janeiro . . .

Did you see the return address? asked Maciel.

Heloísa Dumont.

The owner of the sandal factory, the old whore. I treated her once. She called me to her house, she was sixty-five and wanted a gynecological examination, scared to death of cancer. She lives in an ITU, with employees to clean, sterilize everything; not a speck of dust finds its way into the house, the walls are made with special insulation, it's all very crazy. She handed me imported gloves to examine her with, she's got a well-formed pussy, alive, pink, putting out so much helped.

Why did she write Antenor?

Dear son, it says here.

Son? What kind of story is that?

We went on reading, and I was astonished. How did the two of them manage to keep the relationship hidden? And why did Heloísa go along? Fear of the Godfather, she said. He threatened her, thought that Antenor wasn't his son but the son of Efrahim's father, a complication. Not to harm the son, she said repeatedly, without the son knowing who his mother was.[*]

So we discovered everything. We read for hours, and only when it got dark outside and it started to rain, that rain that always falls in August in Arealva, did we gather up the letters and leave.

Better they stay with me, Maciel said.

What are you going to do?

Nothing, hold on to them, they may come in handy one day. I'm going to scan them, copy them onto diskettes, keep one, give you one, and a third one to someone we trust. We have to protect ourselves.

Are you going to stick it to Antenor?

---

[*] It seems as if the entire city knows the secret. Can this be an open secret?

246

Could be, he's been sticking it to me all his life. He killed my daughter and helped Valéria cuckold me.

Everything had been over between Antenor and me for a long time . . .

The enchantment of the early times, that sensitive man who would go every day to the cemetery to visit his mother's tomb, had changed. But what the fuck kind of tomb was that, if Heloísa was his mother, and everyone knew she was still alive?

Maciel kept the letters. I don't know why he never tried anything against Evandro before, it must have been the confusion, Maciel's brain cells were burned out, even if from time to time some of them fired and he became lucid . . .

Maciel wanted me to turn over to him everything the Godfather had given me. He pressured me, implored, threatened, he became dangerous. He said they were things I owed him, that he was going to go back to being the old Maciel, dancing with all the women . . .

They are all gone out of the way, they are together become unprofitable; there is none that doeth good, no, not one . . .*

(The recorder was turned off.) This is the interesting part. Later, Evandro said, Maciel stopped by the pharmacy for Prozac. He took it, had some whiskey, and left. Manuela shoved me into the car and we followed him. He went to the Nove de Julho, where he waited in the lobby. We saw Antenor go upstairs with him in the elevator. They took a long time. Maciel came down with a satisfied expression on his face, then Antenor, who went into the restaurant and left by the rear door, the one leading to the area where tires are stored.

---

* Paul, Epistle to the Romans.

"Maciel was negotiating with Antenor. And I'll bet that Antenor is heading home to see if the letters are where they're supposed to be. He's going to discover everything. And if he does, he'll kill me! Those letters were my tickets to freedom, I was going to use them to bargain with Antenor, it was the only way he'd let me go. Now he's going to kill me. And I don't want to die, I want to get away, to live a different life somewhere."

"There's nothing can be done, you can't escape!"

We scouted around and found Maciel heading to Shoeshine Man's house. We knew he'd do that, he was desperate and looking to score some drugs. Of course Shoeshine Man refused, but Manuela bought a dose. Maciel calmed down and Shoeshine Man left.

"I want the letters," she said.

"I don't have them, they're with Efrahim."

"Efrahim?"

"I traded for them, he gave me a pile of blow, but I have another diskette hidden in the Shoeshine Man's boxes."

I was startled, despite being used to it. Manuela raised her gun and fired into Maciel's chest. One sharp, direct shot, what aim! He fell, his back resting against a wall, his head hanging. He died without knowing what hit him. At that moment Efrahim arrived, he must've been looking for product to sell in the café. He was pissed at the Shoeshine Man, who was supposed to make deliveries but hadn't shown up. He saw Maciel, he wasn't stupid, saw the revolver in Manuela's hand, and guessed what had happened. She was in a trance, we practically had to carry her to the café owner's car. "I'll take care of this," I said, "I don't know what to do with Maciel's body, but I'll get Manuela out of it. Go search the house, get the diskettes, his address book, make it look like a common burglary, then go to the pharmacy and I'll meet you there." He showed up in the middle of the storm with Manuela's body and said:

"She was the one the Godfather loved best. It's over."

He was high without having taken anything. Efrahim never was one for drugs or alcohol. He was happy. A huge weight had been taken off his shoulders. At the same time, he was terrified. It was all too much for him. He acted without planning, did what he had to do, it'd have been better if he had hired us, the Good-Bye Angel accepts commissions.

At that moment it started raining like crazy, I looked at the square and saw the Whale Ship and got the idea. I told Efrahim to turn the car around, the thunderstorm was so violent that no one would see what was going on, he threw the body behind the bush. I felt sorry for Manuela, but not all that sorry, I'm not the kind who worries about such things. I felt bad for Evangelina, she was crying and saying, "Efrahim did what he had to do. There's something I have to do myself, and the time is now. Do you know where Maciel is?"

"At the Shoeshine Man's house, high as a kite."*

We went there, saw the doctor leaning against the wall, it was still raining, she shot and stabbed him. With the Good-Bye Angel's knife, which she kept in the glove compartment. We carried the body to a spot behind the clump of lemon verbena trees where it wouldn't be found for days. For the first time in her life, Evangelina didn't have the heart to carve up the cadaver. After all, Maciel was the only person who ever loved Evangelina.

"There's something that doesn't fit, that I just can't get my head around. You fainted when you saw Manuela dead."

---

* Nobody makes sense!

"Tension. I loved the woman, but she was like a zombie in this city. I'm human, sensitive, things get to me."

"Tell me one thing, since I'm about to die. There's something between you and Evangelina, you can't hide it."

"We're like brother and sister, partners, accomplices, we adore each other, we're angels, there can't be anything but faithfulness, angels don't touch, and as angels we have the protections of other angels. Come take a look at the table."

He led Pedro Quimera to a small dining room and turned on the lights. There was a table set for fourteen people, seven on each side. Everything prepared as if dinner would be served in a minute.

"What does it mean?" asked Quimera.

"When they see the table set, all the angels kneel to provide our safety. It's a sacred time. They pray for us before God and nothing happens to us. For eleven years, every night at eight o'clock we come here to renew the banquet. That's why we've never been caught. The Good-Bye Angel has their protection. Now I'll tell you about Evangelina and Maciel."

2

In May, years ago, don't ask me the date, Evangelina bought a dress for the presentation of the Chorale at Casa Branca, during the week dedicated to the writer Ganymédes José. The store was packed, everything was getting ready for Mother's Day. It took a long time for the package to arrive, and when she got home she saw it wasn't her dress. In the box was a very delicate Yoji Yamamoto blouse, with a card. From Maciel to Manuela. She went looking for the doctor

and found him at the bank in the Bosque das Amendoeiras, a reserve on the outskirts of the city planted by Japanese immigrants at
the turn of the century. A cool place, redolent of humid forest.

"This box belongs to you."

"And yours is at my house."

She was surprised, she had never imagined him as having a
house. Evangelina was taken* to an apartment complex near the
bus station. Two clean, modest rooms. In one corner, a stack of
medical books, old magazines, inscribed photos of patients and
their children.

"On Mother's Day I used to receive hundreds of presents, that's
how grateful they were."

"You're a nice person, Dr. Maciel."

"Don't give me that, girl. Don't pity me, I like the way I am."

"You do? 'Cause it strikes me as hard to take."

"What's hard to take is having to put up with those people. I
found out what it's like to be the other and I got out. There's just
one person who understands me, who accepts me. Manuela. That's
why the blouse."

"Yamamoto. One of the most expensive."

"A rubber check."

"If you want me to, I can cover it and you can repay me when
you can."

"You don't know me. I'll never repay."

"Maybe someday . . . Give me hope . . . However small, so I
won't feel I've been taken."

"Taking you would be if I promised to pay you back. If you want
to give me the money, go ahead. I'll accept it, I'm not proud."

---

* They went by bus; she was exceedingly proud.

"I'll go the store and make good on the check. I'm not giving you the money."

"You're throwing your money away. When they accepted the check, they knew. Who doesn't know? I gave the manager a song and dance. Any business with me, they just write off."

"Things are strange with you, people still like you, despite everything."

"The manager had two sons, when she couldn't have any. I treated her, I was good, damned good. It was because I liked it, a GYN has to like pussies and take good care of them. A lot of people pity me, and naturally I take advantage of it. Why not?"

"But what if the manager has to pay? Or if the store decides to take back Manuela's clothes? You wouldn't like that; after all, it was an affectionate gesture."

"Your problem, young lady, is that you experience right now the problems of day after tomorrow. Manuela has been hurt so much that she's grown accustomed to it. At least for the moment she receives it, she'll be happy. Besides which, no store would have the courage to take back anything from her. They'd rather lose a little money than lose the customer!"

Idle talk, nothing made sense where Maciel was involved, no one could make heads or tails of anything he said.

"Except that . . . that . . . a present on Mother's Day? It'll hurt her. It's not that long ago her son died and she returned from her trip. They say she tried to kill herself. She's still in a state of shock, you were involved . . . I know because I'm a friend of Evandro the pharmacist."

"I know you . . . They involved me, girl, they involved me. That lawyer, Bradío, is a whore, he does whatever Antenor tells him. Who believes in me?"

"I do."

"What good is that? I arranged that son for her! Would I kill him? You think killing is that easy? It's difficult, it brings about all kinds of torment . . ."

"It's still all up in the air, no one really knows what happened!"

"Antenor suffered because of the presence of the boy. Let's cut him some slack. The boy was a Mongoloid. It hurt, and Antenor was ashamed. The rich Antenor, handsome Antenor, powerful Antenor, the husband of Manuela, the most desirable woman in the city, father of a Mongoloid."

"She had a complicated pregnancy, she was in the hospital in São Paulo."

"What pregnancy? Manuela is sterile. That son was arranged. When she disappeared, Manuela went into seclusion in Areia, Paraíba. The son was Lindorley's. I swear, when I attended to the cleaning woman's pregnancy, everything was normal. I examined the child and there were no problems. It showed up at six months. Antenor went crazy, less over love of the baby than over the effect on his image. No one's more vain than him. It was a calculated decision. He invited me over that afternoon, and we sat around drinking. Manuela went upstairs, he grabbed the child, threw it in the water, and pointed a revolver at me. I've always been afraid of guns, I was scared shitless, I watched the baby thrashing in the water, drowning, and something strange took hold of me. I couldn't move, speak, shout, nothing, and I remembered Anna Karenina being killed inside the car, murdered by Antenor, or at least I believe it was him, and I felt the tissues inside my head being torn apart, I saw Manuela approaching then, I pointed to the pool, she jumped in, I got out of there. Antenor had snorted three or four hefty lines, almost died of an overdose but was saved by the doctors who showed up to examine the child. Afterward, it's what everybody knows, because that's what they were told. Bradío tried to implicate me, but Manuela came to my defense, swearing it was an accident, to this day I don't know why. She must've suffered amnesia, because everything pointed to me as the killer. I never killed anyone, I could've gotten rich at the clinic, performing abortions. There wasn't a rich woman in the city who hadn't come to me. They ended up going to Lindorley to have it done. That's why she was shot in the legs by an enraged father."

Evangelina was in love but knew she had no chance. She's a wonderful person, but what good does that do? Ugly and ungainly! What everyone looks at is the packaging, everything needs a pretty design in order to be consumed. No, don't tell me she became the Good-Bye Angel because of problems of rejection or because society marginalized her. She was never marginalized, she's the best singer in the region, in all of Brazil, she could've been a professional, but she decided to stay here, withdrawn. That's the way she is, she likes her protective shell. Otherwise, she'd have to face envy, competition, ugly squabbles, for what? To be famous? No, she loves singing and can do it on her own, she doesn't need a public, her name in magazines, she doesn't need television programs. She sings for herself! Just look at how things are, Maciel approached her and insinuated himself, and they ended up involved, and that's where Evangelina's resentment began. Because she gave herself, unable to believe she was having sex with the most desired man in Arealva, it was like a dream. She felt herself envied, even if no one actually envied anymore, because Maciel was a shell of his former self, a remnant of the man he had been. But in her head what mattered was the fantasy, what she herself had created. Maciel was the first and certainly the last. What happened yesterday was necessary so she could regain her self-esteem, reaffirm herself as a woman, as a person, emerge from the abyss and depression. Killing Maciel was compensation, the first debt she ever collected. The affair between them lasted for months, until the day she asked a question. She shouldn't have asked, there are things we should accept without looking for the reason why, live and just let things go. But no, we insist, we want to know, we need to go deeper! We're all alike, bound by routine, predictable. She asked Maciel so often, and all she wanted to hear was one of those commonplace phrases uttered by people in love.

She would ask, insistently, feverishly, "Why do you like me? What did you see in me? What was it, why me out of so many women?"

Down deep, she only wanted an answer that would reassure her, affirm her as a woman, distinguish her.

Evangelina screamed, "No, don't tell him, never ever repeat what only you and I know. Don't you dare, or I'll kill you." She howled, unhinged, out of her mind, but Evandro continued, seeming to take pleasure in what he was doing.

"And Maciel said—listen to what he said: 'You! Do you know why I chose you? To be sure. It was my last chance to prove something. It was always very easy to be a man with the beautiful, perfumed women who surrounded me. But one day I started to have doubts . . .'"

"No! Stop, stop! Don't say anything, don't do this to me, my angel brother!" screamed Evangelina, wishing to take her fingernails to Evandro's face.

"'I needed to prove I was a man for any situation. I proved it,' Maciel answered. 'Managing to go to bed with you, having sex so many times—because that's all it was, sex, there was never love—was an experiment. A test, proof I could screw even the ugliest woman, the most ungainly and awkward animal in the world, a monster. Not even your breasts are desirable, they smell like an old woman's farts. If I can go to bed with you, I can go to bed with any woman.'"

Evangelina shot Evandro in the forehead. "I told you, I told you," she said, "I warned you, nobody, nobody could find out about that, I was going to take that insult to my grave. I don't die because I'm already dead. And so are you, you shitheel reporter."

Pedro Quimera shot first.

A single shot. There was one last bullet in Efrahim's revolver. He wiped off his fingerprints and placed the weapon in Evandro's hand, as he had seen done in movies. A fine school. He went out, the haze blanketing everything, Sunday night had begun. Walking through the streets, he could hear the theme music from the *Fantástico* show in every house. In all the houses in Brazil.

THE GODFATHER HOPES
HIS SON WILL DIE OF AIDS

The Godfather stopped at the How Come Pharmacy only to find it closed, the first time that had ever happened. He knocked on the door of the two-story house where Idalina, the needle woman, lived. She didn't wake up, having taken a triple dose of tranquilizers; Manuela's death had left her nervous. The Godfather then went to the Nighttime Shoeshine Man's house, which the police had sealed off and where two members of the Municipal Corporation stood watch. The dead dog was still in the same place, as no one was concerned with the poor animal. "Can I bury it?" he asked, and one of the sentries said no. "Why such meanness?" asked the Godfather. A bill of a hundred changed the man's mind. The dog was beginning to stink; he placed it in the Vemaguet's trunk. The Godfather drove around the city. He was restless, overcome by a great emptiness, enraged because a totally normal Sunday night had swept him up. It didn't seem possible that Manuela was dead.

People were arriving at the bus stops, on their way to shopping centers. Cheap perfume permeated the air. At the door of the Crystal Night, a small crowd was waiting for the café to open. Efrahim hadn't shown up, and there was no answer at his home. The Vemaguet headed in the direction of Hydrangea Gardens, where the multitude had dispersed after learning that no one would be allowed to see Manuela's body. Only a group of reporters were on duty, waiting for what? Some were rereading the extra editions. The Godfather bought several copies from a young black boy sitting in the gutter:

MYSTERY IN DEATH
OF SOCIALITE

NOT WHAT THE DOCTOR ORDERED:
A BULLET IN THE HEART

AREALVA ROCKED:
WHO KILLED THE
BELLE DO JOUR?

CAFÉ OWNER VANISHES

ALSO MISSING, THE POPULAR
NIGHTTIME SHOESHINE MAN,
COLORFUL STREET FIGURE

A profusion of photos of Manuela illustrated the newspapers' pages. The Godfather returned to the Snooker. He didn't see Lindorley, who usually slept on a sofa in the main room. He went to the office, turned on the 30-inch television set to TV Spain, where the corridas were already under way. A bullfighter was sticking colorful banderillas into a bleeding bull. The Godfather watched in boredom a few faenas with the muleta, waiting for the kill. The estocada was perfect, the bull fell with its legs up, convulsing. The Godfather got a pair of scissors and cut out all the photos of Manuela from the newspapers. Patiently, he removed the frames from the pictures of boxers that lined the walls. And put Manuela in their place, aided by masking tape. He finished and stood contemplating the mural. Everything else he tossed into the trashcan, then opened a bottle of alcohol. Not one of them is real, he thought, all of them were montages done in Ribeirão Preto, many of them poorly, because there were no computers in those days. I never boxed a round in my life, never got into the ring, I'm not dumb enough to put my face on public view, I just wanted to be a hero to my boy, wanted him to take the photos with him. Heloísa insisted, we've got to get him out of Arealva, this city would throw it up to him, forever, that he was the son of a whore and a crook. They all think I'm a crook, they won't have anything to do with me, except when they're broke and need money, they take my money and curse me. But we came up with a flawed plan with her sister, in that boardinghouse, the bitch spent all the money we sent and treated the boy terribly. I had to kill her when I found out.

He rummaged through the drawer for his lighter.

Antenor had to take Manuela away from me. I discovered her, shared with her a passion for pool cues. She was happy those afternoons, helping me fleece suckers. She would distract everyone's attention, the players were fascinated, we were an unbeatable pair. I wanted to screw her at any cost, she would shy away one day and lead me on the next, I tried, she would open up and close down, I'd never seen such a game. She wasn't at all afraid of me, it was me who was afraid of her. Afraid she'd go away. Just the way I came I'll leave, she would say. And Antenor fell in love with her, because it was impossible not to, it happened to me and I thought I had a chance despite being much older. She needed someone old and strong. But Antenor came along and the two of them hooked up. I knew my son, it wouldn't last a month, he would screw her and dump her, and then I would protect her. But no! They fell in love. He took her away from me! The last passion of my life. My time was running out, she would bring me extra life. But no, he took her! My son took away the possibility of staying alive! He'll pay, he'll suffer. I don't know why he killed Manuela, but he shouldn't have done it, he thrust a dagger into his father. I'll see him rot in a cell for the rest of his life. I'm already leaving clues, there'll be a lot that he won't be able to explain. I bought Ruy Banguela and Bradío, I'm looking for witnesses, I've got my newspapers, that bastard Luisão owes me a pile of money, there are reporters eating out of my hand, even that fat piece of shit Quimera is going to go along. I'm going to wipe out Antenor, toss him into a cell to rot alongside killers, guys with AIDS, TB, I want them to cornhole him, I want him to die in a prison riot. I'm going to take Heloísa to see her son rotting away, he's going to meet his mother in a glorious encounter. No one will help him, and if a judge lets him off I'll kill the judge . . .

The office was empty. He went to the window, from the house across the way came the sound of the *Fantástico* theme, a couple was having sex in the shadows of the parking lot. The Godfather opened the window, threw a heavy ceramic ashtray at the man's head and quickly hid from sight. The man fell, the woman screamed and bent over the body, her skirt still above her waist. The Godfather attempted to light a fire, but the lighter didn't work, it was out of fluid, he looked for a match, found a box from the Crystal Night and tossed the lit match into the basket of alcohol-soaked papers.*

He descended the stairs, got into the Vemaguet, and went to Evandro's house. The lights were on. He pushed open the gate, noticed that the door was ajar, went in, and saw the two bodies. Evandro dead. Evangelina moaned when she heard the noise. Painfully, she opened her eyes.

"Godfather?"

"What a massacre! What went down here?"

"The reporter, Quimera. He killed Evandro and tried to kill me. Go after him. He's going to get you . . ."

"That fat guy? A killer? Try again!"

---

* The alcohol was pure water. The flask had been open for a long time, and Lindorley, who was senile, didn't take care of the cleaning products, leading to fights with the miserly Godfather. The match went out. The Godfather had better luck at Evandro's house.

"He . . . Now he's headed somewhere, he wants to talk to a woman . . . Mariúsa . . ."

"Mariúsa . . . He's after Mariúsa?"

"Save me, Godfather, I don't want to die, save me. I need to put on the Good-Bye Angel exhibition.[*] Evandro's paintings . . ."

"Exhibition . . . What goddamn exhibition is that?"

"Quick, Godfather, save me!"

"And just why should I save you, big tits? It won't be easy to get you out of here, explain to the hospital, I'm not exactly a guy above suspicion. Stay there, I'm going to make an anonymous phone call. Right! I'm going to say I'm the Good-Bye Angel. I've got experience. I once was."

"You were? When?"[**]

The Godfather turned his back, went to the kitchen, took a container of yogurt from the refrigerator, and made his way through the house, startled by the paintings. He ran his fingers over his lips, a habit of his when some idea was forming. He grabbed the smaller canvases and began taking them to the Vemaguet. He removed the fetid dog and left it in the yard. He filled the backseat and the trunk; later he would return with the Veraneio. He sat down, observing Evangelina in extremis.

"Sing! Sing and I'll save you! Sing 'Che Gelida Manina.' Or 'Una Furtiva Lagrima.' Sing!"

And the singing filled the room, fragile, her voice a thread. The Godfather dragged Evandro's body to the rear of the backyard, the ground was covered with round pebbles forming a Japanese

---

[*] In extremis, people find any reason to justify their life.

[**] Could he have been? When? This remains a mystery to both author and readers.

garden with dwarf plants. He rested the pharmacist's head in the reflection pond and went to get Evangelina, fondling her breasts. Then he brought out the bloody canvases and arranged them. He placed the dead dog on Evangelina's breasts. It'll make nice photos, the press will thank me, TV will go wild. We have to think of the media when we do things. Just one more item. He searched through the house until he found alcohol, thinner, and a gallon of gasoline.* He spread everything around, especially on the furniture, capes, towels, and began striking matches.

With the Vemaguet full of paintings, he drove around the city in search of a place that was well trafficked but deserted. The plaza where Manuela had been found and where Edevair had set himself on fire was empty; there was no traffic there on Sunday night. The How Come Pharmacy was closed. The Godfather removed the paintings and leaned them against the wall of the Cathedral. Surely Evandro would place them in a certain order, there was a chronological sequence of murdered people. There, where Father Gaetano had cursed Arealva, the city would contemplate the works of the Good-Bye Angel. Woe unto thee, City of Blood, the newspaper headlines would say. He heard the sirens of fire trucks and smiled, knowing what it was. Now there was one more job to be done. He got in the Vemaguet and headed for the bus station.

By 4:00 A.M. nothing remained of the former gas station, Evandro's home and atelier. It was an old wooden construction, dried out. The flames devoured everything like children's tongues licking pineapple ice cream on a summer afternoon.

---

* Evandro always kept a gallon on hand in case of the need to cremate a corpse.

The fire merited a small photo, but the images of Evangelina and Evandro dead amidst the canvases of *The Good-Bye Angel* series shocked Arealva, still reeling from the previous day. And the city would remember that weekend as that of the Five Deaths,* as Iramar Alcifes termed it in his Monday afternoon program, half an hour after Manuela was buried.

---

* The body of the Nighttime Shoeshine Man in the Focal tunnel was never found. Or it would have been six deaths.

WHAT IF PEDRO QUIMERA WINS THE LOTTERY?

At 8:00 A.M., Pedro Quimera got off the bus midway to Bauru. He was sweating, his T-shirt was soaked. Television had predicted scattered storms. In front of him, a yellow sign read Floral Mansion, three kilometers. If you had asked, they'd come to pick you up, said the driver. As he crossed the asphalt, the softened pitch yielded beneath his feet. Pedro was afraid he'd be stuck there while a truck ran over him. A recurring nightmare in his life since the age of twelve. A tractor-trailer carrying sanitation equipment had run over him and he had been trapped among porcelain basins, his throat cut, everything soaked in blood. And people laughed. Nothing more ridiculous than dying surrounded by toilets, even if they had never been used.

He walked slowly, tired, he felt disgusted at sweating so much. It took him an hour to arrive at the site, surrounded by green wires overgrown with vines. A silent place, landscaped, with a brook running through it. The rear gate, Efrahim had advised. He felt as if he were in some movie serial. He found the first gate, but the key he had gotten from the box at the Crystal Night didn't work. There must be another. He moved on, the land was extensive. The second gate, with foul-smelling plastic bags, offal from the remains of diets, also wouldn't open. Efrahim must've played a trick on him, it was a prank. In one corner, at the curve of the wire fence, was a small door covered by vegetation. For midgets or dogs, thought Quimera. Whatever it was, it opened.

He rested in the shade and took a short nap, sleeping comfortably. He awoke to the sound of a power lawn mower. He headed in the direction of the building surrounded by porches and pergolas, covered with vines. He crossed paths with orderlies and greeted them. A lot of people must come and go, they were used to unfamiliar faces, Quimera surmised. He didn't see that behind his back two of them were eying him suspiciously. Pedro continued to the main hall. It was full, with people everywhere, dressed in sweatsuits. They seemed happy to be losing weight. Which one was Mariúsa? Where was she? A name like that wasn't common, someone would know her. Why complicate things?* He went to the reception desk. The receptionist had a rosy complexion, the typical "girl next door."

"Mariúsa? And you are—?"

"Her uncle. Didn't you let her know I was coming?"

She checked in the computer. Quimera didn't notice that as she read the information on the screen she raised her eyes and signaled to someone behind him.

"Apartment 23231, C wing. You're in the A wing. The building is shaped like an H. Would you like someone to go with you?"

"No, I'm taking a look around. This is a charming place."

He went down corridors, passing by workout rooms where elderly people were lifting weights, chatting, sipping juice from delicate long glasses, all of it accompanied by ambient, relaxing, classical music. Smetana's *The Moldau*. He could feel the river flowing, the rhythm increasing. If he stayed here for a time, taking off the flab, Yvonne wouldn't recognize him. Speaking of her, I'm not going to look for her, I'm not going back to Arealva, I'm going to hike along the highways, discover Brazil, "on the road," *The Long Haul*.

He knocked at the door of 23231. Adds up to 11, a powerful number, auspicious. The words this place conjures up! He knocked louder, then tried the knob. The door opened. In the dimly lit room was a woman tied to a bed by wide leather straps.

"Mariúsa?"

She didn't answer, merely stared at him, terrified.

---

* Actually, we have abbreviated Pedro's odyssey at the spa to avoid boring the reader. It took him hours, walking, inquiring, until he decided to go to the reception desk. He sensed intuitively that he shouldn't go through the lobby. He was right.

"Are you Mariúsa? I'm a friend. A friend of Manuela's."

"Manuela? What are you doing here? Did he have you committed too?"

"He?"

"The Godfather. Antenor. Efrahim. Maciel. The gang."

"None of them. I'm a reporter, I'm taking a risk, I need a good story. To put an end to those people."

"How'd you get in? Nobody gets in here except the Godfather's people. You're one of them. What do they want this time?"

"Efrahim gave me the key to get in."

"The Count? That doesn't help any."

"He's dead."

"Dead? Was it Antenor?"

"No, a woman named Evangelina."

"That busty woman from the Chorale? Why?"

Her voice was strong, metallic.

"He knew something she didn't want him to tell."

"It sounds like a soap opera. As far as I'm concerned, they can all die. They stuck me in this shit hole! Why don't you get me out of here?"

Pedro Quimera realized that the situation was absurd, for he was accepting as natural the fact that she was tied up, and he hadn't even asked why. What if she was flat-out crazy? She didn't seem to be. But crazy people don't seem crazy, if they did they wouldn't be crazy, because a shrewd crazy knows how to fake it, how to appear normal. Pedro looked for a way to untie the knots; the straps were secured by small padlocks.

"I don't know how to undo this."

"Then leave! Go to the police, bring your friends, get me out of here."

"After you tell me about Manuela. Your name and telephone number were in Dr. Maciel's pocket."

"It's been six years since I heard anything about Maciel, so why would my number be in his pocket? You think I have a telephone here?"

"Maciel was killed."

"Him too? Who are you, an obituary editor? Who else did they kill? Give me the names . . ."

"I don't know, I'm still investigating, it was yesterday."

He preferred not to say that it had been Manuela. And Evangelina.

"All I know is that when I got there I found the Godfather. He searched the guy and took out a piece of paper with your name on it."

"He didn't take out anything. The Godfather is full of tricks. Clever like nothing you ever saw. He wanted you to find my name."

"Why?"

"Because he hates Antenor."

"He hates his own son? This isn't the first time I've heard that. Very odd. Why should he hate his son?"

"Because of Manuela."

"I don't understand his game."

"The Godfather's like that. It's his life, there's no alternative, no other way of being. He's just like a shark. Can you say the shark is bad? No, that's how he was created, he does what he does because he must to survive. The Godfather is like that shark . . . You haven't told me your name."

"Pedro. Pedro Quimera."

She managed a laugh. It was obvious that she wanted to talk.

"Sorry . . . It's an odd name. And Manuela?"

"She was murdered."

"Murdered? Damn, damn, he finished his work."

"He?"

"The Godfather. The Godfather, who else? He was going to kill her one day. The poor girl, in the hands of those two. Damn the day she showed up in Arealva. It's the fault of the storm, it started suddenly and she didn't have anywhere to take shelter. Did she have to go into the Snooker, did she have to be right in front of it?"

Manuela left the bus station, suitcase in hand, and went up Rua do Ao Comércio Elegante. She hadn't imagined the city would be so hot, expecting that the waters of the Tietê and the lakes would temper the climate. Her feet, clad in red shoes, were sweating. When she disembarked in Arealva, she left nothing behind. The house had been repossessed, her father had disappeared, her mother eaten up by osteoporosis and bedridden, shrinking away until she was buried measuring only fifteen inches. A child's coffin was enough.

Arealva had been the most distant place to which her scant money had allowed her to travel. The street in the old downtown was desolate, every tree had been removed. On the narrow sidewalk the concrete lampposts took up all the space.* Storeowners and youths came to the door to watch her pass by in her tight

---

* Successive mayors had widened the streets of Arealva to make room for cars. They did away with the trees, sold off the historical cobblestones, and pocketed fat kickbacks from the paving work.

miniskirt. She loved the sharp tickle the looks provoked, for it meant they would go on thinking about her. Like the guy in the next seat on the bus, who tried to lean against her all night and had masturbated covered by a worsted jacket that smelled of oregano. When she got off the bus, the guy followed her, whispering whore, whore. She was used to it, it had always been like that. What they didn't know was that no man had ever laid a hand on her. Manuela had never yielded, though she had done everything to arouse, to see men act like pigs in a sty, snorting. Men were ridiculous snorting in heat.

The rain began quickly, clouds gathered, and it became night at 11:00 A.M. The windstorm turned awnings inside out, thick drops became hail, and Manuela, soaked through after two minutes of rain, saw the door, a flight of stairs, a neon sign: THE CRYSTAL CUE: BILLIARDS. She felt an attraction, went inside to find shelter, and since the rain was blowing in through the doorway, began climbing the stairs. She noticed an odd smell. Sixty-five steps, she had the habit of counting stair steps, before reaching the huge half-lit room, where the cleaning woman was scrubbing the floor with a dirty mop. In the rear, she could make out a tall man sitting by the window. Manuela counted the billiard tables, more than forty. She deposited on the wide boards of the hardwood floor her suitcase full of postcards from her father. She heard "Susanna" (the radio or a player in the Snooker itself?) by the Art Company, the most popular music in the dance hall in Macedônia. She began dancing, slowly, her eyes closed. And as the rhythm accelerated, she became more excited, dancing was what she liked more than anything. Before the end, the music began again, someone had restarted it. Manuela didn't open her eyes, feeling her lace dress clinging to her body. Her mother had gotten married in that dress, and Manuela had asked her to keep it; the two women had the same body. She was constantly afraid, wondering whether she would get the same disease. At the first sign of pain she would stuff herself with aspirin and several other analgesics; no day went by without her going to pharmacies and scrutinizing the shelves. The music ended, she went on dancing, she heard applause and grumbles, opened her eyes, saw the lanky and attractive old man, very tall and wiry, white eyebrows. He was smiling and applauding, a narrow smile, his lips barely parted, but his eyes were shining, and Manuela felt both uneasy and pleased because her dress was clinging so tightly to her body. That was what the man was gazing at, and she liked it, who knows why, she liked it. The grumbles came from the cleaning woman, standing with her hand on her waist.

"Where do you think you are, you tramp? Beat it."

"How can you say that, Lindorley? What lack of manners! Leave the girl alone. It's raining like crazy out there!"

"It started raining, I got wet, the door was open, I came in. I'll go now."

"Do you have to go?"

"I don't have to, and I don't not have to. I don't have anywhere to go or anywhere to return to."

Drops were staining the green felt of one of the pool tables. Manuela could smell the odor of musty things mixed with that of cleaning products. The man, with his cunning ratlike eyes, gave off a strange undeniable perfume that awoke fantasies.

"I'm the Godfather."

"I'm Manuela."

"Last name?"

"What for?"

"Where are you from?"

"Why?"

"Just asking."

"What for?"

"That one will twist you around her finger, you dirty old man. You're already getting ideas," grumbled the cleaning woman.

"Are you the owner, sir? Care for a game?"

"No *sir*, just Godfather. Do you know how to play?"

"Do you?"

"Girl, I'm the 316."

"316?"

"That's how many matches I've won in a row. A record. Registered with *Guinness*. Come, I'll show you the book."

"A book? I don't really know how to read all that well.* Give me a cue."

"How many points should I spot you?"

"How many do *I* spot *you*?!"

They played all afternoon, stopping to have ham sandwiches with onion sauce, brought by the ill-humored cleaning woman who tossed the tray on the table and withdrew, grumbling. The Godfather ate with care, not allowing the juicy sauce to run down the corners of his mouth. His gestures were studied. They played again the next day, after Manuela had slept for fourteen straight

---

* A strange reference to Manuela's semi-illiteracy. To date, no one has commented on the fact.

hours. They played the third day, and the Godfather didn't win a single time. Calmly, he studied Manuela, let her win, the cleaning woman was unresigned. "What about your title?" she asked. "Is the 316 over? There's something fishy going on! Something fishy, and I see that glint in your eyes and I don't like it one bit!" It was apparent that the Godfather was impatient, not wanting to admit he had fallen in love the moment she had come in. He wouldn't win a single game, his cue wasn't obeying. Beating her might drive her away. They bet money, and after a week Manuela had won a bundle, even if she had noticed something was going on, but why not take advantage of it? She advised that she would go to a hotel, a boardinghouse, and he said no, the storage room is going to be your apartment, I'll order everything changed.

Manuela would disappear when the place opened at five in the afternoon, withdrawing. The Godfather had made Lindorley straighten up the storeroom, had purchased satin sheets, feather pillows, and a white hand-tied rug. By then it was known in the city, or at least in part of the city, that at the Crystal Cue the God-father was hiding a mysterious and beautiful woman, his bastard daughter just arrived from Lichtenstein.*

In the afternoon the pair engaged in aggressive contests, and the Godfather came to realize that it was impossible to defeat her; he tried everything, without success. His decades of cunning and trickery, his encyclopedic knowledge of what it was possible to do with each ball, each stroke of the cue, was of no avail. Manuela destroyed his game on those hot afternoons when the Snooker's

---

* People of the interior love to create fantasies. Where did that Lichtenstein, such an unknown country, come from?

blinds were drawn and the haze penetrated through narrow openings that filtered the light. Manuela was sweating, and the Godfather approached, pretending to move around the table while desperate with desire, longing to touch her but fearful he would be rebuffed. He couldn't understand her, she didn't talk, didn't say where she came from, why she had come, what her plans were. She must be eighteen or twenty, but was indefinable.* He realized that she provoked subtly, without letting her guard down. In earlier days, he would have grabbed Manuela, thrown her onto the worn green felt. However, now he was deterred by her coldness, the eyes that simultaneously rejected and beckoned, leaving him in a state of confusion. Maybe he was too old for such things. Two months went by, with the Godfather captive of those afternoons, even suggesting, "If you like, I can close down the main room and we can play till we drop dead, till we collapse from fatigue, we're exhausted, I don't need this space, I don't need anything, just you." He insisted, fired up when he spoke of death.

One afternoon she stayed in the main room after five, seeing the young men who arrived. The Snooker was a meeting place, an in spot, aided by Iramar Alcifes, who denounced it: there the ivory balls weren't the only attraction. Adolescents knew that the Godfather had something hidden in the storeroom where Manuela slept: marijuana, cocaine. Only later, quite recently, did crack and amphetamines come on the scene. That day, the son of Cyro, the owner of the wheat mills, spent an hour and a half playing with Manuela, who thought he was cute. They played and leaned against one another, smiled and winked, drank a lot, and then he

---

* Manuela's age was always the subject of discussion in the city.

grabbed her and lifted her skirt to her waist so rapidly that the Godfather had no time to react, paralyzed by hatred and desire. Manuela's legs were a more beautiful sight than sinking the eight ball blindfolded. He became excited at seeing the youth opening his fly, he wanted to see her taken right in front of him, and in the blink of an eye he heard a shout, the boy fell, his skull cracked open. Manuela was holding a bloody cue. Who does he think he is, he's the richest kid in town, he was, now he's gone, how could he do that? Ask him why he tried to do that, what gave him the idea he could? They went on talking mad, crazy talk, the Godfather was stunned—and for that old man to be stunned he would've had to see the devil on good terms with God. They carried the body to the storage room, he told Lindorley to clean up the blood, and they waited for nightfall, when they drove the boy in his car to the highway and threw him into a cane field, then abandoned the car a long way off, without its tape player, ripping the seats, removing the magnesium hubcaps. The Godfather phoned Luisão, "Got a good story for you, if you hurry. I was driving along the highway, the body of Cyro's son is there, he was robbed, tell the police and keep me out of it."

("And how do you know these things?" Pedro Quimera asked, and Mariúsa replied that Lindorley was there, she never let the Godfather out of her sight, she was crazy about the old man. The child was theirs, the boy who years later was taken for Antenor and Manuela to adopt because the couple was sterile and Manuela had vowed she would leave Antenor if they didn't have a child, even an adopted one. She wanted a clean adoption, with the mother handing over the baby and disappearing. Lindorley, despite her jealousy, liked Manuela after she rejected the Godfather's advances. "You mean he finally did make advances?")

That night, as they returned from the highway, he thought Manuela would be grateful and proposed staying with her. "No, no, no, never with you. Why do you have to ruin everything?" From that moment on, the Godfather was impotent, it was over for him, and that was agony. He couldn't do anything, no matter who he was with. He tried herbal remedies, went to voodoo rites, frequented Santo Daime, bought American vitamins, contemplated a silicone implant. The doctors swore it was psychological, he should see an analyst! That's not a manly thing, he shouted, and he started using drugs for the first time, wandering around the Snooker and spying on Manuela as she played by herself. Since that night she had refused to play against him, "If you want me to go, I will, I'll go somewhere, it's easy to leave when you don't have anywhere to go, when you come from nowhere."

That was when Antenor appeared. He had been in the Northeast for six months dealing with a land matter. He planned to plant cashew trees in Arealva, which has good soil, and take advantage of the excellent European market for juices and nuts. He met Manuela and would spend his afternoons at the Snooker as if waiting in ambush, drinking margaritas with Mexican tequila and finely chopped ice, the only person in Arealva who knew how to prepare the drink. On Mother's Day in 1983, as he was leaving, he met her at the door.

"Want to go to the cemetery?"

"To do what?"

"To visit my mother's tomb."

They began visiting the tomb on a daily basis. In the deserted cemetery, the sun withering the flowers, they wandered among abandoned sepulchers. Manuela was moved by the fortyish man kneeling before his mother's grave, a pretty brunette with enormous golden earrings in the color photograph on the tombstone. She had never seen a color photo on a sepulcher, it struck her as a good idea. Before she realized it, she was in love with Antenor. There's nothing more attractive and more moving than a man who visits his mother's grave, she said. At the cemetery, she would often see in the distance, hiding among the cypresses and bougainvilleas, a woman in dark glasses observing them. She told Antenor, who had also noticed her. The woman quickly disappeared. Who could be watching them? Unless it was someone sent by the Godfather, who was reticent, jealous, ever since Manuela had started seeing Antenor.

It was Antenor who took her out of the storage room and installed her in the Hotel Nove de Julho, in the suite where President Juscelino Kubitschek had slept two nights following the inauguration of Brasilia. Within seven months they were married, and Manuela invited the Godfather to the wedding, which he didn't attend. He drank for an entire week, hit four customers at the Snooker, put the Crystal Cue up for sale, and announced he would be leaving Arealva. He stayed. He contented himself with spying; no one had never seen such passion. Manuela explained to Antenor that there was one condition: she would continue to play by herself every afternoon. She had inherited the game from her father. She had spent her childhood in pool halls, where her father, a professional, made a living with his cue, going from city to city, and he had taught his daughter the secrets. No lessons of life, advice, behavior, or examples, none of the things fathers usually teach their children. Just how to win big matches.

"And where is he now?" asked Antenor.

"In prison. He went to Mexico, then immigrated illegally to Texas, living here and there, always winning, making lots of money. He would send me a postcard from each place, they're in my suitcase. The last one came from Tennessee, he was probably arrested right afterwards. Promise me we'll go to the United States to look for my father!"

He promised. Because Manuela was different. Besides everything else, he had become curious about her father, who must be an honest cheat, a first-class con man and con men add spice to life.

"How was Manuela different?" Pedro asked.

"She would go to Evandro's pharmacy wearing torn jeans, showing skin. A real turn-on."

"Incredible legs. It was her way, offering herself and then shutting down, defiant, I don't know if you understand."

"She passed by me a thousand times, as I didn't even exist. I would get crazy with rage, I don't know what got her attention."

"There was something in Manuela that attracted people. Her mouth, the changes in the color of her eyes, sometimes brown, sometimes black, vulnerable or hostile. We wanted to decipher her, find out what she was thinking, how to please her. Antenor used to give her a jewel on the seventeenth of every month, the day they met. Once, they were already married, when Antenor was traveling, she received an enormous bouquet of roses. But where was the jewel? Flowers are for cemeteries. She threw them

in the garbage. When he returned, she discovered that the flowers' stems were bound with a sapphire necklace. It caused a huge
quarrel."

"And the son in the pool. What happened?"

"She wanted a child, wanted one badly, but nothing happened.
It became an obsession. Obsession, isn't that a lovely word? Obsession. They ran tests, and both of them were sterile. Antenor
wouldn't admit it; machos aren't sterile, it's her fault. That's how
it began. Then Maciel offered them a baby. She accepted. Later I
saw it, a deal set up by the Godfather, well planned, he was looking to hurt his son. Antenor had taken Manuela from him, or so
he imagined, the old man never was all there, always by himself
at the Snooker."

"What was there between her and the old man? Is there anything weird in the story?"

"Nothing, nothing! She told me everything. There was never
anything. It beats me if there was. I won't hold my hand over the
flame even for a saint."

"What about Maciel? How did he come into the picture?"

"Because of drugs and money. To try for a comeback. Did you
know the doctor? Very proud, I never saw anything like it. Vain.
Living in poverty was humiliating, and that business of his daughter murdered in the parking lot destroyed him. It might have been
Antenor, the Godfather, some petty thief, Maciel, there are some
who say it was his wife, Valéria, when she caught him trying to
have sex with his daughter. Valéria dropped out of sight. Could it
be true? Maciel adored Anna Karenina, he was preparing a plan
to make her a Miss. Except that between him and the world was

Arealva. It's the city, Pedro. It's destructive! Get away from Arealva. The whale bones don't exist."

Quimera felt that Mariúsa was confused, maybe the years in Floral Mansion had left her out of touch with reality. She seemed chaotic, they must have her pumped full of medication.

"Maciel and the Godfather plotted the whole thing?"

"Manuela spent months away from Arealva. When she got back, she announced that in a Hungarian clinic* she had managed to get pregnant. The son that Lindorley swore was hers by the Godfather appeared. Efrahim was the intermediary, linked to Maciel. Efrahim devoted himself to adoptions and had connections to Italians and Germans. Months later came the revelation: the boy was Mongoloid. Manuela was tormented, she changed completely, as if an aneurism had burst in her head. She would spend hours just looking at the boy. She stopped talking. Torn apart by enormous pain. I could tell, I was with her constantly, the pain surrounded her like a saint's halo.** She had love, dedication, counted on the boy recovering, forgot everything else. She wouldn't let Antenor touch her, they hadn't had sex for two years.*** It drove him crazy. She was more and more isolated, she would spend hours at the How Come Pharmacy, and wouldn't let me go with her. It was rumored in the city that she was on everything, Prozac, Ecstasy, that her ass was like a pincushion from shooting heroin. Lies! She never needed anything to bear up, she punished herself."

---

* This doesn't jibe with Maciel's account. But what account jibes with another? The fact is that Manuela disappeared from the city.
** Mariúsa utters some curious phrases. She has her poetry.
*** So, did they have sex? This book is nearly over and the truth about Manuela and sex has yet to be discovered. Everyone contradicts one another.

Short of breath, Mariúsa paused. Quimera had the impression she had everything caught in her throat, ready to explode.

"Until that afternoon at the pool. She used to sit in the sun with the little boy, who was getting no better despite having doctors brought in from outside. You know medicine in Arealva is shitty, it attracts nothing but businessmen. She would stay there until sundown, the doctors had recommended water, air, exercise. In those days the condominium wasn't yet finished, Antenor was the first to move there, a peaceful place, it was only later that it filled up, went crazy, everybody scared, wanting safety, fleeing the city. The area is a fortress, an enormous solitude, a pain, you can't take two steps without a security guard after you. Antenor was sleeping, it must've been five o'clock, a long holiday, or a Sunday, I don't know. He had binged on rum, one drink after another. The little boy was there, with that enormous head of his, those large eyes. Quiet in his crib, watched over by Manuela. She had been absorbed for weeks, concentrating on the child. Antenor woke up and looked at the woman, who was wearing a tight-fitting one-piece swimsuit, her thighs dampened with sparkling mineral water, a skin treatment that had been recommended to her; she took care of herself. I started to steal away, looking back. He jumped on her, in a struggle or fight or horseplay, and took off his clothes. Manuela jumped in the water and tossed out her swimsuit. They stayed in the pool, I shouldn't have looked, but who can resist? It's life. It's fun to watch others do it. They came out of the water and rolled on the grass, and she was screaming, No, no, I said never again, be careful of the boy. And he said, You even took off your clothes, you bitch! He cursed Manuela, struck her, accused her of giving birth to a sickly child, despite it not being her fault, he went so wild that he thought they had actually had a child, and that it wasn't adopted. Antenor smells, it comes from his mother, whores were sick, they went with anyone, they didn't practice hygiene, I'm a nurse, I know about that. I decided it was time for me to go away, leave that house once and for all, but I adored Manuela, I felt good at her side. The happiest times in my life were those afternoons in the Snooker, with her teaching me how to play. We enjoyed ourselves, it was the hours when the Mongoloid was in the hospital and the Godfather served chilled Frascati. He treated her well, she was the only person he wasn't a sonofabitch with. The best afternoons of my life were in that game room, she said, and she was happy and unhappy. She didn't know why she didn't leave the city and take the boy, far away from everything, there was something that attracted her, held her back. She kept to herself, it was hard for her to make friends with women. Maybe because she was different, no one likes people who are different. Her passion for Antenor had ended. A fury that had passed, burned out. A strange passion, because she never gave herself to him, I'm sure of it, I swear it. That's what she said, and I believed it, she never lied. 'I'll kill you, I'll kill you, be with me, at least once, for the sake of your son,' Antenor screamed. The sun bearing down on my face and I saw him kneeling over her with a broken glass in his hand, threatening to slice her face. But a shrewd woman knows what to do, she kicked him in the balls, Antenor fell, he was already hammered, she grabbed the glass and cut him in the neck; I was paralyzed. What if she had hit the jugular? Manuela got up, went to the crib and lifted the little boy out, hugged him, and started to dance.

She really enjoyed dancing, did I mention that? She used to dance at the Getúlio Vargas, she could dance the samba better than the blacks, she would dance at the Regattas until nine in the morning, back in the days when dances lasted all night long and would get more lively around breakfast time. The stereo was playing "Yes Sir, I Can Boogie," dance hall music, I remember it well, how could I forget? It was lovely, Manuela dancing in the sun with the boy, hugging him, I wished I had a camera. I forgot Antenor lying there, I didn't care. And I felt an odd sensation, as if I were outside my body, watching myself, in a pleasant torpor. Maciel used that word a lot. Torpor. It's good to live in a torpor, he used to say. Then she jumped into the pool, grasping the boy, what was he called, what was his name? From where I was I could see her dancing in the water, but I didn't see the boy, she had her back to me, and I ran. Manuela was standing in the shallow end, not moving, bent over, with the boy completely underwater, that infernal music, today I find it infernal, *I can boogie, I can boogie*. I saw she was crying, and she moved away, the boy was floating, floating without moving. I understood and screamed, screamed."

A lovely scene, thought Pedro Quimera. Maybe I could write a screenplay. It would begin that way, the body of a dead person floating in the swimming pool, with the camera placed at the bottom of the water.*

"Then she said, 'I'll meet you later, my son!' She left the pool, I came out of my torpor, Manuela turned around, her face was like Medusa, she hit me and I fell down. She's gone completely mad, I

---

* Has Pedro, who is such a fan of cinema, forgotten that this is the beginning of *Sunset Boulevard* (1950)?

thought, everything's exploded in her head. I could think of nothing but saving the boy, and Manuela was struggling with me, saying 'Leave him, leave him, it's better this way, better for him, better for us, I won't have the strength to see him like this my whole life, let it be now while I can stand it, now, now.' She cried, laughed, spit on me, while Antenor was bleeding. Manuela let me go and sat down in a wicker chair, looking at the little floating body. I threw myself into the water, too late, too late! Nothing could be done! I managed to get him out, put him on the side of the pool, and called Maciel. The only thing that occurred to me."

"How did you call him? Didn't he live here and there in the city, without any fixed address?"

"He still used a clandestine clinic—they had taken away his license—where he treated the poor. He attended to Manuela, after checking the boy and seeing nothing could be done. I called the ambulance, and Bradío came too, I don't have the slightest idea how he found out, because there weren't any servants that day, it was a big holiday, a Sunday. Antenor spent an hour at the hospital, the wound had been minor, just a scratch, and found Manuela in a catatonic state. That was when they took that long trip to Bali. He brought back hundreds of colorful one-piece bathing suits and pareus, nobody had ever seen anything like it, he sold them all, it was a hit. Bradío accused Maciel, just a smoke screen to confuse. The police, under orders, called it an accident. Antenor and the Godfather, to protect Manuela, had me committed here. I had gone totally crazy, threatening to tell the whole story. I suffered, I suffered, no one can imagine how much, I can never forget the little boy floating, drowning is the most horrible thing there is. Do you suppose he suffered a lot, did he? I was lucky they didn't kill me. In any case, everything ended between Manuela and Antenor, even though they kept up appearances. He held on, all he could think about was a career in politics. Did he run? In public they were one thing, in their private life they never spoke. Besides that, he didn't keep his promise to take her to Tennessee[*] to help look for her father—if the father ever existed."

"What about the woman at the cemetery?"

"Manuela knew only that she was brunette, with very large earrings, and closely resembled the woman in the photograph on the gravestone."

"How is it you know so much?"

"Lindorley is my sister, I was Maciel's nurse for many years. I took care of the Mongoloid, and I treated the child as if he were her son and mine."

"You liked him that much? Did you know from the start that he was sick?"

"Yes! Yes, I knew!"

"And you got involved in all that because of Manuela? Is it possible for a woman to be so enchanting?"

"Do you want to know the truth? Do you?"

Mariúsa seemed beside herself, drooling, unable to move, desperate.

"Hasn't it been more than long enough? You say you're a reporter? Well, you're going to have a wonderful story! Get me out of here, we're going to tell it in your paper for all of Arealva to hear.

---

[*] The author was at the Tennessee State Prison but found no reference to a Brazilian prisoner having been there.

I've got nothing to lose. They can kill me, but people are going to know. I bore this pain too."

"What is it that's so sensational?"

"The Godfather may kill you."

Quimera patted his pocket, looking for Efrahim's revolver, then remembered he'd left it beside Evandro. His confidence vanished, but even so he stammered, "Spit it out, for Chrissake!"

Mariúsa didn't have much confidence in his certainty.

"That was my son!"

"Yours?"

"Why do you think I suffered so much? Why did they stick me in here? Because the boy was mine, by Maciel. Mine! Not Lindorley's. He was mine! Maciel thought he could take the place of Anna Karenina. We had the boy, we never imagined that what happened would happen."

"How was it yours? What a bunch of crazies!"

Besides the article, I'm going to write the next seven o'clock soap, thought Quimera. And no one will believe it, they'll criticize me as melodramatic.

"Maciel knew as soon as the child was born. When he told me, he already had the plan to deliver it to Manuela. We decided it was better for him to be raised by someone who could take care of him. To me, handing him over to Manuela was like seeing Moses discovered by Pharaoh's daughter. I agreed to the deal, I would be able to leave Brazil, two hundred thousand dollars, two hundred thousand for a lovely newborn! Understand? Do you understand? Take me away from here, I want to shout it to the world! Look! I'm going to tell you something no one knows, the great secret of

Arealva. It will rock the city much more than Manuela's death. Know why she couldn't have children? Do you know? Do you have any idea? You don't, you couldn't. Manuela was a man. A man so marvelous that he could only be a woman. Beautiful, delicate. That's why Antenor fell in love. He wouldn't let her have an operation, he liked her just as she was, a man-woman, a woman-man. Antenor was absolutely crazy about her. Obsessed. Only he, Evangelina, Maciel, the pharmacist, and I knew."

Absorbed, they hadn't noticed the Godfather and three savage orderlies[*] enter the apartment. Pedro Quimera was immobilized, Mariúsa's mouth was covered, and one of the orderlies injected her in the neck; she lost consciousness. They untied the woman, gagged Quimera and placed him in the bed. He struggled, but the men were strong. They strapped him down, snapped the locks shut.

"I don't have anything against you and that's why I'm leaving you here. It's a nice place, good food, you're going to come out thin, if you ever do come out. Isn't it better this way? You don't pay anything. A free diet plan."

Without understanding what the Godfather was saying, Pedro asked, "Why? Why did you give me the lead to Mariúsa?"

"Because if she kept her part of the bargain, you'd leave here and head straight to the newspaper. Luisão would run a big head-line: *Mystery of Hydrangea Gardens Pool Solved*. No one ever re-ally swallowed the accident story. All that people needed was a pretext for someone to come see Mariúsa and get the story out of her. Then she would disappear with a shitload of money."

---

[*] They weren't orderlies, they were only dressed as such.

"Or just disappear. Without a penny."

"I couldn't just say: I know a woman who's going to tell you the truth. They wouldn't have believed me. When Manuela died, I thought there would be an investigation, someone from the press would come to me or Antenor. Everybody always thought it was Manuela who did the killing, I needed to clear her name. My homage. I was the only one who lifted a finger to clear the memory of the woman. When I left Antenor at home, last night, after we crossed the lake, I dashed here, made a deal with that piece of crap nurse. For her to say that Maciel, in an act of love, threw my grandson into the pool and killed him. The city knew about Maciel's passion for her and would buy it."

"What about Morimoto? The coroner will talk. Manuela a man. What a juicy dish for Iramar. And Portella will love the news."

"Let's say Mortummoto."

"But you did everything to implicate Antenor. Your son. It doesn't make sense."

"My daughter! Antenor was a woman! That's what Maciel discovered in the letters. That's what we've kept hidden all these years. It drove me mad! When he strangled Manuela, he put an end to me and to him. Or should I say her?"

"It wasn't him. It was Efrahim."

"Efrahim? He doesn't even kill the roaches in that café of his."

"He killed to get at you. The last act of his life.[*] I know, Evandro knows, Evangelina, the Nighttime Shoeshine Man."

The Godfather had a moment of indecision. Then he shouted, "Evandro and the woman with big tits are dead! Shoeshine Man!

---

[*] An imposing phrase at the end is always good.

We can still get to Shoeshine Man! I need to know. What about Efrahim? That pustule disappeared, he's scared."

"Efrahim is going to confess . . ."

"I'll draw and quarter him! Cut him into a thousand pieces. Carve him up like a holiday turkey. Him and his daughter, wherever she is."

"In pieces? Who do you think you are, the Good-Bye Angel?"

"Me? It's me. Of course I am!"

"What are you going to do with Mariúsa?"

"She's not going to tell anybody anything. There are certain truths that can't be known. She helped take the sick child to my son. She destroyed my son's life. She ruined him!"

"But you hate Antenor!"

"I love him."

The four men carried Mariúsa away and he heard the door being locked from the outside. Once the initial shock passed, Pedro Quimera was happy they hadn't searched his pockets and taken the lottery ticket. And mentally he checked the numbers again.

BIBLIOGRAPHY

Barros, Laert Elzio and Rodolfo Telarolli. *A História da Focal* (*aspectos da Economia dos Imigrantes em Arealva*). Edições UNESP-Arealva, 1988.

A Bíblia de Jerusalém. Edições Paulinas, 1981.

Lourcelles, Jacques. *Dictionnaire du Cinéma*. Paris: Editions Robert Laffont, 1992, pp. 1479–1480.

Pontes, Alderabã. *Drogas e Jogo em Arealva*. Press Prize, 1994, published in *O Expresso*, 1995. The book that aroused envy in Pedro Quimera.

Torres, Armando. *Sociologia da Nova Burguesia Interiorana de São Paulo*. São Paulo: Edições do Autor, 1985.

Newspapers and magazines

Caras, complete collection 1994–95.

O Cruzeiro, June and August 1956.

Economia ao Alcance de Todos, No. 85, Year 8 (January 1994), pp. 45 ff.: "The Most Developed Cities of the Interior."

O Estado de São Paulo, January 1932, August and October 1944, 1956, 1957, 1990, 1991, and 1993, complete.

O Expresso, complete collection since its founding.

Folha de S. Paulo, collections for 1936, 1941, 1967, 1995.

IstoÉ, January and February 1995.

A Lista, complete collection.
Manchete, complete collection since its founding.
Veja, January, February, March 1995.

Interviews

Adriano Portella (courtesy Golfin Air: two flights daily to Miami),
Candido de Assumpção (leader of the Black Liberation Move-
ment of Arealva, in relation to documentation about attempts to
purchase the Coral Whale), Christina Priscilla Portella, Dorneles
Moura and Draílton Susten (locomotive engineers on fruit trains
who saw apparitions in the Focal tunnel), Idalina Alves (known as
Idalina, the needle woman), Hans of the Deluge, Iramar Alcifes,
Dr. Ivo Pitanguy, a judge (who prefers to remain anonymous),
Lindorley Santana (in the paupers' home), Matthew Silber (warden of the Tennessee State Penitentiary, at least he told me he was
the warden), Rita Capuano.

Audio- and videotapes

Programs of Iramar Alcifes, ceded by court order. Television pro-
grams from stations in São Paulo (capital), by special courtesy.
Recordings of lectures by the Leader of Profitable Knowledge.
Videotapes recorded in Apartment 316 of the Hotel Nove de
Julho (it was necessary to pay the manager three thousand dol-
lars). Tapes that Evandro the pharmacist recorded with Manuela

in the antibiotics storeroom. They were in the possession of Idalina, the needle woman. She charged to listen to the nine hours of tape. At the end, she asked, "Would you like me to masturbate you a bit?" I agreed, and she proved to be very adept. Statements from the evangelicals who, on a Sunday morning, saw Antenor, the Godfather, and Pedro Quimera in the Shoeshine Man's backyard. They requested anonymity for religious reasons. Statements from all the singers in the Gilda Parisi Chorale, deeply traumatized. The Chorale disbanded.

Documents from the Lev Gadelha Museum.

A copy of the Shoeshine Man's notebook.

Reading of Heloísa's letters to her son. They provided the bulk of the information about the Godfather's activities.

Reports from the Morgue and investigations of the deaths of Anna Karenina, Edevair Castelli Lopes, Evandro the pharmacist, Evangelina the singer, Efrahim Capuano, Luisão, Maciel, the Godfather, and Yvonne.

Notes by Pedro Quimera in a spiral notebook, made in the Floral Mansion, from which he fled.

Files of the Municipal Council relating to the change of the name of the city.

Photos from Ruy Banguela's files.

The Meteorological Institute confirmed its monitoring of Saturday's weather and the intermittent showers on Sunday.

There is no record of Pedro Quimera being committed to the Floral Mansion. In fact, I was received with hostility at the institution.

*This book took a long time to be completed, as the research was done without a sponsor and the author frequently was obliged to suspend writing in order to do freelance work as journalist, real estate broker, computer salesman for a rival firm of Antenor's (who refused to hire the writer, which surely influenced the frankly negative depiction of the character), press agent, and refrigerator painter during the recession in the second half of 1995, jobs that made it possible to gather the necessary capital. The publisher thinks it desirable to emphasize that, despite the author having been urged to file a lawsuit against the federal government to receive a pension for having been persecuted for years under the military dictatorship, he refused on the grounds of personal integrity. He stressed that, in reality, the only harm he suffered in those years was having lost a glass of whiskey. He was at a table in a bar when the Federal Police burst into the place in search of a terrorism suspect. Everyone ran, and when the author returned, he saw a policeman finishing his whiskey, a single malt scotch. Despite his protests, the establishment charged him anyway. In today's money it would be equal to fifteen reais. If the current administration sees fit to reimburse me, that's all the author asks. He still has the receipt.**

---

* This publishing house, denying any responsibility, deems it desirable to stipulate that it has its doubts about the receipt, suspecting it to be a fake, since the alleged bar only opened for business two years after the date the whiskey was consumed.

D O R I A N   J O R G E   F R E I R E today lives in Mossoró and spends most of his time sitting on the veranda of his house on Praça da Redenção, calmly conversing with his muse Maria Candida and with friends who come to visit, like the book dealer Gonzaga, Rabbi Auerbach, Pastor Gioia, the theatrical producer Arley Pereira, the psychoanalyst and sexologist Roberto Freyre, Senator João Ribeiro during congressional recesses, and the exiled journalist Loyola Brandão. Dorian plans to write *The Physiology of Love Among Women-Men*, based on the documentation he has collected about Manuela and Roberta Close. He also has completed the first drafts of *The Secret History of Corruption in Arealva* and *Mystical Aspects of Georges Bernanos*. The present author expresses his gratitude to Dorian for opening his files, with photos, notes, documents, as well as copies of the scathing and courageous articles he published about the Godfather, Antenor, Adriano Portella, and Bradío. It was he who found the body of the coroner Morimoto buried at the Focal. Threatened with death and having suffered physical attacks, he reluctantly took his family's advice to return to Mossoró, where he has become one of the stars of the city.

IGNÁCIO DE LOYOLA BRANDÃO began his career writing film reviews and went on to work for one of the principal newspapers in São Paulo. Initially banned in Brazil, his novel *Zero* went on to win the prestigious Brasilia Prize and become a controversial best seller. Brandão is the author of more than a half dozen works of fiction.

CLIFFORD E. LANDERS has translated works from Brazilian Portuguese by such authors as Jorge Amado, João Ubaldo Ribeiro, and Osman Lins. His *Literary Translation: A Practical Guide* was published by Multilingual Matters Ltd. in 2001.

SELECTED DALKEY ARCHIVE PAPERBACKS

PETROS ABATZOGLOU, *What Does Mrs.*
Freeman Want?
MICHAL AJVAZ, *The Golden Age.*
The Other City.
PIERRE ALBERT-BIROT, *Grabinoulor.*
YUZ ALESHKOVSKY, *Kangaroo.*
FELIPE ALFAU, *Chromos.*
Locos.
IVAN ÂNGELO, *The Celebration.*
The Tower of Glass.
DAVID ANTIN, *Talking.*
ANTÓNIO LOBO ANTUNES,
Knowledge of Hell.
ALAIN ARIAS-MISSON, *Theatre of Incest.*
IFTIKHAR ARIF AND WAQAS KHWAJA, EDS.,
Modern Poetry of Pakistan.
JOHN ASHBERY AND JAMES SCHUYLER,
A Nest of Ninnies.
HEIMRAD BÄCKER, *transcript.*
DJUNA BARNES, *Ladies Almanack.*
Ryder.
JOHN BARTH, *LETTERS.*
Sabbatical.
DONALD BARTHELME, *The King.*
Paradise.
SVETISLAV BASARA, *Chinese Letter.*
RENÉ BELLETTO, *Dying.*
MARK BINELLI, *Sacco and Vanzetti*
Must Die!
ANDREI BITOV, *Pushkin House.*
ANDREJ BLATNIK, *You Do Understand.*
LOUIS PAUL BOON, *Chapel Road.*
My Little War.
Summer in Termuren.
ROGER BOYLAN, *Killoyle.*
IGNÁCIO DE LOYOLA BRANDÃO,
Anonymous Celebrity.
The Good-Bye Angel.
Teeth under the Sun.
Zero.
BONNIE BREMSER,
Troia: Mexican Memoirs.
CHRISTINE BROOKE-ROSE, *Amalgamemnon.*
BRIGID BROPHY, *In Transit.*
MEREDITH BROSNAN, *Mr. Dynamite.*
GERALD L. BRUNS, *Modern Poetry and*
the Idea of Language.
EVGENY BUNIMOVICH AND J. KATES, EDS.,
Contemporary Russian Poetry:
An Anthology.
GABRIELLE BURTON, *Heartbreak Hotel.*
MICHEL BUTOR, *Degrees.*
Mobile.
Portrait of the Artist as a Young Ape.
G. CABRERA INFANTE, *Infante's Inferno.*
Three Trapped Tigers.
JULIETA CAMPOS,
The Fear of Losing Eurydice.
ANNE CARSON, *Eros the Bittersweet.*
ORLY CASTEL-BLOOM, *Dolly City.*
CAMILO JOSÉ CELA, *Christ versus Arizona.*
The Family of Pascual Duarte.
The Hive.
LOUIS-FERDINAND CÉLINE, *Castle to Castle.*
Conversations with Professor Y.
London Bridge.

Normance.
North.
Rigadoon.
HUGO CHARTERIS, *The Tide Is Right.*
JEROME CHARYN, *The Tar Baby.*
MARC CHOLODENKO, *Mordechai Schamz.*
JOSHUA COHEN, *Witz.*
EMILY HOLMES COLEMAN, *The Shutter*
of Snow.
ROBERT COOVER, *A Night at the Movies.*
STANLEY CRAWFORD, *Log of the S.S. The*
Mrs Unguentine.
Some Instructions to My Wife.
ROBERT CREELEY, *Collected Prose.*
RENÉ CREVEL, *Putting My Foot in It.*
RALPH CUSACK, *Cadenza.*
SUSAN DAITCH, *L.C.*
Storytown.
NICHOLAS DELBANCO,
The Count of Concord.
NIGEL DENNIS, *Cards of Identity.*
PETER DIMOCK, *A Short Rhetoric for*
Leaving the Family.
ARIEL DORFMAN, *Konfidenz.*
COLEMAN DOWELL,
The Houses of Children.
Island People.
Too Much Flesh and Jabez.
ARKADII DRAGOMOSHCHENKO, *Dust.*
RIKKI DUCORNET, *The Complete*
Butcher's Tales.
The Fountains of Neptune.
The Jade Cabinet.
The One Marvelous Thing.
Phosphor in Dreamland.
The Stain.
The Word "Desire."
WILLIAM EASTLAKE, *The Bamboo Bed.*
Castle Keep.
Lyric of the Circle Heart.
JEAN ECHENOZ, *Chopin's Move.*
STANLEY ELKIN, *A Bad Man.*
Boswell: A Modern Comedy.
Criers and Kibitzers, Kibitzers
and Criers.
The Dick Gibson Show.
The Franchiser.
George Mills.
The Living End.
The MacGuffin.
The Magic Kingdom.
Mrs. Ted Bliss.
The Rabbi of Lud.
Van Gogh's Room at Arles.
ANNIE ERNAUX, *Cleaned Out.*
LAUREN FAIRBANKS, *Muzzle Thyself.*
Sister Carrie.
LESLIE A. FIEDLER, *Love and Death in*
the American Novel.
JUAN FILLOY, *Op Oloop.*
GUSTAVE FLAUBERT, *Bouvard and Pécuchet.*
KASS FLEISHER, *Talking out of School.*
FORD MADOX FORD,
The March of Literature.
JON FOSSE, *Aliss at the Fire.*
Melancholy.

FOR A FULL LIST OF PUBLICATIONS, VISIT:
www.dalkeyarchive.com

MAX FRISCH, *I'm Not Stiller.*
Man in the Holocene.
CARLOS FUENTES, *Christopher Unborn.*
Distant Relations.
Terra Nostra.
Where the Air Is Clear.
JANICE GALLOWAY, *Foreign Parts.*
The Trick Is to Keep Breathing.
WILLIAM H. GASS, *Cartesian Sonata and Other Novellas.*
Finding a Form.
A Temple of Texts.
The Tunnel.
Willie Masters' Lonesome Wife.
GÉRARD GAVARRY, *Hoppla! 1 2 3.*
ETIENNE GILSON,
The Arts of the Beautiful.
Forms and Substances in the Arts.
C. S. GISCOMBE, *Giscome Road.*
Here.
Prairie Style.
DOUGLAS GLOVER, *Bad News of the Heart.*
The Enamoured Knight.
WITOLD GOMBROWICZ,
A Kind of Testament.
KAREN ELIZABETH GORDON,
The Red Shoes.
GEORGI GOSPODINOV, *Natural Novel.*
JUAN GOYTISOLO, *Count Julian.*
Juan the Landless.
Makbara.
Marks of Identity.
PATRICK GRAINVILLE, *The Cave of Heaven.*
HENRY GREEN, *Back.*
Blindness.
Concluding.
Doting.
Nothing.
JIŘÍ GRUŠA, *The Questionnaire.*
GABRIEL GUDDING,
Rhode Island Notebook.
MELA HARTWIG, *Am I a Redundant Human Being?*
JOHN HAWKES, *The Passion Artist.*
Whistlejacket.
ALEKSANDAR HEMON, ED.,
Best European Fiction.
AIDAN HIGGINS, *A Bestiary.*
Balcony of Europe.
Bornholm Night-Ferry.
Darkling Plain: Texts for the Air.
Flotsam and Jetsam.
Langrishe, Go Down.
Scenes from a Receding Past.
Windy Arbours.
KEIZO HINO, *Isle of Dreams.*
ALDOUS HUXLEY, *Antic Hay.*
Crome Yellow.
Point Counter Point.
Those Barren Leaves.
Time Must Have a Stop.
MIKHAIL IOSSEL AND JEFF PARKER, EDS.,
Amerika: Russian Writers View the United States.
GERT JONKE, *The Distant Sound.*
Geometric Regional Novel.

Homage to Czerny.
The System of Vienna.
JACQUES JOUET, *Mountain R.*
Savage.
CHARLES JULIET, *Conversations with Samuel Beckett and Bram van Velde.*
MIEKO KANAI, *The Word Book.*
YORAM KANIUK, *Life on Sandpaper.*
HUGH KENNER, *The Counterfeiters.*
Flaubert, Joyce and Beckett: The Stoic Comedians.
Joyce's Voices.
DANILO KIŠ, *Garden, Ashes.*
A Tomb for Boris Davidovich.
ANITA KONKKA, *A Fool's Paradise.*
GEORGE KONRÁD, *The City Builder.*
TADEUSZ KONWICKI, *A Minor Apocalypse.*
The Polish Complex.
MENIS KOUMANDAREAS, *Koula.*
ELAINE KRAF, *The Princess of 72nd Street.*
JIM KRUSOE, *Iceland.*
EWA KURYLUK, *Century 21.*
EMILIO LASCANO TEGUI, *On Elegance While Sleeping.*
ERIC LAURRENT, *Do Not Touch.*
VIOLETTE LEDUC, *La Bâtarde.*
SUZANNE JILL LEVINE, *The Subversive Scribe: Translating Latin American Fiction.*
DEBORAH LEVY, *Billy and Girl.*
Pillow Talk in Europe and Other Places.
JOSÉ LEZAMA LIMA, *Paradiso.*
ROSA LIKSOM, *Dark Paradise.*
OSMAN LINS, *Avalovara.*
The Queen of the Prisons of Greece.
ALF MAC LOCHLAINN,
The Corpus in the Library.
Out of Focus.
RON LOEWINSOHN, *Magnetic Field(s).*
BRIAN LYNCH, *The Winner of Sorrow.*
D. KEITH MANO, *Take Five.*
MICHELINE AHARONIAN MARCOM,
The Mirror in the Well.
BEN MARCUS,
The Age of Wire and String.
WALLACE MARKFIELD,
Teitlebaum's Window.
To an Early Grave.
DAVID MARKSON, *Reader's Block.*
Springer's Progress.
Wittgenstein's Mistress.
CAROLE MASO, *AVA.*
LADISLAV MATEJKA AND KRYSTYNA
POMORSKA, EDS.,
Readings in Russian Poetics: Formalist and Structuralist Views.
HARRY MATHEWS,
The Case of the Persevering Maltese: Collected Essays.
Cigarettes.
The Conversions.
The Human Country: New and Collected Stories.
The Journalist.

My Life in CIA.
Singular Pleasures.
The Sinking of the Odradek
 Stadium.
Tlooth.
20 Lines a Day.
JOSEPH MCELROY,
 Night Soul and Other Stories.
ROBERT L. MCLAUGHLIN, ED.,
 Innovations: An Anthology of
  Modern & Contemporary Fiction.
HERMAN MELVILLE, *The Confidence-Man.*
AMANDA MICHALOPOULOU, *I'd Like.*
STEVEN MILLHAUSER,
 The Barnum Museum.
 In the Penny Arcade.
RALPH J. MILLS, JR.,
 Essays on Poetry.
MOMUS, *The Book of Jokes.*
CHRISTINE MONTALBETTI, *Western.*
OLIVE MOORE, *Spleen.*
NICHOLAS MOSLEY, *Accident.*
 Assassins.
 Catastrophe Practice.
 Children of Darkness and Light.
 Experience and Religion.
 God's Hazard.
 The Hesperides Tree.
 Hopeful Monsters.
 Imago Bird.
 Impossible Object.
 Inventing God.
 Judith.
 Look at the Dark.
 Natalie Natalia.
 Paradoxes of Peace.
 Serpent.
 Time at War.
 The Uses of Slime Mould:
  Essays of Four Decades.
WARREN MOTTE,
 Fables of the Novel: French Fiction
  since 1990.
 Fiction Now: The French Novel in
  the 21st Century.
 Oulipo: A Primer of Potential
  Literature.
YVES NAVARRE, *Our Share of Time.*
 Sweet Tooth.
DOROTHY NELSON, *In Night's City.*
 Tar and Feathers.
ESHKOL NEVO, *Homesick.*
WILFRIDO D. NOLLEDO,
 But for the Lovers.
FLANN O'BRIEN,
 At Swim-Two-Birds.
 At War.
 The Best of Myles.
 The Dalkey Archive.
 Further Cuttings.
 The Hard Life.
 The Poor Mouth.
 The Third Policeman.
CLAUDE OLLIER, *The Mise-en-Scène.*
PATRIK OUŘEDNÍK, *Europeana.*
BORIS PAHOR, *Necropolis.*

FERNANDO DEL PASO,
 News from the Empire.
 Palinuro of Mexico.
ROBERT PINGET, *The Inquisitory.*
 Mahu or The Material.
 Trio.
MANUEL PUIG,
 Betrayed by Rita Hayworth.
 The Buenos Aires Affair.
 Heartbreak Tango.
RAYMOND QUENEAU, *The Last Days.*
 Odile.
 Pierrot Mon Ami.
 Saint Glinglin.
ANN QUIN, *Berg.*
 Passages.
 Three.
 Tripticks.
ISHMAEL REED,
 The Free-Lance Pallbearers.
 The Last Days of Louisiana Red.
 Ishmael Reed: The Plays.
 Reckless Eyeballing.
 The Terrible Threes.
 The Terrible Twos.
 Yellow Back Radio Broke-Down.
JEAN RICARDOU, *Place Names.*
RAINER MARIA RILKE, *The Notebooks of*
 Malte Laurids Brigge.
JULIÁN RÍOS, *The House of Ulysses.*
 Larva: A Midsummer Night's Babel.
 Poundemonium.
AUGUSTO ROA BASTOS, *I the Supreme.*
DANIËL ROBBERECHTS,
 Arriving in Avignon.
OLIVIER ROLIN, *Hotel Crystal.*
ALIX CLEO ROUBAUD, *Alix's Journal.*
JACQUES ROUBAUD, *The Form of a*
 City Changes Faster, Alas, Than
 the Human Heart.
 The Great Fire of London.
 Hortense in Exile.
 Hortense Is Abducted.
 The Loop.
 The Plurality of Worlds of Lewis.
 The Princess Hoppy.
 Some Thing Black.
LEON S. ROUDIEZ,
 French Fiction Revisited.
VEDRANA RUDAN, *Night.*
STIG SÆTERBAKKEN, *Siamese.*
LYDIE SALVAYRE, *The Company of Ghosts.*
 Everyday Life.
 The Lecture.
 Portrait of the Writer as a
  Domesticated Animal.
 The Power of Flies.
LUIS RAFAEL SÁNCHEZ,
 Macho Camacho's Beat.
SEVERO SARDUY, *Cobra & Maitreya.*
NATHALIE SARRAUTE,
 Do You Hear Them?
 Martereau.
 The Planetarium.
ARNO SCHMIDT, *Collected Stories.*
 Nobodaddy's Children.